The Golden Ass

The Transformations of Lucius

Otherwise Known as

THE

GOLDEN ASS

A New Translation by

ROBERT GRAVES

from Apuleius

Farrar, Straus and Giroux   New York

Farrar, Straus and Giroux
18 West 18th Street, New York 10011

Copyright © 1951 and renewed 1979 by Robert Graves
All rights reserved
Printed in the United States of America
Published in 1951 by Farrar, Straus and Young
This paperback edition, 2009

Library of Congress Control Number: 2008937713
Paperback ISBN-13: 978-0-3745-3181-2
Paperback ISBN-10: 0-374-53181-1

www.fsgbooks.com

13 15 17 19 20 18 16 14

Contents

Contents

Apuleius's Address to the Reader

IF YOU are not put off by the Egyptian story-telling convention which allows humans to be changed into animals and, after various adventures, restored to their proper shapes, you should be amused by this queer novel, a string of anecdotes in the popular Milesian style, but intended only for your private ear, which I call my *Transformations.*

Let me briefly introduce myself as Lucius Apuleius, a native of Madaura in North Africa, but of ancient Greek stock. Various ancestors of mine lived on Mount Hymettus near Athens; in Ephyra, as the province of Corinth was once called; and at Taenarus in Laconia—all of them places immortalized by more famous writers than myself. I was brought to Athens as a child to learn Attic Greek, and later went to Rome where I set myself to study Latin—a painful task, because I was a stranger there and had no regular schoolmasters. You will, I hope, forgive me for not having thoroughly Romanized my literary style; after all, this story with its temperamental shifts and changes is so Greek in character that I should have done wrong to write it in academic Latin. Now read on and enjoy yourself!

Introduction

THE ORIGINAL TITLE of this book, *The Transformation of Lucius Apuleius of Madaura*, was early shortened to *The Golden Ass* because Apuleius had written it in the style of the professional story-tellers who, as Pliny mentions in one of his letters, used to preface their street-corner entertainments with: 'Give me a copper and I'll tell you a golden story.' So 'golden' conveys an indulgent smile rather than genuine appreciation.

William Adlington, in whose vigorous early-Elizabethan translation the book is still best known, remarks in his introduction that Apuleius wrote 'in so dark and high a style, in so strange and absurd words and in such new invented phrases, as he seemed rather to set it forth to show his magnificent prose than to participate his doings to others'. Adlington has missed the point: Apuleius, who could write a good plain prose when he chose, as his *Discourse on Magic* and his *God of Socrates* prove, was parodying the extravagant language which the 'Milesian' story-tellers used, like barkers at country fairs today, as a means of impressing simple-minded audiences. The professional story-teller, or *sgéalai,* is still found in the West of Ireland. I have heard one complimented as 'speaking such fine hard Irish that Devil two words together in it would any man understand'; but this hard Irish, like Apuleius's hard Latin, is always genuinely archaic, not humorously coined for the occasion.

Why did Apuleius choose to write in this eccentric style? For the same reason that Rabelais did. The parallel is close. Both were priests—pious, lively, exceptionally learned, provincial priests—who found that the popular tale gave them a wider field for their descriptions of contemporary morals and manners, punctuated by philosophical asides, than any more respectable literary form.

In my translation I have made no attempt to bring out the oddness of the Latin by writing in a style, say, somewhere between Lyly's *Euphues* and Amanda Ros's *Irene Iddesleigh;* paradoxically, the effect of oddness is best achieved in convulsed times like the present by writing in as easy and sedate an English as possible. Here is the same sentence from Cupid's address to Psyche as translated by Adlington, by the anonymous Victorian author of the *Bohn's Classical Library* version (1881) and by myself:

Et hic adhuc infantilis uterus gestat nobis infantem alium, si texeris nostra secreta silentio, divinum, si profanaveris, mortalem.

Thou hast a young and tender child couched in this young and tender belly of thine, who shall be made if thou conceal my secret, an immortal god, but otherwise a mortal creature.

Adlington.

Infantine as you are, you are pregnant with another infant which if you preserve my secret in silence, will be born divine, but if you profane it, it will be mortal.

Bohn's Victorian.

Though you are still only a child, you will soon have a child of your own which shall be born divine if you keep our secret, but mortal if you divulge it.

R.G.

When one tries to make the English rendering of any Latin text convey the sense of the original, the same problem of impersonation arises as when one tries to broadcast another's lecture or preach another's sermon. It is essentially a moral problem: how much is owed to the letter, and how much to the spirit. 'Stick strictly to the script', and the effect of authenticity is lost. Here I have sometimes felt obliged to alter the order not only of phrases but of sentences, where English prose logic differs from Latin; and to avoid the nuisance of footnotes I have brought their substance up into the story itself whenever it reads obscurely. Adlington often did the same.

Adlington was a pretty good scholar, but the text he used had not yet been critically examined and emended, and no reliable Latin dictionary had yet been published, so he often made bad mistakes. But at least he realized that *The Transformations* was, above all, a religious novel:

'Since this book of Lucius is a figure of man's life and toucheth the nature and manners of mortal man, egging them forward from their asinal form to their human and perfect shape (beside the pleasant and delectable jests therein contained) . . . I trust that the matter shall be esteemed by such as not only delight to please their fancies in recording the same, but also take a pattern thereby to regenerate their minds from brutal and beastly custom.'

However, though Lucius's conversion at the close of the story is a real and moving one (unlike the perfunctory conversions with which Defoe, for reasons of policy, ended his low-life novels of *Roxana* and *Moll Flanders*), it is unlikely that many readers have ever spent much time over it. The book's popularity, ever since it was written, has rested almost wholly on its 'pleasant and delectable jest', especially the bawdy ones.

The main religious principles that Apuleius was inculcating were wholly opposed to those of the Christianity of his day. The first was that men are far from equal in the sight of Heaven, its favour being reserved for the well-born and well-educated, in so far as they are conscious of the moral responsibilities of their station: that only such can be admitted into the divine mysteries and so mitigate their fear of death by a hope of preferential treatment in the after-world. Slaves and freedmen cannot possibly acquire the virtue, intelligence or discretion needed to qualify them for initiation into these mysteries, even if they could afford to pay the high fees demanded. Slavery carries a stigma of moral baseness; and Apuleius's slaves are always cowardly, wicked, deceitful or treacherous.

To be abjectly poor, though free, he regarded as a sign not necessarily of moral baseness but of ill-luck, and his second main religious principle was that ill-luck is catching. The virtuous nobleman does not set his dogs on the poor man, and there is nothing to prevent him from sending a slave round to relieve his immediate distresses; but, like the priest and the Levite in Jesus's parable of the Samaritan, he should carefully avoid all personal contact with ill-luck. Thus when Aristomenes the provision merchant, in Apuleius's opening story, found his old friend Socrates in such a shocking plight at Hypata, he should have been content to toss him a coin or two, spit in his own bosom for luck, and leave him to his fate; instead of officiously trying to rescue and reform him—actually dragging the reluctant wretch into the baths and scrubbing his filthy body with his own hands! Socrates was in any case fated to die miserably, and his bad luck fastened securely on Aristomenes, who soon found himself in Socrates's position—forced to change his name, abandon his wife and family, and become a hunted exile in daily terror of death.

The fault which involved Lucius in all his miseries was that, though a nobleman, he decided on a frivolous love-affair with a slave-girl. A slave-girl is necessarily base; baseness is unlucky; ill-luck is catching. He also transgressed the third main religious principle: he meddled with the supernatural. His ulterior motive in making love to the girl was to persuade her to betray the magical secrets of her mistress, who was a witch. Yet he had been plainly warned against this fault in Byrrhaena's house at Hypata by being shown a wonderful statue of Actaeon's transformation into a stag, his punishment for prying into the mysteries of Diana. A nobleman should not play with black magic: he should satisfy his spiritual needs by being initiated into a respectable mystery cult along with men of his own station; even then he should not thrust himself on the gods but patiently await their summons. Lucius's punishment was to be temporarily transformed not into an owl, as he had hoped, but into an ass.

The owl was a bird of wisdom. The ass, as the Goddess Isis herself reminded Lucius at Cenchreae, was the most hateful to her of all beasts in existence; but she did not account for her aversion. Adlington's explanation, that the ass is a notoriously stupid brute, does not go far enough. The ass was in fact sacred to the God Set, whom the Greeks knew as Typhon, her ancient persecutor and the murderer of her husband Osiris. In Apuleius's day the ass typified lust, cruelty and wickedness, and Plutarch—from whom he claimed descent—had recorded an Egyptian festival in which asses and men with Typhonic colouring (*i.e.*, sandy-red like a wild ass's coat) were triumphantly pushed over cliffs in vengeance for Osiris's murder. When Charitë, in Apuleius's story of the bandits' cave, escapes and rides home on ass-back, he remarks that this is an extraordinary sight—a virgin riding in triumph on an ass. He means: 'dominating the lusts of the flesh without whip or bridle'.

Yet originally the ass had been so holy a beast that its ears, conventionalized as twin feathers sprouting from the end of a sceptre, became the mark of sovereignty in the hand of every Egyptian deity: and the existence of an early Italian ass-cult is proved by the cognomens Asina and Asellus in the distinguished Scipionian, Claudian and Annian families at Rome. That Lucius was eventually initiated into the rites of Osiris by a Roman priest called Asinius was an amusing coincidence. Asses are connected in western European folklore, especially French, with the mid-winter Saturnalia at the conclusion of which the ass-eared god, later the Christmas Fool with his ass-eared cap, was killed by his rival, the Spirit of the New Year—the child Horus, or Harpocrates, or the infant Zeus. That there was an eastern European tradition identifying Saturn's counterpart Cronos with the ass is proved by the anonymous Byzantine scholar of the twelfth century (quoted by Piccolomini in the *Rivista di Filologia,* ii, 159) who in drawing up a list of metals, colours, flowers and beasts appropriate to the seven planetary gods gives Cronos's attributes as lead, blue, the hyacinth, and the ass. This explains the otherwise unaccountable

popular connection between asses and fools; asses are really far
more sagacious than horses.

Until nearly the end of his life as an ass, in the course of which
he gets involved in the hysterical and fraudulent popular rites of
the Syrian Goddess, Lucius is a beast of ill-luck. And ill-luck is
catching: each of his masters in turn either dies violently, is locked
up in gaol or suffers some lesser misfortune. The spell begins to
lift only when he enters the household of Thyasus, the Corinthian
judge, and is there encouraged slowly to reassert his humanity.

The seasonal transformations of the variously-named god of
the mystery-cults, the Spirit of the Year, were epitomized in the
Athenian *Lenaea* festival and corresponding performances
throughout the ancient world, including north-western Europe.
The initiate identified himself with the god, and seems to have
undergone twelve emblematic transformations—represented by
Lucius's 'twelve stoles'—as he passed through the successive
Houses of the Zodiac before undergoing his ritual death and rebirth. 'Transformations' therefore conveys the secondary sense of
'spiritual autobiography'; and Lucius had spent twelve months
in his ass's skin, from one rose-season to the next, constantly
changing his House, until his death as an ass and rebirth as a
devotee of Isis.

The literal story of Apuleius's adventures in Greece can be re-
constructed only in vague outline. It is known that he was a rich
and well-connected young man born at Madaura, a Roman col-
ony in the interior of Morocco, early in the second century A.D.;
his father had been a duumvir, or provincial magistrate, who on
his death left his two sons two million sesterces, about £20,000
in gold, between them. Apuleius went first to Carthage Univer-

sity, and afterwards to Athens where he studied Platonic philosophy. While still at Athens, if the story of Thelyphron the student is in part autobiographical, he ran short of money after a visit to the Olympic Games and was forced for awhile to live on his wits. Perhaps he had run through his allowance by drinking and whoring in the brothels and getting mixed up with the criminal classes like the debaunched young nobleman Thrasyllus (in the story of the bandits' cave). At all events, when he finally reached Corinth and was given a helping hand by Thyasus, he was pretty well down at heel and ripe for repentance and conversion.

After his initiation into the mysteries of Isis, he went to Rome where he studied Latin oratory and made a success at the Bar. Later he travelled widely in Asia Minor and Egypt, studying philosophy and religion. While on a visit to Alexandria by way of Libya, he fell ill at Oea, on the shores of the Gulf of Sirte, where a young man named Sicinius Pontianus who had been his contemporary at Athens University nursed him back to health. Apuleius grew friendly with Pontianus's mother Pudentilla, and Pontianus begged him to marry her, despite the great disparity of their ages, on the ground that fourteen years of widowhood had given her a nervous complaint for which the doctors assured her that marriage was the only remedy. Apuleius consented, but when Pudentilla, who was very rich, made over all her money to him and Pontianus died soon afterwards, the rest of the family charged him with having poisoned him and gained her affections by magic. Apuleius's successful and very amusing speech in his own defense, *A Discourse on Magic,* survives. I should like to have been present in court to hear him sum up a part of his argument with the ludicrously dry: 'I have now stated, Gentlemen, why in my opinion there is nothing at all in common between magicians and fish.'

Though the charge that he used magic failed, it was enough to make ignorant people, including many prominent Christians, believe later that *The Transformations* was to be read as literal truth. Even St Augustine writes doubtfully: 'Apuleius either reported or invented his transformation into asinal shape'; and Lactantius in his *Divine Institutes* is distressed that the miracles of Apuleius, like those of the gymnosophist Apollonius of Tyana, are quoted by anti-Christian controversialists as more wonderful than those of Jesus Christ.

Evidently St Augustine and his credulous contemporaries had not read Lucius of Patra's popular novel *The Ass*, now lost, or Lucian of Samosata's *Lucius, or the Ass,* still extant, which is based on it; otherwise, they would have realized that Apuleius had borrowed the plot of *The Transformations* from one or other of these two sources. (Lucius's date is unknown; but Lucian and Apuleius were close contemporaries). Lucian's novel* is shorter and balder than *The Transformations*. His slave-girl Palaestra has none of the charm that excuses Apuleius's intimate account of the love-affair with her counterpart Fotis; she merely plays the female drill-sergeant, initiating her recruit into the discipline of sex as one teaches arms-drill by numbers. Lucian includes none of Apuleius's incidental stories, such as the stories of Aristomenes, Thelyphron, Cupid and Psyche; nor the Festival of Laughter episode—there really was such a festival at Hypata—nor the hoodooing of the baker; and his hero returns to human shape at Thessalonica, not Corinth, during his exhibition in the amphi-

* See appendix.

theatre, when without divine assistance he manages to grab some roses from one of the attendants. The comic climax of Lucian's story comes when the ex-ass returns hopefully to the rich woman who has recently played Pasiphaë with him and proposes to renew their intimacy: she throws him out of her house, greatly aggrieved that he is now a mere man, quite incapable of satisfying her needs. Lucian's stories all leave a bad taste in the mouth; Apuleius's do not, even when he is handling the same bawdy situation. His rich Pasiphaë, for example, is no mere bestialist, but shows her genuine love for the ass by planting pure, sincere, wholly unmeretricious kisses on his scented nose.

Apuleius constantly uses a device now known on the variety stage as the 'double take'. The audience applauds, but finds that it has applauded too soon; the real point, either funnier or more macabre than anyone expected, was yet to come. The brilliance of his showmanship suggests that he turned professional story-teller during his wanderings in Greece, using Lucius of Patra's *Ass* as his stock piece—he felt its relevance to his case and Lucius happened to be his own name—and stringing a number of popular stories to it. Perhaps one day Thyasus, the Corinthian judge, heard a huge shout of laughter from the servants' quarters of his house and, going along to investigate, stopped to listen to one of Apuleius's droll stories; and so befriended him without at first knowing who he was.

It is unlikely, by the way, that Apuleius really had relatives at Hypata; the incident of his meeting with Byrrhaena there is also found in Lucian's novel. It is equally unlikely that Greek was his mother-tongue, and his reference to family connections with Ephyra (Corinth), Mount Hymettus, celebrated for its honey, and Taenarus the main Greek entrance to the Underworld, are clearly allegorical. These places are chosen as ancient cult-centres of the Triple Goddess whom he adored in her successive aspects as the sovereign of Life, Love and Death.

He probably invented none of his stories, though it is clear that he improved them. The story of Cupid and Psyche is still widely current as a primitive folk-tale in countries as far apart as Scotland and Hindustan; but taking hints from passages in Plato's *Phaedo* and *Republic* he turned it into a neat philosophical allegory of the progress of the rational soul towards intellectual love. This feat won him the approval even of the better sort of Christians, including Synnesius, the early fifth-century Bishop of Ptolemais; and *Cupid and Psyche* is still Apuleius's best known, though by no means his most golden, story. His devotion to Platonic philosophy is shown in the *God of Socrates*, which St Augustine attacked violently.

St Augustine's dislike of his fellow-countryman Apuleius seems to have sprung from an uncomfortable recognition that they would one day come up together for the judgement of posterity. He was born near Madaura, Apuleius's birthplace, whose inhabitants he addresses in his 232nd Epistle as 'my fathers', and went to school there; then, like Apuleius, he went on to Carthage University. Book II of his *Confessions* begins: 'I will now call to mind my past foulness and the carnal corruption of my soul . . . In that sixteenth year of the age of my flesh, when the madness of unlicensed lust took rule over me and I resigned myself wholly to it . . . I walked the streets of Babylon and wallowed in the mire thereof as if in a bed of spices and precious ointments.' He goes on to describe how he took up with a gang of young Mohocks (like

xix

the ones that terrorized Hypata) and so fell into the mortal sin of theft. Still following the footsteps of Apuleius, he studied oratory at Rome. It is not until Book VIII that after a severe struggle with himself he hears a voice from Heaven directing him to read a text from St. Paul, becomes suddenly converted, once more like Apuleius, and determines to devote his life to God.

His father Patricius, a nominal Christian, was a violent, vulgar fellow from whom he inherited neither rank, money nor a predisposition to virtue; so that even had he wished to become a priest of Isis he could not have qualified for the houour. But the Christian mysteries were open to everyone, slave or noble, of good or evil life, and the greater the sinner the warmer his welcome to the fold. Though his conversion was as genuine as that of Apuleius, it does not seem to have made his life nearly so happy. Tormented by the memory of his sins, he flaunts his dirty linen for our detestation: 'Alas, terrible Judge, I began by robbing a peartree, I ended in adultery ·and the hateful Manichaean heresy!' Apuleius does nothing of the sort. His *Transformations* is as moral a work as the *Confessions;* but he presents his errors in humorous allegory, not as a literal record, and admits that he learned a great deal from them which has since stood him in good stead: granted, his love affair with Fotis was a mistake, and he paid dearly for it, but it would be hypocritical to pretend that it was not a charming and instructive experience while it lasted.

St Augustine described with horror the fascination that the amphitheatre and the study of oratory had held for him in his unregenerate days. Apuleius, though a priest of Osiris, continued to practise as a barrister and in later life organized the gladiatorial and wild-beast shows for the whole province of Africa. St Augustine rejected Platonic philosophy as insufficient for salvation; Apuleius was true to it and showed his scorn of contemporary Christianity by making the most wicked of his characters, the baker's wife, 'reject all true religion in favour of the fantastic and blasphemous cult of an Only God' and use the Christian Love-feast as 'an excuse for getting drunk quite early in the day and playing the whore at all hours.* One of St Augustine's biographers, E. de Pressensé, has written approvingly: 'He kept dragging along the chain of guilt . . . and unlike his fellow-countryman Apuleius whose greatest pleasure was to arrange words in harmonious order and who had no desire beyond that of calling forth applause . . . still felt sick at heart.' This is unfair to Apuleius. His greatest desire was not applause: it was to show his gratitude to the Goddess whom he adored, by living a life worthy of her favour—a serene, honourable and useful life, with no secret worm of guilt gnawing at his heart as though he had withheld some confession from her or mistrusted her compassion.

Recent researches into the history of witchcraft show that Apuleius had a first-hand knowledge of the subject. The Thessalian witches preserved the pre-Aryan tradition of a 'left-hand', or destructive, magic performed in honour of the Triple Moon-goddess in her character of Hecate; the 'right-hand', or beneficent, magic performed in honour of the same Goddess being now concentrated in the pure mysteries of Isis and Demeter. It must be remembered that in St Augustine's day the sovereignty of the indivisible male Trinity had not yet been encroached upon by

---

* The Inquisition was very hot against the book and succeeded in mutilating all the editions except the Editio Princeps Andrew, Bishop of Aleria published in Rome in 1469.

Mariolatry, and Apuleius's splendid address to Isis could not therefore be read with indulgence as an anticipation of the *Litany of the Blessed Virgin* with which it has much in common. Apuleius did not deny the power of the left-hand cult, any more than the Christians denied the power of the Devil: but he knew that honourable men like himself ought to leave it alone and that if they kept strictly to the right-hand cult, the devotees of the left-hand could have no power over them. On one point, at least, besides the need for practising virtue in preparation for the afterlife, he agreed with the Christians: his rejection of the official Olympian mythology, which Plato had long before discredited as a barbaric survival, appears in *Cupid and Psyche,* where the gods and goddesses behave like naughty children. But he wrote of them humorously and affectionately as Apollonius Rhodius had done in his *Argonautica,* not in the scoffing style of Lucian's *Dialogues.*

Nothing much more of importance remains to be said about Apuleius except that he became a priest of Aesculapius, the God of Medicine, as well as of Isis and Osiris, and was also a poet and a historian; unfortunately his histories and poems have not survived.

Now: LECTOR INTENDE, LAETABERIS.

R.G.

Deyá,
Majorca, 1947

The Golden Ass

1

The Story of Aristomenes

BUSINESS once took me to Thessaly, where my mother's family originated; I have, by the way, the distinction of being descended through her from the famous Plutarch. One morning after I had ridden over a high range of hills, down a slippery track into the valley beyond, across dewy pastures and soggy ploughland, my horse, a white Thessalian thoroughbred, began to puff and slacken his pace. Feeling tired myself from sitting so long cramped in the saddle, I jumped off, carefully wiped his sweating forehead with a handful of leaves, stroked his ears, threw the reins over his neck, and walked slowly beside him, letting him relax and recover his wind at leisure. While he breakfasted, snatching a mouthful of grass from this side or that of the track which wound through the meadows, I saw two men trudging along together a short distance ahead of me, deep in conversation. I walked a little faster, curious to know what they were talking about, and just as I drew abreast one of them burst into a loud laugh and said to the other: 'Stop, stop! Not another word! I can't bear to hear any more of your absurd and monstrous lies.'

This was promising. I said to the story-teller: 'Please don't think me impertinent or inquisitive, sir, but I'm always anxious to improve my education, and few subjects fail to interest me. If you would kindly go back to the beginning of your story and tell me the whole of it I should be most grateful. It sounds as if it would help me pleasantly up this next steep hill.'

The man who had laughed went on: 'I want no more of that nonsense, do you hear? You might as well say that magic can make rivers run backwards, freeze the ocean, and paralyze the winds. Or that the sun can be stopped by magic in mid-course, the moon made to drop a poisonous dew, and the stars charmed from their proper spheres. Why, you might as well say that day can be magically annihilated and replaced by perpetual night.'

But I persisted: 'No, sir, don't be put off. Finish your story, please finish it; unless this is asking too much of you.' Then, turning to the other, I said: 'As for you, sir, are you sure that it isn't either natural dullness or cultivated obstinacy that prevents you from recognizing the truth of what your friend has been trying to tell you? Stupid people always dismiss as untrue anything that happens only very seldom, or anything that their minds cannot readily grasp; yet when these things are carefully inquired into they are often found not only possible but probable. Tell me, for instance, what you make of this. Last night at supper I was challenged to an eating race by some people at my table and tried to swallow too large a mouthful of polenta cheese. It was so doughy and soft that it stuck half-way down my throat, blocking my windpipe, and I nearly choked to death. Yet only a few days before, at the Painted Porch in Athens, I had watched a juggler actually swallow a sharp cavalry sabre, point downwards too; after which, he collected a few coins from us bystanders and swallowed a hunting spear in the same astonishing way. We watched him tilt his head backwards with the handle sticking out from his throat into the air; and presently, believe it or not, a beautiful boy began to wriggle up that handle with such slippery movements that you might have mistaken him for the royal serpent coiled on the roughly-trimmed olive club carried by the God of Medicine; he seemed to have neither bone nor sinew in his whole body.' Then I turned once more to the other man: 'Come, sir, out with your story! I undertake not only to believe it, even though your friend will not, but to show my gratitude for your kindness by standing you a meal at the next inn.'

'Many thanks for a most generous offer,' he said, 'but I need no reward for telling you my experiences, every word of which —I swear to you by the Sun who sees everything—is absolutely true. And this afternoon when we reach Hypata, the most important town in Thessaly, you will no longer need to make the least mental reservation about its truth, because everyone there knows the story of what happened to me. It was by no means a private affair, you see. I must begin with some particulars about myself—my name, business and so on. I am an Aeginetan, in the wholesale provision trade, and I travel regularly through Thessaly, Aetolia and Boeotia buying honey, cheese and goods of that sort—the name is Aristomenes, at your service! Well, news reached me one day from Hypata that a large stock of prime cheeses was being offered there at a very tempting price. I hurried off at once but, as happens only too often in the trade, my trip was an unlucky one. I found as soon as I arrived that a fellow named Lupus, a merchant in a big way, had cornered the market only the day before. Depressed by having travelled so fast and to so little purpose, I went along early that evening to the public baths; and there, to my astonishment, whom should I meet but my old friend Socrates. I hardly recognized him, he looked so miserably pale and thin, sitting on the ground half-covered with a filthy, tattered old cloak, just like a street beggar. Though we had once been on the most intimate terms I hesitated a little before greeting him.

' "Why, dear Socrates," I said at last, "what in the world is the meaning of this? Why are you sitting here in such a frightful state? Have you committed some crime? Don't you know that you have been officially listed as dead, and that your family have gone into mourning and paid you their last devotions? Your children are now wards of the provincial court, and your poor wife, who has ruined her looks by crying herself nearly blind for you, is being worried by her parents to re-marry and put the family on its feet again. And here you turn up like a ghost! Really, it is most upsetting."

' "Oh, but Aristomenes," he replied, "if only you knew what extraordinarily unkind tricks Fortune can play on a man, you would never speak to me like that." He blushed and pulled his rags over his face, which had the unfortunate effect of uncovering the lower part of his body from the naval downwards.

'I could bear it no longer. Catching hold of him, I tried to pull him up from the ground, but he resisted me and groaned: "Leave me alone, leave me alone! Let Fortune have her way and enjoy her triumph over me for as long as she pleases." However, in the end he promised to come along, so I pulled off one of the two garments I was wearing and put it on him. Then I hurried him into a private bath, where I gave him a good scrubbing and took off several layers of filth. Finally, though exhausted myself, I managed to drag him along to my inn, where I made him lie down on a mattress and gave him plenty of food, plenty of wine and all the latest news from home. After a time he brightened up and we began to laugh and joke together and got very noisy —until all of a sudden he heaved a passionate sigh, beat his forehead with his fists and cried: "Oh, how miserable I am! It all started with my wanting to watch that much advertised gladiatorial display near Larissa. I had gone to Macedonia on business, as you probably know, and I was coming home after ten months with a tidy sum of money when, just before reaching Larissa, I was waylaid by bandits in a wild valley and robbed of practically everything but my life. Well, I managed to get away from them in the end and, almost at my last gasp, reached this town. Here I went to an inn run by a woman named Meroë. She was no longer young but extraordinarily attractive, and when I told her my sad story and explained how anxious I was to return home after my long absence, she pretended to be deeply sympathetic, cooked me a grand supper for which she charged me nothing, and afterwards pressed me to sleep with her. But from the moment that I first climbed into her bed my mind began to sicken and my will-power to fail. While I was still well enough to work for a living I gave her what little money I picked up by carrying bags, and then, as I grew weaker, I even presented her with the clothes that the kind robbers had left me to cover my nakedness. And now you see the condition into which bad luck and a charming woman have brought me."

' "Good God," I said, "you deserve all this and more, if possible, for having deserted your home and children and made yourself a slave to an old bitch like that!"

' "Hush, hush," he cried, a forefinger to his lips, looking wildly round in case we were overheard. "Say nothing against that marvellous woman, or your tongue may be your ruin."

' "Really!" I said. "Then what sort of inn-keeper can she be? From the way you talk, anyone would think that she was an absolute empress possessed of supernatural powers."

' "I tell you, Aristomenes," he answered in lugubrious tones, "my Meroë is able, if she pleases, to pull down the heavens or uplift the earth; to petrify the running stream or dissolve the rocky mountain; to raise the spectral dead or hurl the gods from their thrones; to quench the bright stars or illuminate the dark Land of Shadows."

' "Come, come, Socrates, this is the language of melodrama! Ring down the curtain for pity's sake and let me have the story in plain words."

'He answered: "Will a single instance of her powers convince you? Or must you have two, or more? Her ability to make men fall passionately in love with her—not only Greeks, but Indians, and eastern and western Egyptians and even, if she pleases, the mythical inhabitants of the Antipodes—this is only a slight sample of her powers. If you want to hear of the greater feats that she has performed in the presence of reliable witnesses, I will mention a few. Well, first of all, one of her lovers dared have an affair with another woman; she only needed to pronounce a single word and he was transformed into a beaver."

' "Why a beaver?"

' "Because the beaver, when alarmed by the hunt, bites off its

8

own testicles and leaves them lying by the river bank to put the hounds off the scent; and Meroë hoped that this would happen to him. Then there was the old inn-keeper, her neighbour and rival, whom she transformed into a frog; and now the poor fellow swims around in one of his own wine casks, or buries himself in the lees, croaking hoarsely to his old customers: 'Walk up! Walk up!' And the barrister who had once been briefed to prosecute her: his punishment was ram's horns, and now you can see him any day in court bleating his case and making learned rebuttals, with the horrible things curling from his forehead. Finally, when the wife of another of her lovers spoke nastily about her, Meroë condemned her to perpetual pregnancy by putting a charm on her womb that prevented the child from being born. This was about eight years ago; and now the poor woman swells bigger and bigger every month until you would believe her to be on the point of bearing a young elephant."

' "But when all these things came to be generally known?"

' "Why, then there was a public indignation meeting, at which it was decided to stone her to death the next day. This single day's grace was enough for Meroë, just as it was for Medea when King Creon ordered her to quit Corinth. Medea, you remember, set fire to her supplanter's bridal head-dress; soon the whole palace was alight, and the new bride and Creon himself were both burned to death. But Meroë, as she confided to me the next morning when drunk, dug a trench and performed certain rites over it, and by the dark power of the spirits that she invoked, she laid a spell on the gates and doors of every house in Hypata, so that for forty-eight hours nobody could come out into the streets, not even by tunnelling through a house wall. In the end

9

the whole town had to appeal to her from their windows, promising if she freed them never to molest her again but, on the contrary, always to defend her against harm; then she relented and removed the spell. But she took her revenge on the chairman of the meeting by spiriting away his house at midnight—walls, floors, foundations and all, with himself inside—to a town a hundred miles off. This place stood on the top of a waterless hill —the townspeople had to rely on rain-water for all purposes—and the buildings were so closely crowded together that there was no space to fit the house in; so she ordered it to be flung down outside the town gates."

' "My dear Socrates," I said, "these are certainly very wonderful and terrible stories and I am beginning to feel a little scared myself; in fact, really frightened. Suppose that your old woman were informed by her familiar spirits of all that we have been saying? But what do you say to going to sleep at once? The night is still young and we could make an early start tomorrow morning, getting as far away from this damned hole as our legs will take us."

'While I was speaking, poor Socrates suddenly fell asleep, and began snoring loudly: the natural effect of a good meal and plenty of wine on a man in his exhausted condition. I locked and barred the bedroom door, pushed the head of my bed against the hinge, shook up the mattress and lay down. For a time I could not sleep, because of Socrates's uncanny stories, but about midnight when I had comfortably dozed off, I was awakened by a sudden crash and the door burst open with greater force than if a pack of bandits had run at it with their shoulders. Lock, bar and hinges all gave way together and my bed, which was a worm-eaten old camp-bed, a bit short for me and with one damaged leg, was tossed into the air and fell upside down, pinning me underneath it.

'Emotions are contradictory things. You know how sometimes one weeps for joy: well now, after this terrible awakening, I found myself grinning and joking to myself: "Why, Aristomenes, you have been transformed into a tortoise!" Though knocked flat, I felt fairly safe under the bed and poked my head out sideways, like a tortoise peeping from under his shell, to watch what would happen next. Presently in came two terrible old women, one of them carried a lighted torch in her hand, the other a sponge and a drawn sword. They stood over Socrates, who was still asleep, and the one with the sword said to the other: "Look, sister Panthia, here is the man whom I chose to be my sweetheart —as condescendingly as the Goddess Diana chose the shepherd Endymion, or Olympian Jove chose that pretty little Ganymede. And a wonderfully hot time I gave him, too. But he never really returned my girlish passion and fooled me day and night. Now I have caught him not only spreading scandal about me but actually planning to run off! He fancies himself an Odysseus, does he, and expects me to howl and sob like Calypso when she awoke and found herself alone on her island?" Then she pointed at me and said: "And this creature peeping at us from under the bed is Aristomenes, who put him up to his mischief; but if he hopes to get safely away from me he is making the mistake of his life. I'll see that he repents too late of all the nasty insulting things he said about me earlier tonight, and of this new impertinent prying."

'I broke into a cold sweat and began to tremble so violently that my spasms made the bed rattle and dance over me. But Panthia said to Meroë—she could only have been Meroë: "Sister, shall we tear him to pieces at once, or shall we first tie strong twine around his privates and haul him up to a rafter and watch them being slowly cut through?"

' "No, no, dear, nothing of that sort! Let him be for awhile. My darling Socrates will be needing a sexton tomorrow to dig a little hole for him somewhere or other." Still speaking, she turned Socrates's head on the pillow and I watched her drive the sword up to the hilt through the left side of his neck. Blood spurted out, but she had a small bladder ready and caught every drop as it fell. Socrates's windpipe had been sliced through, but he uttered a sort of cry, or indistinct gurgle, and then was silent. To complete the sacrificial rite in what, I suppose, was her usual manner, this charming woman thrust her hand through the wound, deep into my poor friend's body, groped about inside and at length pulled out the heart. But Panthia took the sponge from her and stopped the gaping wound with it, muttering as she did so:

> *Sponge, sponge, from salt sea took,*
> *Pass not over the running brook!*

Then they came across the room to me, lifted away the bed, squatted over me and stared long and vigorously in my face.

'After this they left me; and no sooner had they crossed the threshold than the door rose up by itself and bar, lock and hinges miraculously refixed themselves in their original positions. I lay prostrate on the floor, naked, cold, and clammy with loathsome urine. "A new-born child must feel like this," I said to myself.

"Yet how different his prospects are! I have my whole life behind me, not in front of me. Yes, I'm as good as dead, like a criminal on his way to the cross. For what will become of me tomorrow morning when they find Socrates's corpse with his throat cut? Nobody will believe my story. 'You ought at least to have cried out for help if you were no match for the women,' they will tell me. 'A big, strong man like you, allowing a friend's throat to be cut before your eyes and not uttering a word!' And: 'How do you explain being left alive yourself? Why didn't they kill you, as a witness to the crime, to destroy all evidence against them? Your punishment for being alive to tell the tale must be death.'" My mind circled around what seemed to me at the time an almost posthumous chain of reasoning. But the night was now nearly over and at last I made up my mind to steal out of the inn before daylight and run off. I took up my bundle of belongings, drew the bolts of the door and put the key in its lock, but the honest old door which during the night had opened of its own accord to let my enemies in, now refused to let me out until I had turned the key this way and that a score of times and rattled hard at the handle. Once outside in the courtyard I called out: "Hey, porter, where are you? Open the gate, I want to be off before daybreak."

'He was lying naked on the bare ground beside the gate and answered, still half-asleep: "Who's that? Who's asking to get off at this time of night? Don't you know, whoever you are, that the roads are swarming with bandits? You may be tired of life, or you may have some crime on your conscience, but don't think that I'm such a pumpkin-headed idiot as to risk my life for yours by opening the gate and letting them in."

'I protested: "But it's almost morning. And anyhow, what harm could bandits do you? Certainly I think you are an idiot to be afraid of them. A team of ten professional wrestlers couldn't take anything worth having from a man as naked as you are."

'He grunted, turned over on his other side and asked drowsily: "How do I know that you haven't murdered the man you brought in yesterday afternoon—running off at this unearthly hour?"

'I shall never forget how I felt when he said this. I had a vision of Hell gaping for me and the old three-headed Dog snarling hungrily. I was convinced that Meroë had refrained from cutting my throat only because of her vicious intention to get me crucified. I went back to my room, determined to kill myself in my own way. But how was I to set about it? I should have to call on my bed to help me. So I began talking to it. I said coaxingly: "Listen, bed, dear little bed, the only true friend that I have left in this cruel world, my fellow-sufferer and the sole witness of my innocence—please bed, lend me some clean, wholesome instrument to put me out of my misery. For I long to die, dear bed!" Anticipating the bed's reply, I began to tug out a length of the rope with which its frame was corded, made one end fast to a rafter which stuck out above the window, and knotted the other into a running noose. I climbed on the bed, put my neck into the noose, and then kicked the bed away.

'My attempt at suicide was a failure. The rope was old and rotten and broke under my weight. Down I tumbled. I rolled gasping and choking against the body of Socrates which was lying on its mattress not far off. And at that instant in came the porter and shouted: "Hey you, you who a moment ago were rearing to get off in such frantic haste, what are you doing here, wallowing on that mattress and grunting like a pig?"

'Before I could answer, Socrates sprang up, as if suddenly awakened—whether by my fall or the porter's hoarse voice was not clear—and said sternly: "I have often heard travellers cursing at porters and their surly ways, and upon my word, they have every right to do so. I was tired out, and now this damned fellow bursts into the room and shouts at us—I am sure with the notion of stealing something while our attention is distracted—and spoils the deepest sleep that I have had for months."

'At the sound of Socrates's voice I jumped up in an ecstasy of relief and cried: "No, no, you are the best porter in the whole wide world, and honest as the day! But look, look, here's the man whom in your drunken daze just now you accused me of murdering—my friend, whom I love as dearly as a father or brother." I hugged and kissed Socrates, but he pushed me away crossly, saying: "Ugh, you stink like the bottom of a sewer!" and began offering unkind suggestions as to how I came to be in such a mess. In my confusion I made him some sort of lame excuse—I forget what—and turned the conversation as soon as possible. Catching hold of his hand, I cried: "What are we waiting for? Why not start at once and enjoy the freshness of the early morning air?"

' "Why not?" he sniffed. So I shouldered my bundle once more, settled my bill with the porter, and soon Socrates and I were out on the road.

'When we had gone some little distance from the town and the whole countryside stood out clear in the rising sun, I took a long careful look at Socrates's throat to see where, if at all, the sword had gone in. But nothing showed and I thought: "Here's Socrates as well as he ever was and without a scratch on him.

15

No wound, no sponge, not even a scar to show where the sword went burrowing in, only a couple of hours ago. What a vivid and fantastic dream! I was mad to drink so much." And I said aloud: "The doctors are right. If you stuff your stomach the last thing at night and then flood it with drink you are bound to have nightmares. That was why I slept so poorly last night after our celebration; I had such a frightful dream that I still feel as though I were spattered with human blood."

'Socrates laughed. "Blood indeed! The plain truth is that you soaked your bed and still stink of it. But I agree with you about the cause of nightmares. Last night I had a terrible one myself, now I come to remember it: I dreamed that my throat was cut and I had all the sensations of agony from the wound, and then someone pulled my heart out, which was such an unspeakable experience that it makes me feel ill even to think of it. My knees are trembling so violently now that I must sit down. Have you anything for me to eat?"

'I opened my haversack and took out some bread and cheese. "What about breakfast under that big plane-tree over there?" I asked.

'As we sat down together I noticed that his healthy looks had faded and that, though he ate ravenously, his face was turning the colour of boxwood. I must have looked almost as pale myself because the vision of that terrible pair of furies had repossessed my mind, and all the terrors of the night returned with a sudden rush. I took a small bite of bread, but it stuck in my gullet and I could neither swallow it nor cough it up. I grew more and more anxious. Would Socrates survive? By this time a number of people were about, and when two men are travelling together and one dies mysteriously by the roadside suspicion naturally falls upon the other. He ate a huge meal, a great deal of bread and nearly a whole cheese, and then complained of thirst. A few yards off, out of sight of the road, a brook ran gently past the roots of the tree. It was bright as silver, clear as crystal, placid as a pond. "Come here, Socrates," I said. "This looks better than milk. Have a good drink of it." He got up, walked along the shelving bank until he found a place that suited him, knelt down, bent his head forward, and begin to drink greedily. But hardly had his lips touched the water when the wound in his throat opened wide and the sponge dropped out into the water, followed by a small trickle of blood. He would have fallen in after it, if I had not caught at one leg and lugged him up to the top of the bank. He was stone dead when I got him there.

'After a hurried funeral-service I scraped away the sandy soil and laid him in his eternal resting place, there by the brookside. Then, trembling and sweating with fear, I ran across the fields, continually changing my direction, stumbling on and on, always making for the wildest and most desolate country . . .

'I never returned to Aegina. With a conscience as bad as any murderer's, I abandoned my business, my home, my wife, my children, and exiled myself to Aetolia. There I married again.'

*

That was the end of Aristomenes's story. His friend, who from the first had obstinately refused to believe a word of it, said to me at once: 'Well now, honestly, I have never in all my life heard so many nonsensical falsehoods told at one time. This is worse even than the stories the priests tell. You are an educated man, to judge by your dress and general appearance; surely you didn't believe a word?'

I answered: 'I refuse to admit, in theory, that anything in this world is impossible; to do so would be to set myself above the Power that pre-destines all human experience. And, in practice, things do occasionally happen to you and me, as to everybody else, which are so outrageous that we can hardly believe in them ourselves, and which any ordinary person would certainly reject as mere fiction. As a matter of fact, I do believe Aristomenes's story and I'm most grateful to him for having entertained me so well; I hardly noticed the roughness and steepness of the hill. And look over there: those must be the town gates! It seems almost impossible that I have got here so easily, not on horseback but towed along by my ears. My horse, I am sure, will gratefully second my hearty vote of thanks; Aristomenes has saved him a long, tiresome trot.'

Here our ways parted. They turned off towards a group of houses to the left of the road; I went straight on.

2

At Milo's House

I knocked at the door of the first inn I saw. An old woman opened it. 'Good afternoon, Mother,' I said. 'Is this the town of Hypata?'

She nodded without speaking.

'You know a man named Milo, one of the first citizens of the place?'

'Well, you might call him that, I suppose,' she answered with a grin, 'because his house is one of the first that you come to. It's built in the space, just outside the city walls, where the official auspices are taken.'

'Joking apart, would you mind letting me know what sort of a man he is and telling me how to reach his house?'

'Do you see that last row of windows facing the city, with a gate on the other side opening on a blind alley? That's where Milo lives—a fabulously rich old man and a disgrace to the whole district—the meanest, most miserly, dirtiest fellow you ever saw. He's a money-lender—high interest is the only thing that has ever interested him highly—and lives shut up there in that big bare house, gloating all day over his stacks of coin. Nobody lives with him except his unfortunate wife and one slave-girl; and when, very occasionally, he does go out, he dresses like a common beggar.'

As I rode off I laughed to myself: 'My friend Demeas has certainly given me a valuable letter of introduction. While I'm staying with Milo I need not at least be afraid of smoky fires or pervasive kitchen smells.'

Soon I reached the gate at which the old woman had pointed and found it stoutly barred. I banged at it and shouted 'Hullo, hullo there!'

After a time the slave-girl came out and asked: 'Was it you who made that dreadful noise?'

'It was I who knocked.'

'Well, where's your gold or silver? You must be the only man in Hypata who doesn't know our terms: no cash advanced, except on a pledge of equal weight in precious metal.'

'Not at all the way to speak to visitors,' I said severely. 'Is your master at home?'

'Of course he is. But what's your business?'

'I have come with a letter of introduction to him from Demeas the Corinthian.'

'Wait here, while I give him your message.' She barred the gate again and went back into the house. Presently she reappeared: 'My master says, will you please come in?'

I found Milo in his dining-room, stretched out on a very narrow couch and just beginning his dinner. His wife sat perched precariously at his feet.

He waved a hand at the almost bare table and said: 'Just in time for a meal.'

I thanked him and handed him the letter, which he hurriedly read. 'I'm grateful to Demeas,' he said, 'for giving me an opportunity to meet so fine a young man as yourself.' Then, apparently because there was dinner enough only for two, he sent his wife away and asked me to sit down in her place. Naturally I hesitated, but he caught hold of my tunic and steered me to the seat. 'Sit down, sit down, my lord,' he said. 'You will excuse the inconvenient shortage of chairs and other furniture. It's a necessary precaution against burglary.'

I sat down.

'I guessed at once from the neatness of your dress and the correctness of your behaviour that you must be a man of good family, and from Demeas's letter I now see that I was right; but please don't despise our little cottage. The spare bedroom which adjoins this room is at your disposal; if you can manage to make yourself comfortable there you will be doing us a great honour, and at the same time earning credit such as the famous Theseus earned—I notice that your father's name is Theseus too—when he condescended to accept the hospitality of poor old Hecale.'

Before I had the opportunity of eating anything he called the girl: 'Fotis, take this gentleman's bag into the spare bedroom and lay it carefully down somewhere. Then fetch a towel from the cupboard, and a little flask of toilet-oil, and take him along to the nearest public baths. He must be hot and tired after his long journey.'

I saw at once how extraordinarily mean Milo was, but decided to humour him. I said: 'Please don't trouble about the oil or the towel. I always carry that sort of thing in my bags, and there's no need for your girl to escort me, either: I can easily find my way to the baths. My only anxiety at the moment is for my horse. He deserves a reward for having carried me here so willingly. Please, Fotis, would you mind buying him a good feed of hay and oats? Here's the money.'

I went into the yard and lounged about until my horse had been fed and Fotis had arranged my things neatly in the bedroom. Then I went towards the baths, first visiting the provision market to buy something for my supper. There was plenty of fish for sale, and though I was first asked two hundred drachmae* a basket, eventually I beat a fishmonger down to twenty, paid him and walked off with my purchase. As I left the market, a man named Pythias, who had been one of my fellow-students at Athens, happened to be walking in the same direction. He recognized me first and gave me a most friendly embrace.

'Why, if it isn't my friend Lucius! Heavens, what years it seems since we studied together under old Dositheus! And from that day to this I have never heard the least news of you. Tell me, my dear fellow, what in the world brings you here?'

'We must have a long talk tomorrow. But, Pythias, what's this I see? A magistrate's robe, and a posse of constables armed with truncheons marching behind you? My heartiest congratulations!'

He explained: 'I am now Inspector-General of Markets, so if I can be of any service in helping you to buy something for your supper, please call on me.'

---

* There were 25 denarii, or drachmae, in an *aureus*, a gold coin of about the value of an English sovereign or approximately $2.80 in U. S. currency.

'How kind of you! But I have just bought myself a few pounds of fish.'

'Let me have a look at them.' He took the basket from me, shook the fish about so that he could inspect them more closely, and then asked: 'Do you mind telling me what you paid for this refuse?'

'It took me a long time to beat the fishmonger down to twenty drachmae.'

'Which fishmonger? Point him out to me.'

I pointed back at a little old man seated in a corner of the market. Pythias at once began abusing him in his severest official tones: 'Hey, you, is this the way to treat the Inspector-General's friends, or for that matter any visitor at all who comes to buy in the provision market? Asking no less than twenty drachmae, twenty drachmae indeed, for these absurd little tiddlers! Hypata is the most prosperous town in all Thessaly, but with fellows like you forcing up food prices to such a preposterous height we might as well be living in the rocky wilderness. And don't think that you're going to escape with a mere reprimand. By Heaven, I intend to keep you rogues in check, so long as I hold my present appointment.'

He emptied the basket on the ground, ordering one of his constables to jump on the fish and squash them into paste on the pavement. Beaming moral satisfaction with his own severity, Pythias advised me to go home. 'All is well now, Lucius,' he said cheerfully. 'You need say no more. I am satisfied that the little wretch has been sufficiently humiliated.'

My knowledgeable old fellow-student! Flabbergasted at having lost both my supper and my money as the result of his kind intervention, I went on to the baths where I spent the afternoon resting.

At nightfall I returned to Milo's hospitable house, and had not been long in my bedroom before Fotis came in. 'The master is expecting you at the supper-table,' she said.

Remembering Milo's frugal habits I sent him a polite message, begging to be excused: 'Explain to him, please, that I'm so tired after my ride that I need sleep more than food.'

Fotis took my message in and presently Milo himself appeared, grabbed hold of my wrist and politely tried to drag me off with him to the supper room. 'No, no, really, I'm not hungry,' I protested.

'I won't stir from here until you consent to come with me,' he declared, still clutching my wrist and raising his other hand as if he were taking an oath in court. So I had to give in, and he led me again to the same shabby old couch, where he seated me at the foot-end, before lying down himself. Supper had not yet been served.

'Now tell me,' he said. 'How is our mutual friend Demeas? All's well with him, I hope? And how is his wife? Are his children in good health? Any trouble with the servants?'

I answered him in detail. Next, he demanded an exact account of the business affairs that I had come to settle in Hypata, and again I satisfied his curiosity. Still no supper. Then he wanted to know all about conditions in my native province, and asked for full biographical details of all our leading citizens. When he finally started cross-examining me on the personal affairs of our Governor-General, I began to nod—the journey had been wearisome enough but this talk was worse—and kept stopping short in the middle of sentences, or getting my words mixed up. He saw that I was dead tired and kindly allowed me to go to bed.

How glad I was to escape from the smelly old bore! Though I had dined only on conversation, the heavy sleep that was now overpowering me would be as welcome as a heavy meal. I stumbled along to my bedroom and slept like a log.

*

The next morning I awoke early and rose at once. I have an almost morbid interest in everything queer and out of the way, and I remembered that here I was in the heart of Thessaly, a province notorious as the native home of magic and sorcery; and in the very city, too, which had been the scene of Aristomenes's story. So I looked around me with more than usual excitement, carefully examining everything within view. How could I be sure that anything in the whole city was what it seemed to be? Obsessed with the idea that the evil power of witches might have been everywhere at work, I wondered whether the stones I kicked against were really, perhaps, petrified men, and whether the birds I heard singing were people in feathered disguise—like Procne, Tereus and Philomela in the myth—and I began to entertain doubts about the trees around the house, and even about the faucets through which the fountains played. I was quite prepared when I visited the town to see the statues and the images of gods step from their pedestals, or hear the walls speak, have strange news told me by oxen and other cattle; or even to be granted an oracle from the sun in the sky.

In this stupid and overwrought mood, though nowhere finding the least justification for my suspicions, I wandered all round the town from door to door, and at last found myself once again in the provision market. A woman came by with a crowd of servants in attendance; her long jewelled ear-rings and the jewel-studded embroidery on her dress showing her to be of high rank. At her side walked a dignified old man who cried out as soon as he saw me: 'Bless my soul! Here's Lucius.' He came forward and embraced me, and then going back to the lady whispered something in her ear, after which he came forward again and challenged me: 'Come, come, Lucius, why don't you go along and give her an affectionate kiss?'

'I could never take such a liberty with a lady to whom I have not the honour of being introduced,' I stammered, with a deep blush, staying where I was and looking down at my feet. She was staring attentively at me. 'Really,' she exclaimed, 'the resemblance is extraordinary. Salvia had exactly the same slenderness and upright carriage, the same rosy cheeks and delicate skin, the same yellow hair neatly dressed, the same alert, shining grey eyes that used to remind me of an eagle's, the same graceful way of walking.' Then she said: 'I nursed you as a baby, Lucius. But there's nothing so strange about that, because your dear mother and I were not only maternal cousins (the celebrated Plutarch was our grandfather) but foster-sisters, brought up together in the same house. In fact, the only difference in rank between us is that she married a nobleman, I married a commoner. Byrrhaena is my name—your mother must often have mentioned it when telling you about your early childhood. You must come to stay with me at once, and treat my house as your home.'

By this time I had recovered from my embarrassment. I explained that nothing would have given me greater pleasure than to accept her invitation, but that unfortunately I was now Milo's guest and to leave his house for another in the same town would be extremely discourteous. 'But I shall be most happy to see as much of you as my obligations to Milo permit: whenever I come into the town I shall call on you without fail.'

Byrrhaena lived only a short distance away, and I was soon admiring the inner courtyard of her house, with its ornamental pillars at the four corners, surmounted by winged Victories. The figures were extraordinarily life-like, each hovering palm-branch in hand on outspread wings, her dewy feet so lightly poised on a motionless globe that you would never have guessed that they were carved from the same block of stone—they seemed to be on the point of soaring off again. But a sculptured group of Parian marble which stood in the very centre of the court interested me still more and put everything else into proper perspective. It was a Diana with hounds; wonderful work. The Goddess seemed to be striding towards you as you entered, her tunic blown back by the wind, and awing you by the majesty of her presence. The brace of hounds that she held in leash were balanced on their hind legs, ready to bound off in a flash. They looked so menacing with their fierce eyes, pricked ears, dilated nostrils and snarling jaws, that if any other dog near by had suddenly barked you would have thought for the moment that the sound came from their white marble throats. Behind the Goddess was a cavern, its entrance carpeted in moss, grass, fallen leaves and brushwood, with shrubs and creepers growing here and there; the back was a highly polished slab which mirrored her shoulders; and under the lip hung apples and grapes, ripe for eating, so exquisitely carved that you fancied yourself in mid-August. And when you looked down at the rivulet which seemed to spring and ripple from the

27

Goddess's footprints, you found it as life-like as the clusters of grapes. But this was not all: from the tangle of branches appeared the face of Actaeon peeping eagerly out, already half-transformed into a stag—as also showed in the reflection of the scene carved on the surface of the water—which was his punishment for spying on the Goddess when she was about to bathe.

As I was examining the group with delighted curiosity, Byrrhaena said: 'Cousin, this is all for you.' Then she sent off the servants and said to me in a low voice: 'In the name of this Goddess, the Goddess of Chastity, dear Lucius, I beg you to be on your guard. I find it difficult to express my anxiety for you in your present situation; but please understand that my feelings for you are almost as tender as if you were my own son. I must give you a warning, a very solemn warning, against Milo's wife Pamphilë who, I fear, will try to fascinate you by magic. She is a well-known witch and said to be a past mistress of every sort of necromancy: so much so, that merely by breathing on twigs, stones and so on,

> *She can transfer the light, the starry sky,*
> *To the dark depths of Hell and thus restore*
> *The reign of primal Chaos . . .*

She falls in love with every handsome young man she sets eyes on, and at once decides to possess him. She begins her campaign with flattering advances and as a rule makes a quick conquest, after which she binds him to her with the unbreakable fetters of lust; but whenever she meets with resistance, her rage and hatred are so violent that she thinks nothing of petrifying her victim on the spot, or transforming him into a ram or a bull or a wild beast, or killing him out of hand. You can imagine my concern on your

28

behalf, because Pamphilë is a nymphomaniac and you're exactly the type of good-looking young man that would most attract her.'

But I was naturally adventurous, and as soon as Byrrhaena mentioned the black art, which always held a peculiar attraction for me, so far from feeling inclined to be on my guard against Pamphilë I had an irresistible impulse to study magic under her, however much money it might cost me, and take a running leap into the dark abyss against which I had been warned. My mind had taken fire; I disengaged my hand from Byrrhaena's almost as though I were snapping a chain, and left her with an abrupt goodbye. I set off at a run for Milo's house, and as I raced madly through the streets I was saying to myself: 'Now for it, Lucius! But have your wits about you, because here at last you have a chance: your secret ambition has always been to study the laws of magic.* Forget your childish terrors. Face this new undertaking boldly and practically—though of course you must avoid any entanglement with Pamphilë. To go to bed with your worthy host's wife would be a disgraceful failure in good manners. On the other hand, there's no reason why you shouldn't try to seduce Fotis; the girl is not only beautiful, lively and amusing but already half in love with you. Last night when you went to bed, she led you to your room, turned your sheets down, tucked you tenderly in, then gave you a charming good-night kiss and showed quite plainly how sorry she was to leave you. Remember how she kept stopping on her way to the door and looking back at you? The very best of luck to you, then, Lucius; but, whatever may come of it, good or bad, my advice is: go for Fotis.' My mind was now made up, and when I reached Milo's house I marched in as

* I read *tabulis* for *fabulis*.

confidently as a Senator leading the Ayes into the division lobby.

I found nobody at home but my charming Fotis who was preparing pork-rissoles for her master and mistress, while the appetizing smell of haggis-stew drifted to my nostrils from an
earthenware casserole on the stove. She wore a neat white house-
dress, gathered in below the breasts with a red silk band, and as
she alternately stirred the casserole and shaped the rissoles with
her pretty hands, the twisting and turning made her whole body
quiver seductively.

The sight had so powerful an effect on me that for awhile I
stood rooted in admiration; and so did something else. As last I
found my voice. 'Dear Fotis,' I said, 'how daintily, how charm-
ingly you stir that casserole: I love watching you wriggle your
hips. And what a wonderful cook you are! The man whom you
allow to poke his finger into your little casserole is the luckiest
fellow alive. That sort of stew would tickle the most jaded palate.'

She retorted over her shoulder: 'Go away, you scoundrel; keep
clear of my little cooking stove! If you come too near even when
the fire is low, a spark may fly out and set you on fire; and when
that happens nobody but myself will be capable of putting the
flames out. A wonderful cook, am I? Yes, I certainly know how
to tickle a man's . . . well, his palate, if you care to call it that,
and how to keep things nicely on the boil—between the sheets as
well as on a kitchen-stove.'

She turned and laughed at me. I did not leave the kitchen until
I had taken a careful look at her from head to foot. But for the
moment I need only write about her head; the truth is that I have
an obsession about hair. Whenever I meet a pretty woman, the
first thing that catches my eye is her hair; I make a careful mental

picture of it to carry home and brood over in private. This habit of mine I justify on a sound logical principle: that the hair is the most important and conspicuous feature of the body, and that its natural brilliance does for the head what gaily coloured clothes do for the trunk. In fact, it does a great deal more. You know how women, when they want to display their beauty to the full, shed their embroidered wraps and step out of their expensive dresses, and proudly reveal themselves with nothing on at all, aware that even the brightest gold tissue has less effect on a man than the delicate tints of a woman's naked body. But—and here you must excuse a horrible idea which I hope nobody will ever put into practice—if you shaved the head of even the most beautiful woman alive and so deprived her face of its natural setting, then I don't care whether she originally floated down from Heaven, and was reborn from sea-foam like the Goddess Venus—I don't even care whether she were Venus herself, with every one of the Graces and Cupids in attendance, Venus dripping with precious balsam and fragrant as cinnamon, and with the famous girdle of love clasped around her waist—the fact is, that her baldness would leave her completely without attraction even for so devoted a husband as the God Vulcan.

What joy it is to see hair of a beautiful colour caught in the full rays of the sun, or shining with a milder lustre and constantly varying its shade as the light shifts. Golden at one moment, at the next honey-coloured; or black as a raven's wing, but suddenly taking on the pale blueish tints of a dove's neck-feathers. Give it a gloss with spikenard lotion, part it neatly with a finely toothed comb, catch it up with a ribbon behind—and the lover will make it a sort of mirror to reflect his own delighted looks. And oh, when hair is bunched up in a thick luxurious mass on a woman's head or, better still, allowed to flow rippling down her neck in profuse curls! I must content myself by saying baldly that such is the glory of a woman's hair that though she may be wearing the most exquisite clothes and the most expensive jewellery in existence, with everything else in keeping, she cannot look even moderately well dressed unless she has done her hair in proper style.

Fotis, I grant, needed no expert knowledge of hairdressing: she could even indulge an apparent neglect of the art. Her way was to let her long, thick hair hang loosely down her neck, braiding the ends together and catching them up again with a broad ribbon to the top of her head; which was the exact spot where, unable to restrain myself a moment longer, I now printed a long passionate kiss.

She glanced back at me over her shoulder, and her keen eyes seemed to look straight into my heart. 'Oh, you schoolboy!' she said. 'Always greedy for anything sweet, without a thought for the bitter aftertaste. Today I may taste like honey, but I give you fair warning that before long you may feel me burning like gall at the back of your throat.'

'What do I care, you beautiful thing? I give you leave to lay me at full length on this fire and grill me brown, so long as you promise to soothe my agony with only a single kiss.' I threw my arms around her and kissed her again and again until she yielded. Then she returned my embraces with answering passion. Her breath smelled as sweet as cinnamon, and when she put her lips to mine she slipped the tip of her tongue in between them, which was like sampling nectar in Heaven. I gasped out: 'Oh, Fotis, this is killing me! Unless you take pity on me I'm as good as dead.'

Smothering me with kisses, she answered: 'You needn't worry about dying, if you can hold out a little longer. I love you, I'm utterly yours. At torch-time tonight I'll come to your bedroom. Now go away, and keep in good condition for tonight's battle. I'm going to fight you all night long with deadly courage.'

After a good deal more in the same strain, we parted; and about noon a complimentary present arrived from Byrrhaena. It consisted of a fat pig, a brace and a half of chickens, and a jar of vintage wine. I called Fotis. 'Look, darling,' I said. 'We didn't remember to invoke the God of Wine, did we? But he always aids and abets the Goddess of Love, so he's come of his own accord. Let's put the whole of this jar aside for tonight. It will rid us of all embarrassment and supply us with the energy we need for our work. In provisioning the ship of love for a night's cruise, one needs to make certain of two things only: that there's enough oil for the lamp and wine for the cup.'

I spent the afternoon at the baths, and on my return found that my two slaves, who had been following me on foot from Corinth, had just arrived and that Milo was expecting me to join him and Pamphilë at their tiny supper table. Fotis had put part of my gift to immediate use and forced Milo to be generous for once. A couch had been found for me, and with Byrrhaena's warning fresh in my mind I settled back on it so as to keep as far as possible out of Pamphilë's view. But every now and then I stole a frightened glance in her direction, as if she were the deadly Lake of No Birds; but Fotis was waiting on us, so most of the time I followed her with my eyes and felt completely at my ease.

It was now growing dark and the table lamp was lighted. Pam-

33

philë studied the wick * and pronounced: 'Tomorrow it will rain heavily.'

'How do you know that? Milo asked.

'Why, by the lamp.'

Milo laughed: 'We are evidently entertaining a famous Sibyl unawares. Every evening she surveys the universe from the watch tower of her lamp, and foretells what sort of a trip the sun is going to enjoy next day.'

I broke in: 'But is it really to be wondered at that this flame, though small and artificially lighted, should retain sqme memory of its father the sun, the prime source of fire, and so be able to foretell, by divine instinct, what is about to happen in the skies? I regard this as an elementary type of divination, compared with what I came across at Corinth recently. A Chaldaean astrologer had put the whole city in a flutter by his accurate answers to questions he was asked. For a fee he would tell people exactly on what day to marry, or on what day to lay the foundation-stone if they wanted a building to stand for ever, or on what day to conclude a business deal, or on what day to set out on a journey by land or sea. When I questioned him about this expedition of mine, his answers were strange and rather contradictory: he told me, for instance, that it would make me very famous and that I should write a long book about it which nobody, however, would take seriously.'

Milo laughed again: 'What did this Chaldaean of yours look like, and what did he call himself?'

'He was tall and rather dark. His name was Diophanes.'

'The very man who once came here to Hypata and made the

* A cauliflower in the wick portended rain.

same sort of predictions! He earned a lot of money, a small fortune, in fact, but in the end fate proved, well, unpropitious—or, if you like, malicious—or downright vicious. It happened like this. One day Diophanes stood in the middle of a crowd of people, all wanting to hear their own peculiar fates. A business man named Cerdo had just asked him to name a lucky day for travelling. Diophanes gave him the answer and Cerdo opened his purse and began counting out the fee of a hundred drachmae. At that moment a young nobleman came up from behind and tugged at Diophanes's robe. He turned round and they embraced affectionately. "Sit down, do sit down!" said Diophanes, and forgetting all about his pretended omniscience he said: "What a pleasure this is! I never expected to see you in these parts. When did you arrive?" The nobleman answered: "Only last night but, my dear fellow, you must explain your sudden departure from Euboea* and tell me what sort of a journey you had." Then Diophanes, thoroughly off his guard, cried out: "If only all my enemies and ill-wishers could meet with as much bad luck as I did on my way here. Odysseus's ten years' wanderings on his return from Troy were nothing to it. To begin with, our ship was struck by a sudden gale as soon as she put to sea, and tossed about from whirlpool to whirlpool, then both her rudders snapped, and finally just as we made the Thessalian coast she sank like a stone. Some of us managed to struggle ashore, but with the loss of all our belongings, and we had to beg or borrow money to help us on the next stage of our journey. And, as though all this had not been enough, we were attacked by bandits, and my brother Arignotus, who showed fight, was murdered before my very eyes."

* Euboea is separated from Thessaly only by a narrow channel.

'While Diophanes was still telling his sad story, Cerdo picked up his money again and slipped off, and it was only then that he came to himself and realized that he'd given away the whole show; for we were all shouting with laughter. Nevertheless, Lord Lucius, I sincerely hope that what this celebrated Chaldaean told you was the truth, though you may be the only man to whom he ever told it, and that you will continue to have a pleasant and prosperous journey.'

I groaned silently as Milo went maundering on. I was vexed with myself for having started him on a train of anecdotes at a time like this: I saw that I was in danger of losing the best part of the night and all the pleasures that it promised me. At last I yawned shamelessly and said: 'Please don't trouble to tell me any more about Diophanes. It's all the same to me what happens to him or where his bad luck carries him and, honestly, I don't care whether the waves or the bandits get the bigger share of his earnings the next time he's forced to disgorge. The fact is that I'm still suffering from the effects of my day-before-yesterday's ride and feel quite worn out. Please forgive me if I say good night at once and go straight to sleep.'

I rose and went to my bedroom. On the way I noticed that the palliasse which my two slaves shared in the inner courtyard had been moved as far as possible away from my door—evidently Fortis had taken this precaution against their over-hearing our love talk that night—and, inside, I found a feast waiting for me. My bedside table was covered with little dishes of tasty food saved from supper and generous cups of wine, with only just enough room left at the top for the necessary tempering with water, and there was a bell-mouthed decanter, handy for pouring out more wine. The scene suggested a gladiator's breakfast on the morning of a big fight.

By the time that I was in bed, Fotis, who had succeeded in getting her mistress off to sleep quickly, appeared in the doorway with a bunch of roses. A rose in full bloom was tucked between her breasts. She glided towards me, kissed me firmly, wove some of the roses into a garland for my head and sprinkled the bed with the petals of the rest. Then she took a cup of wine, tempered it with hot water and put it to my lips; but before I could drain it she gently pulled it away and, gazing fixedly at me, took little sips at it, like a dove drinking, until it was empty. This performance she repeated two or three times.

The wine went to my head; but it also went to my thighs. I grew restive and, like a fallen soldier displaying a wound, pulled off my nightshirt and gave Fotis visible proof of my impatience. 'Have pity on me,' I said, 'and come quickly to my rescue. As you see I'm well armed and ready for the merciless battle to which you challenged me, the sort of battle in which no herald can intervene to part the combatants. Since the first of Cupid's sharp arrows lodged in my heart this morning, I have been standing to arms all day, and now my bow is strung so tight that I'm afraid something will snap if the Advance isn't sounded pretty soon. However, if you want my battle-ardour to burn more fiercely still, you darling, let your hair down so that it ripples all over your neck and shoulders.'

She snatched away the plates and dishes, pulled off every stitch of clothing, untied her hair and tossed it into happy disorder with a shake of her head. There she stood, transformed into a living statue: the Love-goddess rising from the sea. The flushed hand

37

with which she pretended to screen her mount of Venus showed that she was well aware of the resemblance; certainly it was not held there from modesty.

'Now fight,' she challenged me. 'And you must fight hard, because I shall not retreat one inch, nor turn my back on you. Come on face to face if you're a man, strike home, do your very worst! Take me by storm, kill me, and die in the breach. No quarter given or accepted.'

She climbed into bed, flung one leg over me as I lay on my back, and crouching down like a wrestler, assaulted me with rapid plungings of her thighs and passionate wrigglings of her supple hips. My head swam. It was as though the apple-bough of love had bent down over me and I was gorging myself with the fruit until I could gorge no more; and at last with overpowered senses and dripping limbs Fotis and I fell into a simultaneous clinch, gasping out our lives.

However, after dosing ourselves with more wine, we presently revived and engaged in another style of unarmed combat; and continuously renewed our sleepless struggle, with intervals for refreshment, until daybreak.

This was the first night of many that we spent in the same exhilarating though exhausting sport.

3

The Story of Thelyphron

ONE DAY Byrrhaena sent me a pressing invitation to a supper party, and though I made various excuses she refused to accept any of them. There was nothing for it but to go to Fotis, as one might approach the priestess of an oracular shrine, and ask her advice. She now resented my straying a yard from her company, but I was generously excused my military duties that evening and granted a short pass. However, she warned me: 'Listen, darling! Don't stay too long at the party. Come back as soon as you can, for in the early hours Hypata is terrorized by a gang of Mohocks who think it amusing to murder whoever happens to be passing by and to leave the streets strewn with corpses. They are members of the first families in the town, and the nearest Roman barracks are some miles away, so nothing can be done to end the nuisance. You are in particular danger of being attacked, because these Mohocks have no respect for foreigners. And they'll be all the keener to practise their swordmanship on you when they see that you're dressed as a nobleman.'

'You needn't worry, dearest Fotis,' I told her. 'That supper party has far less attraction for me than our love-banquets here; so I promise to shorten your anxiety by coming home as soon as I can. Besides, I shall wear this sword, which I know very well how to handle in self-defence, and take one of my slaves along with me, too.'

The supper party proved to be a regular banquet. Byrrhaena was the leading hostess of Hypata and everybody was there who was anybody. The tables were made of polished citrus wood richly inlaid with ivory; the couches were upholstered in cloth of gold; each of the large wine-cups, though all were of different workmanship, was a masterpiece of its kind—whether of glass encrusted with fine cameos, or cut rock-crystal, or highly polished silver, or gold, or beautifully carved amber, or whether hollowed from some semi-precious stone. In short, think of anything impossible in the way of cups, and there you had it.

A swarm of liveried waiters darting deftly about kept the tables well supplied with food, while pretty curly-headed pages in handsome clothes ran up and down replenishing those jewels of cups with vintage wines of great age.

It was growing dark, so the lights were brought in, and the conversation began to get lively. Byrrhaena turned to me and asked: 'Well, cousin, what do you think of our beloved Thessaly? So far as I know we are a long way in advance of all other countries in the world, if you judge by temples, baths and other public buildings, and our private houses are incomparably better furnished. Besides, anyone who visits our town is at perfect liberty to choose what sort of time he will have: if he is on business he can enjoy all the bustle of Rome at our Exchanges, and if he wants a thorough rest there are houses here as peaceful as any country manor. Hypata, in fact, has come to be the chief holiday centre of the province.'

I agreed with her warmly. 'Nowhere in all my travels have I ever felt more at home than I do here—though I suppose I ought to qualify this by admitting my terror of the mysterious arts of your local witches, against which there seems to be no known means of protecting oneself. I am told that not even the dead are respected by them—that they rifle graves and funeral pyres in search of bones, and cut pieces of flesh from unburned corpses to use for blasting their neighbours' lives. And that some of these old sorceresses, the moment they smell death anywhere about, run off at top speed and mutilate the corpse before the mourners arrive.'

'There's no doubt at all about that,' said a man at my table, 'and, what's more, they don't even spare the living. Not long ago a fellow whose name I needn't mention got dreadfully bitten about the face by that hell pack.'

An uncontrolled burst of laughter greeted this remark, and everyone turned round to look at a guest reclining inconspicuously at a corner table. The laughter went on and on, and the man, thoroughly embarrassed and muttering angrily to himself, was on the point of walking out when Byrrhaena signalled to him to remain where he was.

'No, no, my dear Thelyphron,' she protested. 'You mustn't rush off like that. Show your usual good humour and tell us that adventure of yours once again; I am anxious that my cousin Lucius, who is as dear to me as a son, should have the pleasure of hearing it from your own lips. It is a wonderful story.'

He answered, still very angry: 'My lady Byrrhaena, you are always the perfect hostess and your goodness of heart never fails; but the insolence of my fellow-guests is past endurance.'

Byrrhaena told him firmly that he would be doing her a great disservice if he went against her wishes, however disagreeable he might find the task that she had set him. So he made a little heap of the coverings of his couch and propped himself up on it with his left elbow: then with his right hand he signalled for attention in oratorical style, protruding the forefinger and middle finger, pointing the thumb upward and folding down the two remaining fingers for good luck.

This was the story he told:

'While I was still a University student at Miletus I came over to attend the Olympian Games. Afterwards, feeling a strong desire to visit northern Greece, I travelled through most of Thessaly. One unlucky day I arrived at Larissa, having run through nearly all the money I had brought with me, and while I was wandering up and down the streets, wondering how to refill my purse, I saw a tall old man standing on a stone block in the middle of the market place. He was making a public announcement at the top of his voice, offering a large reward to anyone who would stand guard over a corpse that night.

'I asked a bystander: "What is the meaning of this? Are the corpses of Larissa in the habit of running away?"

' "Hush, my lad," he answered. "I can see that you are very much of a stranger here, else you would realize that you are in Thessaly where witches are in the habit of gnawing bits of flesh off dead men's faces for use in their magical concoctions."

' "Oh, I see! And would you mind telling me what this guardianship of the dead involves?"

' "Not at all. It means watching attentively the whole night, one's eyes fixed on the corpse without a single sideways glance. You see, these abominable women have the power of changing their shape at pleasure: they turn into birds or dogs or mice, or even flies—disguises that would pass scrutiny even in a Court of Law, and by daylight too—and then charm the guardians asleep. I won't try to tell you all the extraordinarily ingenious tricks that they use when they want to indulge their beastly appetites; at any rate, the usual reward of from a hundred to a hundred and fifty drachmae for the night's job is hardly worth the risk. Oh—I was almost forgetting to tell you that if next morning the guardian fails to hand over the corpse to the undertakers in exactly the same condition as he found it, he is obliged by Law to have bits cut from his own face to supply whatever is missing."

'That did not frighten me. I boldly told the crier that he need not repeat the announcement. "I'm ready to undertake the job," I said. "What fee do they offer?"

' "A thousand drachmae, because this is a job that calls for more than usual alertness against those terrible harpies: the deceased was the son of one of our first citizens."

' "All this nonsense leaves me unmoved," I said. "I am a man of iron, I never trouble to go to sleep, and I have sharper eyesight than Lynceus, the *Argo's* look-out man. In fact, I may say that I am all eyes, like the giant Argus whom Jupiter once put in charge of the nymph Io."

'I had hardly finished recommending myself for the job before the old man hurried me along to a big house with its gates locked and barred. He took me through a small side door and along

43

corridors until I reached a bedroom with closed shutters, where a woman in deep black sat wailing loudly in the half-light.

'The crier went up to her and said: "This man undertakes to guard your husband's body to-night; and he agrees to the fee."

'She pushed back the hair that shaded her beautiful grief-stricken face, and implored me to be vigilant at my post.

' "You need have no anxiety, Madam, if you make it worth my while afterwards."

'Nodding absently, she got up and led me into an adjoining room, where she showed me the corpse lying on a slab and wrapped in a pure white linen shroud. After another fit of weeping, she called in seven mourners as witnesses, also her secretary who had his writing materials with him. Then she said: "Gentlemen, I call you to witness that the nose is undamaged, so are both ears, the eyes are still in their sockets, the lips are whole, the chin the same." She touched each feature as she mentioned it, and the secretary wrote out the inventory, which the witnesses signed and sealed.

'I asked her as she was going away: "Will you be good enough, Madam, to see that I have everything I need for my vigil to-night?"

' "What sort of things?"

' "A good large lamp with enough oil in it to last until daybreak; pots of wine; warm water for tempering; a cup; and a plateful of cold meat and vegetables left over from your supper."

'She shook her head angrily: "What an absurd request! Cooked meat and vegetables indeed in this house of mourning, where no fire has been lighted for days! Do you imagine that you have come here for a jolly supper party? You are expected to mourn and weep like the rest of us." Then, turning to her maid: "Myrrhina, fill the lamp, bring it back at once, shut the door and leave the guardian to his task."

'All alone with the corpse, I fortified my eyes for their vigil by rubbing them hard and kept up my spirits by singing. Twilight shaded into night, and night grew deeper and deeper, blacker and blacker, until my usual bed-time had passed and it was close on midnight. I had been only a little uncomfortable at first, but now I was beginning to feel thoroughly frightened when all of a sudden a weasel squeezed in through a hole in the door, stopped close by me and fixed her eyes intently on mine. The boldness of the creature was most disconcerting, but I managed to shout out: "Get away from here, you filthy little beast, or I'll break your neck. Run off and play hide and seek with your friends the mice. Do you hear me? I mean it."

'She turned tail and skipped out of the room, but as she did so, a sudden deep sleep stole over me and dragged me down with it into bottomless gulfs of dream. I fell on the floor and lay there so dead asleep that not even Delphic Apollo could have readily decided which of us two was the corpse; the body on the slab or the body on the floor. It was almost as though I had actually died and my corpse had been left without a guardian.

'At last the darkness began to fade and

"The sentries of the Crested Watch 'gan shout"

—crowing so loud that I eventually awoke, picked up the lamp and ran in terror to the slab. I pulled back the shroud and examined the corpse's face closely; to my huge relief I found it unmutilated. Almost at once the poor widow came running in, still weeping, with the seven witnesses behind her. She threw herself on the corpse and after kissing it again and again had the lamp brought close to make sure that all was well. Then she turned and called: "Philodespotus, come here!"

'Her steward appeared. "Philodespotus, pay this young man his fee at once. He has kept watch very well."

'As he counted me out the money she said: "Many thanks, young man, for your loyal services; they have earned you the freedom of this house."

'Delighted with my unexpected good luck, I gently tossed the bright gold coins up and down in my hand and answered: "I am much obliged to you, Madam. I shall be only too pleased to help you out again, whenever you may need my services."

'These words were scarcely out of my mouth when the whole household rushed at me with blows and curses, in an attempt to cancel their dreadful ominousness. One punched me in the face with his fists, another dug his elbows into my shoulder, someone else kicked me; my ribs were pummelled, my hair pulled, my clothes torn and before they finally threw me out of the house I felt like Adonis mauled by the wild boar, or Orpheus torn in pieces by the Thracian women.

'When I paused in the next street to collect my senses, and realized what I had said—it had certainly been a most tactless remark—I decided that I had got off lightly enough, all considered.

'By and by, after the customary "last summons", the agonized calling of his name by the relatives in case he might be only in a coma, the dead man was brought out of the house; and since he had been a man of such importance he was honoured with a public procession. As the cortège turned into the market place, an old man came running up, the tears streaming down his face. In a frenzy of grief he tore out tufts of his fine white hair, grabbed hold of the open coffin with both hands and screamed for vengeance.

' "Gentlemen of Hypata!" he cried, his voice choking with sobs, "I appeal to your honour, I appeal to your sense of justice and public duty! Stand by your fellow-citizen, this poor nephew of mine; see that his death is avenged in full on that evil woman, his widow. She, and she alone, is the murderess. To cover up a secret love-affair and to get possession of her husband's estate she killed him—she killed him with a slow poison." He continued to sob and scream, until the crowd was stirred to indignant sympathy, thinking that he probably had good ground for his accusations. Some shouted: "Burn her! Burn her!" and some: "Stone her to death!" and a gang of young hooligans was encouraged to lynch her.

'However, she denied her guilt with oaths and tears (though these carried little conviction), and devout appeals to all the gods and goddesses in Heaven to witness that she was utterly incapable of doing anything so wicked.

' "So be it then," said the old man, "I am willing to refer the case to divine arbitration. And here is Zatchlas the Egyptian, one of the leading necromancers of his country, who has undertaken, for a large fee, to recall my nephew's soul from the Underworld and persuade it to reanimate the corpse for a few brief moments."

'The person whom he introduced to the crowd was dressed in white linen, with palm-leaf sandals on his feet and a tonsured head. The old man kissed his hands and clasped his knees in a formal act of supplication. "Your reverence," he cried, "take pity on me. I implore you by the stars of Heaven, by the gods of the Underworld, by the five elements of nature, by the silence of night, by the dams that the swallows of Isis build about the Coptic island, by the flooding of the Nile, by the mysteries of Memphis, and by the sacred rattle of Pharos—I implore you by these holy things to grant my nephew's soul a brief return to the warmth of the sun, and so re-illumine his eyes that they may open and momentarily regain the sight that he has forfeited by his descent to the Land of the Dead. I do not argue with fate, I do not deny the grave what is her due; my plea is only for a brief leave of absence, during which the dead man may, assist me in avenging his own murder—the only possible consolation I can have in my overwhelming grief."

'The necromancer, yielding to his entreaties, touched the corpse's mouth three times with a certain small herb and laid another on its breast. Then he turned to the east, with a silent prayer to the sacred disk of the rising sun. The whole market place gasped expectantly at the sight of these solemn preparations, and stood prepared for a miracle. I pushed in among the crowd and climbed up on a stone just behind the coffin, from which I watched the whole scene with rising curiosity.

'Presently the breast of the corpse began to heave, blood began to pour again through its veins, breath returned to its nostrils. He sat up and spoke in a querulous voice: "Why do you call me back to the troubles of this transitory life, when I have already drunk of the stream of Lethe and floated on the marshy waters of the Styx? Leave me alone, I say, leave me alone! Let me sleep undisturbed."

'The necromancer raised his voice excitedly: "What? You refuse to address your fellow-citizens here and clear up the mystery of your death? Don't you realize that if you hold back a single detail, I am prepared to call up the dreadful Furies and have your weary limbs tortured on the rack?"

'At this the dead man roused himself again and groaned out to the crowd: "The bed in which I lay only yesterday is no longer empty; my rival sleeps in it. My newly-married wife has bewitched and poisoned me."

'The widow showed remarkable courage in the circumstance. She denied everything with oaths, and began contradicting and arguing with her late husband as though there were no such thing as respect for the dead. The crowd took different sides. Some were for burying the wicked woman alive in the same grave as her victim: but others refused to admit the evidence of a senseless corpse—it was quite untrustworthy, they said.

'The corpse soon settled the dispute. With another hollow groan it said: "I will give you incontrovertible proof that what I say is true, by disclosing something that is known to nobody but myself." Then he pointed up at me and said: "While that learned young student was keeping careful watch over my corpse, the ghoulish witches who were hovering near, waiting for a chance to rob it, did their best to deceive him by changing shape, but he saw through all their tricks. Though the bedroom doors were carefully bolted, they had slipped in through a knot-hole disguised as weasels and mice. But they threw a fog of sleep over him, so that he fell insensible, and then they called me by name, over and over again, trying to make me obey their magical commands. My weakened joints and cold limbs, despite convulsive

49

struggles, could not respond immediately, but this student who had been cast into a trance that was a sort of death, happened to have the same name as I. So when they called: 'Thelyphron, Thelyphron, come!' he answered mechanically. Rising up like a senseless ghost he offered his face for the mutilation that they intended for mine; and they nibbled off first his nose and then his ears. But to divert attention from what they had done, they cleverly fitted him with a wax nose exactly like his own, and a pair of wax ears. The poor fellow remains under the illusion that he has been well rewarded for his vigilance, not meanly compensated for a frightful injury."

'Terrified by this story, I clapped my hand to my face to see if there were any truth in it, and my nose fell off; then I touched my ears, and they fell off too. A hundred fingers pointed at me from the crowd and a great roar of laughter went up. I burst into a cold sweat, leaped down from the stone, and slipped away between their legs like a frightened dog. Mutilated and ridiculous, I have never since cared to return to Miletus; and now I disguise the loss of my ears by growing my hair long and glue this canvas nose on my face for decency's sake.'

The drunken diners laughed as heartily as before when Thelyphron reached the climax of his story, and called for the usual toast to the God of Laughter. Byrrhaena explained. 'At Hypata, ever since the city was founded, we have celebrated a unique festival: the happy celebration of Laughter Day. I do trust you will be present at the ceremony tomorrow, and especially that you will be able to think out some joke of your own as a contribution to the proceedings; you see, Laughter is a god whom we hold in the very greatest esteem.'

'Certainly I'll be there,' I answered cheerfully. 'And I only hope that I'll be able to invent something really good, something so funny that I should not be ashamed to tie it around the neck of your great local deity himself.'

By this time I had drunk as much as I wanted, and when my slave came up to my table and told me that it was now midnight, I took a hasty leave of Byrrhaena and went unsteadily out into the darkness. The slave was carrying a lantern, but a sudden gust of wind extinguished it half way down the first street and we had a difficult time groping our way from door to door, continually catching our toes in the cobbles and falling over. And when at last I reached our lane, I came suddenly on three strapping great men heaving with all their strength at Milo's gate, trying to force their way in. They seemed not in the least alarmed by our arrival, but began using greater violence than before, aiming kicks at the gate as if to burst it off its hinges. I had no doubt that they were house-breakers, desperate ones too, and neither had the slave. Drawing my sword from under my cloak where I was holding it ready for just such an emergency as this, I rushed straight at them, and as they turned to close with me I lunged at each in turn and drove the blade into his body up to the hilt. They fell, and I thrust at them repeatedly as they attempted to rise, until all three gasped out their lives at my feet.

The disturbance woke Fotis, who ran up and opened the gate for me. I crawled into the house, panting for breath and dripping with sweat, and flung myself on my bed. There I fell asleep in a moment, as exhausted by my fight as if I had been battling, like Hercules, with Geryon, the King of Red Island, who had three bodies in one.

4

The Festival of Laughter

DAWN with rosy arm uplifted (as the poets say) had just begun
to urge her gleaming steeds through the morning sky, when I
woke from a tranquil sleep: and it was as though night had
handed me over to the custody of day, for I suddenly remembered
the acts of violence I had committed while it was still dark, and
my mind was in a ferment. I sat hunched up in bed with my feet
crossed and my fingers nervously clasping and unclasping themselves as I hugged my knees. Presently I wept, picturing to myself
the scene in court, my trial and condemnation, my executioner,
my execution. 'How can I hope to find a judge,' I asked myself,
'so mild and understanding as to find me not guilty of deliberately
murdering those three unarmed men? I suppose that this was
what Diophanes the Chaldaean had in mind when he confidently
predicted that my journey was to make me famous!'

I was still brooding on my unlucky adventure and its probable
consequences when I heard a violent knocking and shouting at
the gate. As soon as it was opened, in rushed a great mass of
people, headed by the magistrates and town constables, and occu-

pied every room in the house. Two constables were ordered to arrest me and, though I offered no resistance, I was dragged violently off. When we reached the end of the lane I was astonished to see an enormous crowd waiting for my appearance: the entire population of Hypata seemed to be present. But as I walked miserably along the high road, staring at the ground through which I feared that my spirit must soon descend to the gloomy world below, one thing astonished me still more. For as I glanced up for a moment at the roaring crowd lining the roadside, I could not see a single person among all those many thousands who was not bursting with laughter.

Instead of marching me straight to the Market, where the trial was to take place, they took me along a circuitous processional route, turning corner after corner. It was as though I were the sacrificial victim which is led through all the principal streets of a town when unlucky portents have been observed and a sin-offering is needed to placate the local deities. Eventually I was put into the dock, and the magistrates took their seats on the bench. But when the Clerk of the Court bawled for silence, protests were heard from every side. 'For Heaven's sake stop the proceedings!' 'We're being crushed to death!' 'Try him in the theatre instead!' 'Stop! Stop!' 'Try him in the theatre!'

Since the trial was of such unusual interest the magistrates agreed on a change of venue; and the crowd emptied itself into the theatre with remarkable speed. Every single seat was occupied, every entrance blocked; even the roof was alive with people. Some balanced on the pediments of columns, some clung to statues, some squeezed themselves in at the windows or straddled the rafters; nobody seemed to pay the least attention to his own safety in the general desire to witness my trial. The constables led me across the stage and placed me right in front, close to the orchestra, as if the sin-offering were now being exhibited for public scrutiny.

The Clerk of the Court began bawling again, this time summoning the chief witness for the prosecution to appear. Up stepped an old man, whom I did not know. He was invited to speak for as long as there was water in the clock; this was a hollow globe into which water was poured through a funnel in the neck, and from which it gradually escaped through fine perforations at the base.

He spoke as follows:

'It is my duty today, your Honours, to give evidence on a matter which I regard as of no small importance, because it affects the peace of the whole town; and I trust that your Honours' sentence will be an exemplary one—that your sense of civic dignity will not allow you to condone this bloody multiple murder of your fellow-citizens committed by the villain in the dock. Your Honours must not suspect that I am motivated by any private grudge or feud in bringing this accusation. The fact is that I am the Captain of the Town Watch, and I doubt whether there is a man alive who can charge me with any irregularity in the performance of my duties. So let me report in detail exactly what happened last night. About midnight when I was completing my rounds, having visited every street and made sure that all was correct and in order, my attention was directed to this young man who was running amuck with his sword in a lane just outside the town walls. As I came up with my patrol, three men had just fallen dying at his feet, with blood spouting from their wounds. The murderer at once ran off, apparently well aware of the enormity of his crime, and though it was dark we saw him slip into a house close by, where he lay low all night. We kept the gate under observation, and by the mercy of the gods, who never allow crimes of this sort to go unpunished, we were able to pick him up early this morning before he had managed to escape by a back passage. Now I have fetched him here before your Honours for the sentence that he so richly deserves. He is a murderer in the first degree, caught red-handed, and though he is not a native of Thessaly, I trust that the sentence will be as severe as if his name appeared on the Town register.'

He had hardly finished before the Clerk of the Court jumped up and ordered me to begin my defence at once if I had one to make. At first I could do nothing but weep, not so much because of the ruthlessness of the accusation, as because of my own guilty conscience; but at last I was somehow inspired with enough boldness to plead.

'Your Honours,' I said, 'however truthful an account I give you of the circumstances in which these three fellow-citizens of yours—whose corpses are produced in evidence against me—met their deaths at my hands, I know only too well how difficult it will be to persuade you and the great assembly confronting me that I am innocent of wilful murder.

'However, if you are kind enough to grant me a brief hearing, I undertake to prove that I now stand on trial for my life not because of any criminal propensities in me, but as the accidental result of having given way to righteous anger. This is what happened. I returned from a supper party last night somewhat later than usual, and rather the worse for drink—I admit that—and just as I reached the house of your worthy fellow-citizen Milo, whose guest I am, I saw a gang of ruffians trying to break their way in by wrenching the gate off its hinges. They had already smashed the bars and were now openly threatening to murder every soul in the house. Their leader, a huge fellow who was doing most of the work, shouted out: "Come on, lads, show what stuff you're made of! Once inside, we'll kill every man Jack of them. There's no holding back now. Anyone who resists must be knocked on the head; anyone who stays in bed must be put to sleep for ever. Dead men tell no tales." At that, your Honours, I admit I drew my sword, which I carry as a protection against dangers of this very sort. I thought it my duty to frighten off these bloodthirsty scoundrels by a show of force. However, instead of running away when they saw that I was armed, they audaciously stood their ground and prepared to fight it out. Their captain, if I may call him so, rushed straight at me, grasped my hair with both hands and began forcing my head back. He shouted out: "Quick, a stone! Bash his skull in!" But luckily, before he got what he wanted, I was able to drive my sword sideways into his body and he fell dead at my feet. Another tackled me by the ankles and tried to bite my feet, but I ran him through with a well-aimed thrust under the shoulder blade; then, rapidly disengaging my sword, I received the third one on the point as he rushed at me with his guard down.

'The fight was over, and I began congratulating myself on having preserved the lives of my host and hostess and safeguarded the peace of the town. In fact, I expected not merely to be pardoned for what I had done, but to be given some public reward for my services. Now I am amazed and mystified at this charge of wilful murder. After all, I am a man of high standing in my own country, where I have never been accused of the smallest crime, and value my reputation above all the treasures of this world; nobody in this entire theatre can prove that before last night I had the slightest quarrel with those wicked wretches, or that I was even acquainted with any of them. If I am charged with highway robbery, let the prosecution show you one single article which I am alleged to have taken from their dead bodies. I plead guilty to justifiable homicide alone.'

I burst into tears again and stretching out my hands in a gesture of supplication, appealed to the humanity of the audience. I begged them by all that they held most dear to show me mercy. When I thought that my tears and undeniable misery must have created a favourable impression, I called upon the all-seeing eyes of Justice and the Sun himself to declare my innocence before a full Council of the blessed gods. At last I dared raise my head a little. To my consternation the whole audience was tittering with suppressed merriment—the whole audience, except Milo, my kind host, my friend, my protector who, seated well in front, was unashamedly gasping and crying for laughter.

I thought: 'Merciful Heavens, has he no heart? Has he no conscience? I save his house from robbery, I save him and his family from assassination, yet when I stand here in the dock on a capital charge, he won't raise a finger to save me. He justs sits and cackles with brutal laughter at the prospect of my death!'

Meanwhile a young woman in deep mourning, with a baby at her breast, came hurrying down the central aisle, followed by an old hag dressed in filthy rags. Both were lamenting at the top of their voices, and waving olive branches to show that they were suppliants. They climbed up on the stage, and bending over the bench on which the three corpses lay covered with a sheet, beat their breasts and howled dismally. The hag screeched: 'Your Honours, I appeal to you in the name of pity, I appeal to you in the name of conscience! These fine young men had a mother, a poor widow. She demands vengeance for their brutal murder and will take no denial.' And the younger woman shrieked: 'The eldest of them was my husband and now I too am a poor, destitute widow. But whatever happens to me, your Honours, I beg you at least to remember my little child, who has been orphaned so young. I beg you to blot out with the murderer's blood the terrible crime that has been committed in our law-abiding town of Hypata.'

The senior magistrate rose and addressed the people: 'Since no one, not even the defendant Lucius, can deny that this is a crime calling for the severest punishment, it only remains for us to perform the secondary duty of finding out who were his accomplices in this foul deed. It seems most unlikely that he could have murdered three such powerfully built men as these single-handed. But the slave who escorted the prisoner home from the supper party has mysteriously disappeared and left him as the only material witness of the crime, so we shall have to extract the truth from him by torture. It is imperative that we force him to reveal the names of his gang, if only to set our minds at ease. They may be planning further acts of violence.'

The instruments of torture regularly used in Greece were produced at once: the charcoal brazier for scorching the soles of my feet; the wheel for racking my joints; not to mention a cat-o'-nine-tails and the flogging bench. It doubled my misery to realize that I would not be allowed to die at least unmutilated. But while I was waiting for the torture to begin, the old hag who had spoiled everything by her howling appealed to the magistrates: 'Before you crucify this bandit who has murdered my poor darlings, will your Honours please allow their corpses to be uncovered so that everyone here may see how young and beautiful they were? That will make you all angrier than ever; you will insist on a revenge as cruel as the crime itself.'

Great applause. The magistrates immediately ordered me to go over to the bench and uncover the corpses myself. I refused to do anything of the sort, and struggled against the constables who tried to force me to obedience. The order to relive my crime in public by a display of the victims, I found a terrible one to obey. But they managed to wrench my hand from my side and stretch it over the bodies. There was no help for it: I had to yield, whatever the consequences might be. With fearful reluctance, I grasped the hem of the shroud and drew it back.

But good God! what was this? this most extraordinary sight, this sudden complete change of the whole situation? A moment before I was reckoning myself already a slave of Queen Proserpine's, detailed for duty in the infernal halls of her royal husband; but now, nothing of the kind! I stood goggling dumbly like an idiot, and even today I find it difficult to convey adequately the stupefying effect that the sight produced on me. The three corpses were nothing more than three inflated wine-skins, punctured in several places! And so far as I could recall the details of my fight with the house-breakers, the holes corresponded exactly with my sword-thrusts.

Then the laughter, which had until now been slyly repressed

by the stage-managers of the hoax, burst out uproariously from the whole vast theatre. Part of the audience cheered me exuberantly as a jolly good fellow, but many could do no more than press their hands to their stomachs to relieve the ache. The proceedings ended abruptly and as the great crowd poured out of the theatre, drowned in floods of mirth, every face was turned back for a last hilarious look at me.

From the moment that I pulled back the shroud, I had been standing there as stiff and cold as stone, exactly as if I had been one of the marble columns that supported the roof; and my soul had not yet floated back from the shadows of death, when my host Milo came up and with gentle insistence drew me away with him. Then my tears burst out once more, and I could not restrain my convulsive sobbing; however, he took me home by side-streets and narrow passages to spare me the embarrassment of being recognized. He tried to calm me by cheerful attempts at consolation, but I was now burning with such indignation at having been victimized in this insulting way that he could do nothing with me.

Presently the magistrates arrived at our house in their robes of office and did their utmost to appease me. 'Lord Lucius,' they said, 'we are well aware of your rank and high position, for your mother's family is, of course, famous throughout Greece; so you must not think that it was in wanton insult that we subjected you to the proceedings which you have taken so much to heart. We beg you to forget your momentary anguish. The fact is that today we annually hold a solemn festival in honour of Laughter, the best of all gods, which must always be celebrated with some new practical joke. Laughter will now lovingly accompany you wherever you go and never allow you to be glum, daubing your forehead with the cheerful colours that mark you as his own. Moreover, the town of Hypata has unanimously conferred on you the highest dignity that it can bestow: you are now inscribed on the roll of its most distinguished benefactors and your bronze statue will in due course be unveiled in the market place.'

I replied politely: 'Convey to the citizens of this splendid and unique town how deeply sensible I am of the honour that has been done me; but please forgive me for suggesting that they should reserve their public statuary for older and more worthy persons than myself.' I forced a smile as I took courteous leave of them, and did what I could to give them the impression that I was now perfectly happy.

As soon as they had gone a servant ran in. 'The Lady Byrrhaena's compliments, and will my lord kindly remember her invitation to supper, which he was good enough to accept last night; the guests will be arriving very shortly.'

Shuddering at the very mention of her house, I answered: 'Please assure her ladyship that I would come most willingly, but for an unavoidable engagement. My host Milo has charged me, in the name of the God who presides over today's festivities, to dine with him tonight, and insists that he will neither allow me to leave the house nor come out with me himself. I regret that I must postpone the pleasure to another more suitable evening.'

Milo then took me along to the nearest baths, ordering a slave to follow us with the toilet materials; and it was true that Laughter accompanied me wherever I went. I shrank from the humorous greetings of everyone we met, huddling as close as I could to Milo, appalled with shame at having been made to look such a fool. How I managed to wash, anoint and wipe myself clean at the baths, and how I ever got home again, I really cannot remember; I was so mortified and confused at being stared at, nudged at and pointed at by the whole town.

I swallowed a wretched little meal at Milo's and then told him that so much weeping had given me a severe headache and that I must go to bed at once. Milo readily excused me. So I went along to my room and flung myself on the bed, where I brooded painfully on the events of the day.

Presently my dear, dear Fotis, having got her mistress safely to bed, came stealing in. She was not at all her usual gay, lively self, but frowning and anxious. After a long silence she faltered: 'I have something to confess, Lucius: I am wholly to blame for all your misfortunes of today.' Then she pulled a sort of stock-whip from under her apron and handed it to me. 'Here, take this. Revenge yourself with it on the girl who has betrayed you; yes, flog me as hard as you like and wherever you like. Only don't think for a moment that I purposely caused you so much misery. I call all the gods to witness that I would willingly shed my own blood rather than let you suffer the slightest harm on my account, or feel the least trouble hanging over your head. But bad luck always dogs me; so something that I was ordered to do for quite another reason had the effect of hurting you horribly.'

My curiosity had not been damped by my cruel experiences and I was longing to get to the bottom of the mysterious incident of the wine-skins. I cried indignantly: 'You bring me this wicked, horrible thing and invite me to beat you with it? Before it ever touches your creamy skin, I'll chop and tear it into little bits. But, darling, tell me faithfully, please tell me, just what it was you did that has made me so miserable. I swear to you, I swear by your face which I love so much, that nobody, not even yourself, could make me believe that you ever hurt me deliberately; and it is a principle of justice that no innocent intention must ever be viewed as criminal because it accidentally happens to result in bad luck.'

Her half-closed eyes were moist and tremulous and languid with desire. I began to drink love from them with thirsty kisses; which revived her spirits a little. She said: 'First, I must carefully shut the door in case anyone overhears what I am going to tell you—something very private—and we both get into frightful trouble.' She locked and bolted the door, then came back to the bed and holding my head close to hers, with her hands locked behind it, said in a soft whisper: 'I should be absolutely terrified to let you into the secrets of this house if I didn't have complete trust in your discretion. You come of a noble family, and you have a noble soul, and you are already initiated into various religious mysteries. So I know that you will never reveal to a soul what I am now going to tell you; my deep love for you forces it out of me, and you will be the only person in the world whom I have taken into my confidence. It may seem a trivial story, but you must repay me by keeping it forever tightly locked in the darkest corner of your mind; because it concerns my mistress Pamphilë and the magic arts by which she exacts obedience from ghosts, puts pressure on the stars, blackmails the gods and keeps all the five elements well under her thumb.

'She works at these arts with the most frantic fervour whenever she falls in love with a good-looking young man; which is pretty often. At present she's desperately in love with a young

Boeotian who really is wonderfully handsome, and is using all her best sorceries to seduce him. Yesterday evening I heard her threatening the Sun that if he didn't hurry up and set, to give her more time for her spells, she'd throw a cloud of darkness around him and consign the earth to perpetual night. That was after she had seen the Boeotian having a hair-trim at the barber's and privately ordered me to go into the shop and pick up some of the hair lying about on the floor. Though I took care to attract as little attention as possible, the barber knew that our house has a bad reputation for black magic, so he grabbed me and shouted: "Now really, this is going too far, you little witch. When are you going to stop stealing the hair of my good-looking customers? Unless you end this nonsense pretty soon, I warn you that I'll march you straight off to Court!" Then he rudely felt between my breasts and pulled out the ends of hair already hidden there; he was in a towering rage. I felt very badly about it because I know my mistress only too well: whenever she gets crossed like this she flies into a vile temper and gives me a savage beating. I wondered: "Shall I run away?" But as soon as I thought of you, I decided to do nothing of the sort. As I walked gloomily home I saw a man with a pair of shears trimming the hair off some goat-skins. They were hanging in front of his shop, tightly tied at the necks and well blown up, and it happened that the colour of their hair was yellowish and of exactly the same shade as the Boeotian's. I picked up several strands and brought them back to my mistress, without telling her whose hair it really was.

'When it grew dark, she climbed in a great state of excitement up to the cock-loft at the top of the house, which she finds a convenient place for practising her art in secret; it's open to all the four winds, with a particularly wide view of the eastern sky. She had everything ready there for her deadly rites: all sorts of aromatic incense, metal plaques engraved with secret signs, beaks and claws of ill-omened birds, various bits of corpse-flesh—in one place she had arranged the noses and fingers of crucified men, in another the nails that had been driven through their palms and ankles, with bits of flesh still sticking to them—also little bladders of life-blood saved from the men she had murdered and the skulls of criminals who had been thrown to the wild beasts in the amphitheatre. She began to repeat certain charms over the still warm and quivering entrails of some animal or other, dipping them in turn into jars of spring-water, cow's milk, mountain honey and mead. Then she plaited the hair I had given her, tied it into peculiar knots and threw it with a great deal of incense on her charcoal fire. The power of this charm is irresistible— backed, you must understand, by the blind violence of the gods who have been invoked: the smell of the hair smoking and crackling on the fire compels its owner to come to the place from which he is being summoned. So you see, instead of the Boeotian, the goat-skins came rapping for admittance at our gate, magically endowed with human breath and senses and understanding. Then unluckily you arrived too, pretty drunk, and in the pitch darkness mistook them for burglars. You drew your sword courageously, like Ajax when he went mad and mistook the flock of sheep for his enemies; but yours was a far nobler deed because you never shed a drop even of sheep's blood. So now, darling, here you are, safely back in my arms, after your attack of homicidal—I mean wineskinicidal—mania.'

I joked back: 'Yes, I'm a regular Hercules. This first labour of mine compares well with his slaying of the three-bodied King Geryon, or his capture of the three-headed dog Cerberus. But if you want me to forgive you wholeheartedly for causing me so much anguish, I insist on your doing one thing for me. It is this: I want to be secretly present when next your mistress invokes the infernal gods, and especially when she makes use of her supernatural powers to change herself into some animal. I'm determined to know everything possible about the science of magic. And, by the way, *you* seem to be pretty well grounded in it. Of one thing I'm quite certain: that though I have always shied away from love affairs even with ladies of the highest rank, I'm now a complete slave to your sparkling eyes, your rosy cheeks, your shining hair, your fragrant breasts and those kisses you give me with your parted lips. It is a willing slavery too. I have no notion of leaving you and no regret that I'm so far from home, and I'd give the whole world not to forfeit the joy in store for me tonight.'

'I should love to do as you ask, darling Lucius,' she said, 'but Pamphilë is a surly old beast and when she starts working on spells of this sort it's always in a lonely spot where she can be certain of not being disturbed. All the same, I would risk anything to please you, so I'll keep a careful watch on her movements and let you know when she gets busy again. But remember what I told you: you must promise to keep the most faithful silence about all this.'

Before we had quite finished discussing my plan, a sudden wave of longing swept over us both. We pulled off our clothes and rushed naked together in Bacchic fury; and when I was nearly worn out by the natural consummation of my desire she tempted me to make love to her as though she were a boy; so that when, after long hours of wakefulness, we finally dropped off to sleep, it was broad daylight before we felt like getting up again.

5

Lucius Is Transformed

WE SPENT the next few nights in the same delightful way, and then one morning Fotis ran into my room, trembling with excitement, and told me that her mistress, having made no headway by ordinary means in her affair with the Boeotian, intended that night to become a bird and fly in at his bedroom window, and that I must make careful preparations if I wished to watch the performance.

At twilight, she led me on tip-toe, very, very quietly, up the tower stairs to the door of the cock-loft, where she signed to me to peep through a chink. I obeyed, and watched Pamphilë first undress completely and then open a small cabinet containing several little boxes, one of which she opened. It contained an ointment which she worked about with her fingers and then smeared all over her body from the soles of her feet to the crown of her head. After this she muttered a long charm to her lamp, and shook herself; and, as I watched, her limbs became gradually fledged with feathers, her arms changed into sturdy wings, her nose grew crooked and horny, her nails turned into talons, and

68

soon there was no longer any doubt about it: Pamphilë had become an owl. She gave a querulous hoot and made a few little hopping flights until she was sure enough of her wings to glide off, away over the roof-tops.

Not having been put under any spell myself, I was utterly astonished and stood frozen to the spot. I rubbed my eyes to make sure that I was really Lucius, and that this was no waking dream. Was I perhaps going mad? I recovered my senses after a time, took hold of Fotis's hand and laid it across my eyes. 'Dearest love,' I said, 'I beg you, by these sweet breasts of yours, to grant me a tremendous favour—one which I can never hope to repay—in proof of your perfect love for me. If you do this I promise to be your slave for ever more. Honey, will you try to get hold of a little of that ointment for me? I want to be able to fly. I want to hover around you like a winged Cupid in attendance on his Goddess.'

'H'm,' she said, 'so that is your game, is it, my darling? You want to play me a foxy trick: handing me an axe and persuading me to chop off my own feet? That's all very well, but it hasn't been so easy for me all this time to keep you safe from the she-wolves of Thessaly. You would have been easy meat if I hadn't protected you with my love. Now if you become a bird, how shall I be able to keep track of you? And when will I ever see you again?'

I protested: 'All the gods in Heaven forbid that I'm such a scoundred as you make out. Listen: if I became an eagle and soared across the wide sky as Jupiter's personal courier, his thunderbolt proudly grasped in my claws, do you really suppose that even such winged glory as that would keep me from flying back every night to my love-nest in your arms? By that enchanting knot of hair on your head in which my soul lies helplessly entangled, I swear that I'm incapable by nature of loving any other woman in the whole world but my dearest Fotis. And anyhow, when I come to think of it, if that ointment really does turn me into a bird, I'll have to steer clear of the town; owls are such unlucky birds that when one blunders into a house by mistake, everyone does his best to catch it and nail it with outspread wings to the doorpost. Another thing, if I played truant from you and made love to the ladies in my owl disguise, what sort of a jolly welcome do you think they would give me? But that reminds me: once I'm an owl, what is the spell or antidote for turning me back into myself?'

'You need not worry about that,' she said. 'My mistress has taught me all the magical formulas. Not, of course, because she has a kindly feeling for me, but because when she arrives home from one of her adventures I have to prepare the necessary antidote for her to use. It really is extraordinary with what insignificant herbs one can produce a total transformation: tonight, for instance, she will need only a little anise and laurel leaves steeped in spring-water. She will drink some of the water, wash herself with the rest, and be a woman again at once. You can do the same after your flight.'

I made her reassure me on this point several times before she went, twitching with fear, up the tower stairs and brought me out one of the boxes from the casket. Hugging and kissing it I muttered a little prayer for a successful flight. Then I quickly pulled off my clothes, greedily stuck my fingers into the box and took out a large lump of ointment which I rubbed all over my body.

I stood flapping my arms, first the left and then the right, as I had seen Pamphilë do, but no little feathers appeared on them and they showed no sign of turning into wings. All that happened was that the hair on them grew coarser and coarser and the skin toughened into hide. Next, my fingers bunched together into a hard lump so that my hands became hooves, the same change came over my feet and I felt a long tail sprouting from the base of my spine. Then my face swelled, my mouth widened, my nostrils dilated, my lips hung flabbily down, and my ears shot up long and hairy. The only consoling part of this miserable transformation was the enormous increase in the size of a certain organ of mine; because I was by this time finding it increasingly difficult to meet all Fotis's demands upon it. At last, hopelessly surveying myself all over, I was obliged to face the mortifying fact that I had been transformed not into a bird, but into a plain jackass.

I wanted to curse Fotis for her stupid mistake, but found that I could no longer speak or even gesticulate; so I silently expostulated with her by sagging my lower lip and gazing sideways at her with my large, watery eyes.

When Fotis saw what had happened she beat her own face with both hands in a frenzy of self-condemnation. 'Oh, this is enough to kill me!' she wailed. 'In my flurry and fear I must have mistaken the box; two of them look exactly alike. Still, my poor creature, things are not nearly so bad as they seem, because in this case the antidote is one of the easiest to get hold of; all that you need do is to chew roses, which will at once turn you back into my Lucius. If only I had made my usual rose-garlands this evening! Then you would have been spared the inconvenience of being an ass for even a single night. At the first signs of dawn I promise faithfully to go out and fetch what you need.' Over and over again she cursed her own stupidity and carelessness, but though I was no longer Lucius, and to all appearances a complete ass, a mere beast of burden, I still retained my mental faculties. I had a long and furious debate with myself as to whether or not I ought to bite and kick Fotis to death. She was a witch, wasn't she? And a very evil one, too. But in the end I decided that it would not only be dangerous but stupid to kill the one person who could help me to regain my own shape. Drooping my head and shaking my ears resignedly, I swallowed my rage for the time being and submitted to my cruel fate. I trotted off to the stable, where I would at least have the company of my white thoroughbred who had carried me so well while I was a man.

He was there with another ass, the property of my host—my former host—Milo, and really I did expect that, if dumb beasts have any natural feelings of loyalty, my horse would know me and take pity on my plight, welcoming me to his stable with as much courtesy as if I were a foreign ambassador on a visit to the Imperial Court at Rome. But—O Hospitable Jupiter and all the Gods of Faith and Trust!—my splendid horse and Milo's horrible ass put their heads together at once, suspecting that I had designs on their food, and formed an alliance against me. The moment I approached their manger they laid their ears back, wheeled round, and started kicking me in the face. My own horse! What gratitude! Here was I, driven right away from the very barley which only a few hours before I had measured out for him with my own hands.

As I stood in my lonely corner, banished from the society of my four-footed colleagues and deciding on a bitter revenge on them next morning as soon as I had eaten my roses and become Lucius again, I noticed a little shrine of the Mare-headed Mother, the Goddess Epona, standing in a niche of the post that supported the main beam of the stable. It was wreathed with freshly gathered roses, the very antidote that I needed. I balanced hopefully on my hindlegs, pushed my forelegs as far up the post as they would go, stretched my neck to its fullest extent and shot out my lips. But by a piece of really bad luck, before I could eat any of the roses, my slave who was acting as groom happened to catch me at work. He sprang up angrily from the heap of straw on which he was lying and shouted: 'I've had quite enough trouble from this damned cuddy. First he tries to rob his stablemates and now he plays the same trick on the blessed gods! If I don't flog the sacrilegious brute until he's too lame to stir a hoof . . .' He groped about until he found a bundle of faggots, picked out a thick knobbly one, the biggest of the lot, and began unmercifully whacking my flanks.

A sudden loud pounding and banging on the outer gate. Distant cries of 'Thieves! Thieves!' The groom dropped his faggot and ran off in terror. The next moment, the courtyard gate burst open and armed bandits rushed in. A few neighbours hurried to Milo's assistance but the bandits beat them off easily. Their swords gleamed like the rays of the rising sun in the bright light of the torches that they carried. They had axes with them, too, which they used to break open the heavily barred door of the strong room in the central part of the house. It was stuffed with Milo's valuables, all of which they hauled out and hastily divided into

73

a number of separate packages. However, there were more packages to carry than robbers to carry them, so they had to use their wits. They came into our stable, led the three of us out, loaded us with as many of the heavier packages as they could pile on our backs, and drove us out of the now ransacked house, threatening us with sticks. Then they hurried forward into trackless hill-country, beating us hard all the way. But one of them stayed behind as a spy; he was to follow later and report what steps were taken by the authorities to deal with the crime.

The hills were steep, my load heavy, and the journey interminable; soon I felt more dead than alive. As a Roman citizen I decided to notify the civil power and rescue myself from my dreadful predicament by appealing to the Emperor. It was already broad daylight when, as we passed through a large village where a fair was in progress, I tried to invoke the august name of Caesar in the presence of a crowd of Thessalians. I managed to shout 'O' loudly and distinctly, but that was all; I was unable to pronounce the word 'Caesar'. My discordant bray so annoyed the bandits that they whacked and poked at my miserable hide until it felt hardly fit even to make one of those leather sieves for bolting corn.

At last Jupiter the Deliverer generously offered me a chance to escape. After we had passed several farm buildings and large country houses I saw a charming little garden full of many different sorts of flowers, among them budding roses still wet with the morning dew. I gasped for joy and quickened my pace, and had almost come up to the roses, my mouth watering hopefully, when at the last moment I thought better of my project. If I suddenly ceased to be an ass and became Lucius again, the bandits would

74

be sure to kill me, either because they took me for a wizard or for fear that I might inform against them. For the present I must lay off roses and put up with my misery a little longer by champing my bit like the beast I was.

About midday under a scorching sun, we turned off the road and presently came to a hamlet where we stopped at a private house. Two or three old men came out. Any ass could have seen from the exchange of greetings and embraces and the long conversation which followed that these were friends of the bandits, who gave them some of the plate from a package on my back and whispered what must have been a warning to keep quiet about it. When my horse and Milo's ass and I had all been unloaded, we were turned out to graze in the next paddock, but I was not gregarious enough to enjoy the company of my fellow-beasts, especially as I had not yet got accustomed to eating grass. Feeling half-starved I boldly jumped into a small vegetable patch behind the stable, where I filled my stomach with greens. When I had finished I silently invoked all the gods of Heaven, and had a good look around me. There might happen to be a flowering rose-tree in one of the gardens near by, and this was such a secluded place, well away from the road and hidden by fruit-trees, that if I could find the antidote to my four-footedness and regain my upright posture, it was unlikely that anyone would witness the transformation. While I was excitedly weighing my chances of escape, I saw, a good distance off, what looked like a dip in the ground enclosed by a small plantation of ornamental trees, and against the variegated background of leaves I made out the bright red of roses. In my imagination, which was far from being that of a mere beast, I pictured the place as a grove of Venus and the Three Graces,

75

with the lovely colours of their royal flower glowing from a central shrine. Breathing a silent prayer to the God of Luck I galloped off at such speed that I felt more like a heavily backed race-horse than an ass. But even with this remarkable turn of speed I could not out-distance the fate that dogged my heels; for when I reached the place it was not a dip in the ground after all, but a concealed stream with thickly wooded banks, and the roses were not your fresh tender roses, dripping with honey-dew, that happily laugh at you from their thorny twigs. They were what country people call rose-laurels: cup-shaped red blossoms, growing from a long-leaved bush resembling a laurel, which have no scent at all and are deadly poison to all cattle. Finding myself still entangled in bad luck I resolved, in my despair, to commit suicide by eating these mock-roses.

As I walked hesitantly towards the bush, a young man who must have been the owner of the vegetable patch ran angrily at me with a big stick. He beat me so hard in revenge for the damage I had done that he might have killed me if I had not had the sense to defend myself by raising my rump and letting out with my hind legs. I got my own back with a succession of such hard kicks that I left him lying helpless on the slope of the hill. Then I bolted.

Unfortunately his wife—at least, I suppose she was his wife—happened to be standing higher up on the same hillside and saw him lying below her half-dead. She rushed to his rescue, shrieking: 'Kill that wicked ass! He's nearly murdered my husband!'

Her neighbours at once unchained their dogs and set them at me with: 'Sick him, boy, sick him! Tear him to bits!' It looked as if my last hour had come, because there were several of these dogs, huge mastiffs of the sort used in the amphitheatre for baiting bulls and bears. I took what seemed my last chance of survival: instead of running farther away, I doubled back to the stable as fast as I could. The villagers called off their dogs, but had great difficulty in keeping them away from me. I was tied to a staple with a strong leather strap and fiercely beaten again. That would certainly have been the end of me but for my stupidity in gorging myself on those raw greens: the blows raining on my stomach had the effect of squirting out its half-digested contents in my tormentors' faces. I was terribly loose, and the stench was so disgusting that everyone ran out, cursing and choking.

That same afternoon the bandits loaded us up again, taking care to give me by far the heaviest load to carry. I was exhausted by the long journey and the great weight on my back, my sides ached from the beatings and I could hardly walk because my unshod hooves were worn down to the quick. When we had come a good distance farther I began planning a new way of escape. We were following a road that wound along a valley above a ravine and I decided to fall down with my legs doubled under me and not to budge another inch, though the bandits beat me with sticks or even pricked me with their swords. Surely that would make them realize that I had been over-driven and was now three parts dead? Why shouldn't they grant me an honourable discharge on the grounds of ill-health? I knew that they could not afford any delay and calculated that when they had done their worst to make me get up they would naturally divide my load between the horse and the other ass and then push on, leaving me there by way of further punishment as a prey for the wolves and vultures.

This splendid plan was thwarted by my usual bad luck. Milo's ass somehow guessed what I had in mind and forestalled me: he pretended to be completely worn out, fell sprawling on the road with all his load, and lay there as though dead. He made no attempt to rise in spite of whacks and sword-pricks, not even when the bandits made a concerted effort to haul him up by all four legs, both ears and the tail. Realizing that the case was hopeless they decided after a short discussion not to delay their flight a moment longer for the sake of a foundered ass. 'The brute is as good as dead,' they told one another. They divided his load between the horse and myself, hamstrung him with a sword, dragged him off the road and toppled him down into the ravine.

The fate of my unlucky comrade scared me. I decided to play no more clever tricks and make no more splendid plans, but to show my masters that I was an honest and hard-working ass. Besides, they had been encouraging one another by saying that they were quite near their mountain cave and that their hard journey would soon be over.

One more hill, not a very steep one, and there at last we were at our destination. My horse and I were unloaded and all the treasures stowed safely away in the cave. For want of water, I lay down and rolled in the dust to refresh myself.

Here I must give a close description of the cave and its immediate surroundings. This will be a test of my literary powers and at the same time allow you to judge whether or not I was an ass as regards my ability to size up a situation. To begin with the mountain, then. It was rugged and very high, a powerful natural fortress, covered with dark woods and cut by irregular bramble-choked gullies that ran obliquely across its slopes and were flanked by inaccessible cliffs. From near the peak a spring burst out and ran shining down the sides, breaking into a number of small streams that flooded the meadows below with large sheets of standing water. The cave opened near the foot and above it rose a tall fort, built of wattles fastened on a timber frame. The lower storey was extended on all four sides into a roomy pen for stolen sheep. A quick-set hedge, instead of a wall, surrounded the cave entrance, providing the bandits with a sort of reception hall. There were no other buildings near except a small thatched hut which, as I afterwards found, was used as a listening post. Sentries, chosen by lot, were posted there every night.

6

The Bandits' Cave

THE BANDITS tied us up by our halters outside the cave and one by
one crept in on all fours: I could hear them shouting at the bent
old woman who kept house for them.

'Hey, what are you playing at, you stinking old corpse?'

—'She's not a corpse.'

—'I say she is.'

—'And I say she isn't. Life may be ashamed to own her, but
then so is Death to claim her.'

—'Well, anyhow, look at her sitting on her backside at this
time of night! Hey, you, why don't you get stirring and cook us
a good supper? We need some sort of reward for all our dangers
and troubles. All you do, day and night, you old soak, is to pour
our wine down your leathery old throat.'

She squeaked tremulously: 'Oh no, no, my gallant young gentlemen! Don't you be hard on me. There's all sorts of meat stew-
ing in the pots, very tasty too, you'll find; and any amount of
bread, and nice well-rinsed cups with as much wine as you can
possibly drink. And, as usual, I've heated you the water for a good
wash before supper.'

They all undressed and stood around a great roaring fire where they splashed themselves with hot water, and afterwards rubbed themselves with oil before taking their places at a table heaped with every kind of food.

They had hardly settled down before another larger group of bandits came in, and took their hot wash in the same way. They had obviously been out raiding too, because they brought in another haul of loot; coin, plate and gold-embroidered silk robes. When they joined their comrades at table everyone drew lots as to who should wait on the rest. Heavens, how they ate and drank! The meat was piled up in heaps, the loaves in large mounds, the wine cups were arranged in columns like an army on the march. They bawled songs, yelled obscenities and played practical jokes on one another. I was reminded of the way the Centaurs and Lapiths had behaved in the tale of Pirithoüs's marriage feast. At last the toughest bandit of them all began to make a speech.

'Silence, everyone! I'm speaking for the brave boys at this end of the table who attacked and stormed Milo's house at Hypata. We cleaned the place out properly and not only piled up a fortune in gold and silver but didn't lose a man—in fact, we came back with four pairs of legs to the good, if that's worth mentioning. And we don't think much of you other fellows and your raid into Boeotia. You have come back fewer than you went, and I can tell you one thing: that all the loot you brought in will never make up for the loss of your captain. Lamachus was a wonderfully brave fellow.'

'Much too brave, in fact!' someone agreed, 'and that was his ruin. However, his name will appear in the history books one day along with the names of kings and generals.'

'But you miserable petty thieves, you either sneak around the public baths doing little piddling jobs for the second-hand clothes dealers, or else go creeping into old women's tumble-down cottages in the hope of hooking a thing or two off a shelf.'

The acting captain of the larger party took him up sharply. 'That's all very well, you fool. When are you going to learn that the bigger the house the easier it is to rob? Where there are plenty of slaves about, none of them ever thinks of saving his master's property before his own life. But people who live economically with few slaves not only keep their stuff pretty well hidden, but defend it fiercely at the risk of their lives, even if it isn't particularly valuable. Listen to our story and you'll find that I'm talking sense.

'As we went towards the famous city of Thebes, "Seven-gated Thebes" they call it, we enquired who were the richest men in the district—you'll agree with me that the first rule of our profession is to find out where the money lies—and someone told us of a rich banker named Chryseros who made a great show of being a pauper for fear he might be called on to accept public office. We heard that he lived all alone in a small house, so strongly barred and bolted that it was almost a fortress, where he brooded all day long in dirty clothes over his bags of gold. We decided to pay Chryseros our first call and expected to find little difficulty in relieving him of his money; so many against one. As soon as it was dark we collected outside his door but agreed that it was unsafe to force the lock or break the hinges—it was a double door—because the noise might give the alarm. To smash it down was out of the question. So our brave Lamachus, with his usual confidence and devotion to duty, quietly slipped his arm through an old keyhole which he enlarged by cutting away the rotten wood around it, and tried to unbolt the door from the inside. Unfortunately that disgusting old biped Chryseros had heard us and was on the watch. He crept up to the door very softly with a hammer in one hand and a nail in the other, and with a sudden sharp blow nailed poor Lamachus's hand to a door-panel. He left him writhing there like a criminal on the cross, rushed up to the roof of the filthy little house, and shouted to his neighbours at the top of his voice: "Help, help! Fire, fire! Come quickly, and help me put it out, before it spreads to your own houses!" He appealed to them all by name, and they rushed up in alarm, being anxious, naturally, to localize the blaze.

'This put us in a dilemma. We saw no chance of getting away unless we deserted Lamachus, which was out of the question. So we had to take desperate action: we hacked off his arm at the elbow, with his consent of course, and left it sticking through the hole. Then we bound up the stump tightly, swathed it with rags, for fear that the drops of blood might leave a trail, and rushed off with what was left of our poor captain. By now the whole district was alarmed. We were chased with shouts and cries and had to run so hard that, though we hurried Lamachus along as fast as we could, he couldn't keep up with us. Yet it was death for him to drop behind. He begged us to put him out of his misery and held us to the oath of mutual help which we had all sworn together by the right hand of Mars. He said that we couldn't leave a comrade behind to be gaoled and then crucified, and that his greatest happiness now would be to die at our hands: for how long could a brave bandit survive the loss of a hand that he used for stealing and cutting throats? But however hard he pleaded he couldn't persuade any of us to kill him—that would have been as bad as parricide—so he drew his sword with his left hand and after kissing it repeatedly, plunged it under his breast-bone.

'Lamachus was the bravest man we knew and his death affected us deeply. We carefully wrapped his body in a linen robe and consigned it to the river Ismerius. The river will roll him secretly down to his tomb in the wide salt sea.'

—'May he rest in peace!' everyone sighed. 'It was a heroic end and matched his wonderfully gallant life.'

'We lost Alcimus too, our cleverest planner of burglaries and raids, through another stroke of bad luck. He had broken into an old woman's cottage and got up to the attic bedroom where she was lying asleep; but instead of strangling her at once, as he ought to have done, for some reason or other he left her alone and began throwing her stuff down through the window for us to collect. He cleared the whole room in workmanlike fashion and then, thinking that we might as well have the old girl's bedding while we were about it, pushed her out of bed. He was about to throw down the coverlet after the other things when the wicked old creature clasped him by the knees and cried: "Stop, stop! What are you at, son? Why in the world are you throwing my sticks of furniture and my ragged old coverlet into my rich neighbour's back yard?"

'This fooled Alcimus. He thought he had mistaken the window and instead of throwing the things into the street was really throwing them into someone's back yard. So he went to the window, and not realizing that he was in any danger leant out for a good look around, with a particular eye for the rich neighbour's house, where he hoped to do business later on. Then the old bitch

stole up behind him and gave him a sudden unexpected push—
not a hard push, but he was off his balance at the time and down
he went, head first. It was some little distance to the ground and
he fell sideways on a big stone mounting-block just outside the
house, which smashed his ribs; he lay coughing up streams of
blood. Before he died he managed to tell us in a few broken words
what had happened. So we sent him downstream to follow
Lamachus; yes, he was worthy of the honour.

'This double loss decided us against trying our luck in Thebes
any longer. We trudged up to Plataea, the nearest town of any
size, and there we found everyone talking about a coming gladiatorial show. Demochares, the nobleman who was to produce it,
was as generous as he was rich; his entertainments were always on
a truly noble scale. It's no use trying to describe the lavish preparations made; I couldn't possibly do the man justice. At any rate he
had got together a company of gladiators famous for their wrist-
play, and another of net-and-trident fighters equally famous for
their foot-work, not to mention a gang of criminals who had forfeited the right to live at large and were being fattened up as food
for the wild beasts. Then there were great timber structures on
wheels, with towers and platforms and pictures painted on their
sides, used as movable cages for the extraordinary collection of
wild beasts that he had got together. Many of these were specially
imported from overseas; living graves for the criminals, but what
handsome ones!

'He had a particularly large pack of enormous bears, some of
them trapped by himself on hunting expeditions, some bought
from the dealers at great expense, others sent him by friends who
competed for the honour of presenting him with the largest and

fiercest specimens procurable. He kept them in his luxurious bear-garden where they were looked after with the greatest care. However, though his only motive in making all these preparations was to please the general public, the gods grew jealous. His bears began to pine and waste away, because of the heat and the long confinement and the lack of exercise, and then an epidemic carried them off, one after another, until there was hardly a bear left alive. Soon the streets of Plataea were full of bears turned out to die, like so many stranded hulks, and then the starving people from the slums, who are always ready to cram themselves with any filthy offal that they can pick up for nothing, came flocking around the carcases.

'This inspired Babulus here, and myself, with a brilliant idea. We lugged one of the biggest bears along to the boarding house where we had taken rooms, as though we intended merely to carve it up for food; but what we did was to flay it, claws and all, leaving the head attached to the skin at the back. Then very carefully we scraped the inside of the skin with razors, sprinkled it with wood ash and hung it up to dry in the sun. While it was curing we gorged ourselves on bear-steaks and took an oath to stand by one another through thick and thin. The best man among us, which meant the bravest, would volunteer to put on the skin and pretend to be a bear; the rest of us would take him to Demochares's house as an addition to the pack, where he would wait for an opportunity to open the front-door for us in the middle of the night. Then we would rush in and sack the place.

'The ingenuity of the scheme tickled everyone so much that several candidates came forward for the dangerous honour of playing bear; however, when we put the matter to the vote Thrasyleon was the man we chose. He was perfectly calm as we stitched him into his bear-skin, which was now soft and pliable. We concealed the fine seams by brushing the coarse, shaggy hair over them and fitted his head into the back part of the bear's, which we had cleaned out, leaving ventilation holes around the nostrils and eyes. He made a fine lively bear, and we bought him a cheap cage into which he crawled at once—oh, he was a brave fellow, was Thrasyleon—and then everything was ready for our next act. This was to forge a letter in the name of Nicanor, a Thracian said to be one of Demochares's closest friends. We wrote that he was out on a hunting expedition and "dedicated the first fruits of the chase, this fine bear, to his dear friend Demochares."

'It was late in the evening when we took the letter and the cage, with Thrasyleon inside, to Demachares's house. Demochares was impressed by the huge size of the new bear, and delighted with Nicanor's generosity. The present was so opportune that he told his steward to count us out a reward of ten gold pieces. Meanwhile, of course, the whole household flocked around the cage crying: "Oh, isn't he a beauty? Isn't he huge?" But Thrasyleon had enough sense to discourage their curiosity by making sudden threatening rushes at the side of the cage, so that they kept well away.

'Demochares's friends all congratulated him: what good luck to be able to make up for his previous losses, in part at least, by acquiring this splendid beast. Presently he ordered it to be led out, very carefully, to join what was left of the pack in the bear-garden. But I protested at once: "Excuse me, sir, this animal is still weak after its long, hot journey from Thrace. You must be careful about putting it among creatures that have not yet recovered, I hear, from

87

a dangerous epidemic of bear-fever. You ought to let it lie in some cool part of this house that catches the evening breeze; if possible, near a pool of water. You surely know that when at liberty a bear always makes for a running stream, or a cave with water dripping from the roof?"

'He was impressed by my warning and agreed at once. "Put the cage anywhere you please," he said. Then I added: "If you like, my lord, we are perfectly prepared to stay here by the cage all night, to feed and water him at his usual time. The poor creature has suffered greatly from the heat and the uncomfortable journey." But Demochares said: "No, please do not trouble! Nearly everyone in my household has had plenty of experience of bears and knows all about feeding them."

'So we said goodbye and walked out. We went some little distance out of town until we came to a mausoleum in a lonely spot not far from the main road. We broke in and took the lids off some rotten old coffins—with the mouldering remains of corpses still inside—which would make convenient safes for the loot we hoped soon to bring back. Then we gathered, sword in hand, outside Demochares's gate, all set and ready for the attack; but waiting, as usual, for the dark, moonless part of the night when everyone is sunk in his first and deepest sleep.

'Thrasyleon played his part well. He waited for exactly the right moment before creeping out of his cage and killing all the house-guards, who were lying asleep near by, with one of their own swords. After this he went on to kill the porter, took the key from his belt, opened the front door and let us in. Then he showed us the strong-room into which, not long before, he had noticed a large quantity of silver plate being stored away for the night. We broke it open, and I told my comrades to carry off as much gold and silver as they could handle and hurriedly dump it at the mausoleum in the homes of our thoroughly reliable dead friends; then to come back at once for another load. I volunteered to stay behind and keep guard at the gate until they returned. Thrasyleon was to remain in his disguise; we thought that it would be a great help to have a bear running loose around the place. Any slave who happened to wake up would need to be a pretty bold fellow not to rush away and lock himself in the nearest room, shaking with terror, when he saw the huge beast lumbering about in the gloom.

'Our plan was working out smoothly when, as bad luck would have it, something unforeseen happened. While I was still anxiously waiting for my comrades to come back a slave happened to wake up—I suppose he heard a noise and had an intuition that something unusual was afoot. He tiptoed out of his dormitory, and when he saw the bear roving freely about the house, went back as silently as he had come, roused the other slaves, and told them what he had seen. The next minute they all came pouring out with torches, lanterns, candles, tapers and so forth. The whole inner court was lit up, and everyone was armed with a club, a spear or a drawn sword. They ran to guard all the exits of the court and then unkennelled the boarhounds and mastiffs to pull Thrasyleon down. In the hubbub that followed I stole out and hid behind the gate, from where I watched him put up a wonderful fight against the dogs. It was as though he were struggling against the Hound of Hell itself, with its three grinning jaws. Although he knew he was doomed, he never forgot his honour, or the honour of our band, and acted his part in the most lifelike way, first running off to avoid the dogs' rushes, then standing at bay and beating at their muzzles with his claws, then retreating again until at last he managed to burst through the front gate and out into the road. But he couldn't get clear away because all the dogs in the neighbourhood—there was a large savage pack of them in the next lane—joined in the pursuit.

'It was shocking to see poor Thrasyleon cornered by dozens of maddened dogs, who fastened their teeth into various parts of his body and began pulling him to pieces. Soon I could stand it no longer: I rushed among the crowd and did all I could to rescue the poor fellow. I shouted: "What a wicked shame to kill a beast like that! He's worth pots of money." But no one would listen to me, and suddenly up ran a big man with a levelled spear and thrust Thrasyleon right through the body. When the rest of the gang saw the point sticking out on the other side, they were encouraged to use their swords. Upon my word, Thrasyleon died grandly! Though everything else was lost, he never lost heart and took whatever came to him. When another set of teeth met in his flesh or another sword sliced him, he just growled and bellowed in bear fashion so as not to betray us by shouting or yelling like a man. Yes, he met his fate unflinchingly and kept our secret to the last. It was a glorious fight, and he'd struck such terror into the crowd that nobody laid a finger on his corpse. It was quite late in the morning before a butcher arrived who had more courage than his neighbours. He slit open the paunch and found to his astonishment that he was not flaying a bear, but stripping a brave bandit of his overcoat.

'I went to meet the rest of the band with the news of Thrasyleon's death—but his glory will never die while any of us are still alive to tell the tale—and we returned to the mausoleum. There we packed up the loot that the honest corpses had been guarding for us, and hurried out of the district. It was a hard journey over the hills with our loads, and the loss of our three comrades made us feel pretty despondent. The same fancy haunted us all the way home, that the Goddess of Honesty must have left this upper world, distressed at her bad treatment, and gone to live among ghosts and corpses. However—here we are, and there's the loot.'

They filled gold cups with untempered wine and poured it on the floor of the cave as a libation for the dead. Then they sang hymns in honour of their patron Mars, lay down and went off to sleep.

*

The old woman gave us two beasts such a generous quantity of raw barley that my horse might have fancied himself the guest of honour at a banquet of the Salian College at Rome. He had it all to himself, because though I like barley, I had always eaten it either boiled until tender in a stew, or properly milled and baked into bread. But I found the corner where the remaining loaves were stored and started munching ravenously. My jaws ached with hunger and seemed covered with cobwebs from long disuse.

Late that night the bandits hastily left the cave; some were dressed up as ghosts, others wore ordinary clothes and carried swords. But not even sleep could stop me from chewing on greedily, without a pause. While I was still Lucius I had been able to rise from table satisfied wth a mere loaf or two, but now I had such a large belly to fill that I had nearly finished my third basketful of bread when dawn broke and discovered me still eating; then at last with the proverbial humility of an ass, I left my food—most reluctantly, I admit—and quenched my thirst at a neighbouring stream.

Presently the bandits returned, with very sober faces. Despite their numbers and armed strength they brought back no loot at all, not so much as a ragged cloak; and only a single prisoner, a girl. However, to judge from her clothes, she belonged to one of the first families of the district and was so beautiful that though I was an ass, I swear that I fell deeply in love with her. They brought her into the cave where, in her distress, she began to pull her hair out and tear her clothes. They did what they could to comfort her. 'You are perfectly safe, Madame,' they assured her. 'We have no intention either of hurting you or showing you any discourtesy. Be patient for a few days, if only as a kindness to us: you see, it was poverty that forced us to take up this profession and your close-fisted parents are bound to hurry up with the ransom money. After all, you are their only daughter and they are disgustingly rich.'

Her distress was increased rather than lessened by this rough consolation, and I could not blame her for laying her head between her knees and crying uncontrollably. They told the old woman to sit with the girl and amuse her as best she could, while they went off again on business.

The old woman could do nothing with her. She cried louder than ever, her chest heaving with sobs, until tears of sympathy rolled down my hairy cheeks. She wailed: 'To think of losing everything! Such a lovely home, so many dear friends and kind slaves, and parents whom I love so much. To be kidnapped in this dreadful way and shut up like a criminal in a rocky prison without any of the comforts which I have had all my life! Under constant threat of having my throat cut and in the power of these horrible bloodthirsty bandits! How can you expect me to stop crying? How can you expect me even to stay alive?'

She went on in this strain, until depression, combined with a sore throat and weariness, made her stop: she closed her swollen eyes and dozed off. Soon she awoke again, in greater distress than before, and started beating her beautiful face and pounding her breasts. The old woman begged her to explain this new outburst of sorrow, but she only groaned and said: 'No, there's no longer any doubt about it: I have no hope of escape. All is over. A rope, or a sword, or a handy precipice—it has come to that now.'

The old woman grew very angry. She glowered at the girl and asked: 'Why are you crying, you naughty little thing? Why did you go to sleep, and then wake up almost at once to start this damned nonsense all over again? I'll give you precipices! I suppose you want to defraud my poor boys of the tidy sum they fixed as your ransom fee? If you won't calm down or stop crying— bandits aren't easily impressed by tears—I'll see that they roast you alive, instead.'

That frightened her. She seized the old woman's hand and kissed it: 'Spare me, dear granny, spare me!' she said. 'Only be patient with me. I refuse to believe you incapable of pity, old as you are, because you have such lovely white hair. Please let me tell you all about myself; it's such a sad story.'

The old woman said she didn't mind listening, so the girl began: 'I have a cousin three years older than myself. His name is Tlepolemus. We two have been inseparable since childhood—in fact, we once used to sleep in the same bed—and love each other dearly. He is a nobleman, and everyone in the town wants to see him promoted to the highest offices. We have been engaged for years, and only today our four parents publicly registered our marriage contract; after which he went off with his family and friends to offer the usual sacrifices in the different temples, while I waited for him at home among the laurel-leaves and torches with everyone singing the bridal hymn. My mother had helped me into my wedding-dress and was crying and hugging and kissing me, and had already begun anxiously praying that I would be blessed with children to keep the family name alive, when suddenly the bandits burst in with glittering swords, just like gladiators. They made no attempt at killing or robbing anyone, but went straight for the bridal chamber in a compact body. None of the slaves, or anyone else, offered the least resistance, but let the bandits snatch me, half-dead with fear, from my mother's arms. So the wedding came to a sudden end. It was like the wedding of Hippodamia and Pirithoüs which the Centaurs and Lapiths spoiled by their brawling, or that other one of Laodamia and Protesilaüs, when Protesilaüs was suddenly called away to fight at Troy and was almost the first Greek to be killed. When I went to sleep just now I had a most horrible dream which brought all my misery back, worse than before. I dreamed that I was violently pulled out of my bridal bed, and out of the bedroom and out of the house and carried off through a pathless desert, still calling the name of the poor darling Tlepolemus who had been cheated of my kisses. And in the dream he came after me, still perfumed and garlanded like a bridegroom, following the trail of the bandits and shouting to everyone to help him rescue his beautiful wife who had been stolen from him. This made one of the bandits angry. He picked up a big stone and threw it at the poor boy and killed him. I woke up screaming.'

The old woman sighed sympathetically. 'My pretty dear,' she said, 'you must be cheerful and stop worrying about dreams. The dreams that come in daylight are not to be trusted, everyone knows that, and even night-dreams often go by contraries. For example, that one is weeping or being beaten or even having one's throat cut, is good luck and usually means prosperous change, whereas to dream that one is laughing, stuffing oneself with sweets or having fun under the bedclothes is bad luck and a sure sign of illness or unhappiness. Now let me tell you a fairy tale or two to make you feel a little better.'

7

Cupid and Psyche (I)

'ONCE UPON A TIME there lived a king and queen who had three very beautiful daughters. They were so beautiful, in fact, that it was only just possible to find words of praise for the elder two, and to express the breath-taking loveliness of the youngest, the like of which had never been seen before, was beyond all power of human speech. Every day thousands of her father's subjects came to gaze at her, foreigners too, and were so dumbfounded by the sight that they paid her the homage due to the Goddess Venus alone. They pressed their right thumbs and forefingers together, reverently raised them to their lips and blew kisses towards her. The news of her matchless beauty spread through neighbouring cities and countries. Some reported: "Immortal Venus, born from the deep blue sea and risen to Heaven from its foam, has descended on earth and is now incarnate as a mortal at whom everyone is allowed to gaze." Others: "No, this time the earth, not the sea, has been impregnated by a heavenly emanation and has borne a new Goddess of Love, all the more beautiful because she is still a virgin." The princess's fame was carried farther and farther to distant provinces and still more distant ones and people made long pilgrimages over land and sea to witness the greatest wonder of their age. As a result, no body took the trouble to visit Venus's shrines at Cyprian Paphos or Carian Cnidos or even in the isle of Cythera where her lovely foot first touched dry land; her festivals were neglected, her rites discontinued, the cushions on which her statues had been propped at her sacred temple feasts were kicked about the floor, the statues themselves were left without their usual garlands, her altars were unswept and cluttered with the foul remains of months-old burned sacrifices, her temples were allowed to fall into ruins.

'When the young princess went out on her morning walks through the streets, victims were offered in her honour, sacred feasts spread for her, flowers scattered in her path, and rose garlands presented to her by an adoring crowd of suppliants who addressed her by all the titles that really belonged to the great Goddess of Love herself. This extraordinary transfer of divine honours to a mortal naturally angered the true Venus. Unable to suppress her feelings, she shook her head menacingly and said to herself: "Really now, whoever would have thought that I'd be treated like this? I, all the world's lovely Venus whom the philosophers call 'the Universal Mother' and the original source of all five elements! So I'm expected to share my sovereignty, am I, with a mortal who goes about pretending to be myself? And to watch my bright name, which is registered in Heaven, being dragged through the dirty mud of Earth! Oh, yes, and I must be content, of course, with the reflected glory of worship paid to this girl, grateful for a share in the expiatory sacrifices offered to her instead of me? It meant nothing, I suppose when the shepherd Paris, whose just and honest verdict Jupiter himself confirmed, awarded me the apple of beauty over the heads of my two goddess rivals? No, it's quite absurd. I can't let this silly creature, whoever she may be, usurp my glory any longer. I'll very soon make her sick and sorry about her good looks: they are dead against the rules."

'She at once called her winged son Eros, alias Cupid, that very wicked boy, with neither manners nor respect for the decencies, who spends his time running from building to building all night long with his torch and his arrows, breaking up respectable homes. Somehow he never gets punished for all the harm he does, though he never seems to do anything good in compensation. Venus knew that he was naturally bent on mischief, but she tempted him to still worse behaviour by bringing him to the city where the princess lived—her name, by the way, was Psyche—and telling him the whole story of the new cult that had grown up around her. Groaning with indignation she said: "I implore you, darling, as you love your mother, to use your dear little arrows and that sweet torch of yours against this impudent girl. If you have any respect for me, you'll give me my revenge, revenge in full. You'll see that the princess falls desperately in love with some perfect outcast of a man—someone who has lost rank, fortune, everything, someone who goes about in terror of his life and in such complete degradation that nobody viler can be found in the whole world."

'She kissed him long and tenderly and then went to the near by sea-shore, where she ran along the tops of the waves as they danced foaming towards her. At the touch of her rosy feet the whole sea suddenly calmed, and she had no sooner willed the powers of the deep to appear, than up they bobbed as though she had shouted their names. The Nereids were there, singing a part song; and Neptune, sometimes called Portumnus, with his blueish beard; his wife Salacia, the naughty goddess of the deep sea, with a lapful of aphrodisiac fish; and little Palaemon, their charioteer, riding on a dolphin. After these came troops of Tritons swimming about in all directions, one blowing softly on his conch-shell, another protecting Venus from sunburn with a silk parasol, a third holding a mirror for her to admire herself in, and a whole team of them, yoked two and two, harnessed to her car. When Venus goes for an ocean cruise she's attended by quite an army of retainers.

'Meanwhile Psyche got no satisfaction at all from the honours paid her. Everyone stared at her, everyone praised her, but no commoner, no prince, no king even, dared to make love to her. All wondered at her beauty, but only as they might have wondered at an exquisite statue. Both her less beautiful elder sisters, whose reputation was not so great, had been courted by kings and successfully married to them, but Psyche remained single. She stayed at home feeling very miserable and rather ill, and began to hate the beauty which everyone else adored.

'Her poor father feared that the gods might be angry with him for allowing his subjects to make so much of her, so he went to the ancient oracle of Apollo at Miletus and, after the usual prayers and sacrifices, asked where he was to find a husband for his daughter whom nobody wanted to marry. Apollo, though an

Ionian Greek and the true founder of Miletus, chose to deliver the following oracle in Latin verse:

> *On some high mountain's craggy summit place*
> *The virgin, decked for deadly nuptial rites,*
> *Nor hope a son-in-law of mortal birth*
> *But a dire mischief, viperous and fierce,*
> *Who flies through aether and with fire and sword*
> *Tires and debilitates all things that are,*
> *Terrific to the powers that reign on high,*
> *Great Jupiter himself fears this winged pest*
> *And streams and Stygian shades his power abhor.*

'The king, who until now had been a happy man, came slowly back from the oracle feeling thoroughly depressed and told his queen what an unfavourable answer he had got. They spent several miserable days brooding over their daughter's fate and weeping all the while. But time passed, and the cruel oracle had to be obeyed.

'The hour came when a procession formed up for Psyche's dreadful wedding. The torches chosen were ones that burned low with a sooty, spluttering flame; instead of the happy wedding-march the flutes played a querulous Lydian lament; the marriage-chant ended with funereal howls, and the poor bride wiped the tears from her eyes with the corner of her flame-coloured veil. Everyone turned out, groaning sympathetically at the calamity that had overtaken the royal house, and a day of public mourning was at once proclaimed. But there was no help for it: Apollo's oracle had to be obeyed. So when the preliminaries of this hateful ceremony had been completed in deep grief, the bridal procession moved off, followed by the entire city, and at the head of it walked Psyche with the air of a woman going to her grave, not her bridal bed.

'Her parents, overcome with grief and horror, tried to delay things by holding up the procession, but Psyche herself opposed them. "Poor Father, poor Mother, why torment yourselves by prolonging your grief unnecessarily? You are old enough to know better. Why increase my distress by crying and shrieking yourselves hoarse? Why spoil the two faces that I love best in the world by crying your eyes sore and pulling out your beautiful white hair? Why beat your dear breasts until my own heart aches again? Now, too late, you at last see the reward that my beauty has earned you; the curse of divine jealousy for the extravagant honours paid me. When the people all over the world celebrated me as the New Venus and offered me sacrifices, then was the time for you to grieve and weep as though I were already dead; I see now, I see it as clearly as daylight, that the one cause of all my misery is this blasphemous use of the Goddess's name. So lead me up to the rock of the oracle. I am looking forward to my lucky bridal night and my marvellous husband. Why should I hesitate? Why should I shrink from him, even if he has been born for the destruction of the whole world?

'She walked resolutely forward. The crowds followed her up to the rock at the top of the hill, where they left her. They returned to their homes in deep dejection, extinguishing the wedding-torches with their tears, and throwing them away. Her broken-hearted parents shut themselves up in their palace behind closed doors and heavily curtained windows.

'Psyche was left alone weeping and trembling at the very top of the hill, until a friendly west wind suddenly sprang up. It played around her, gradually swelling out her skirt and veil and cloak until it lifted her off the ground and carried her slowly down into a valley at the foot of the hill, where she found herself gently laid on a bed of the softest turf, starred with flowers.

'It was such a cool, comfortable place to lie that she began to feel rather more composed. She stopped crying and fell asleep, and when she awoke, feeling thoroughly refreshed, it was still daylight. She rose and walked calmly towards the tall trees of a near-by wood, through which a clear stream was flowing. This stream led her to the heart of the wood where she came upon a royal palace, too wonderfully built to be the work of anyone but a god; in fact, as soon as she came in at the gates she knew that some god must be in residence there.

'The ceiling, exquisitely carved in citrus wood and ivory, was supported by golden columns; the walls were sheeted with silver on which figures of all the beasts in the world were embossed and seemed to be running towards Psyche as she came in. They were clearly the work of some demi-god, if not a full god, and the pavement was a mosaic of all kinds of precious stones arranged to form pictures. How lucky, how very lucky anyone would be to have the chance of walking on a jewelled floor like that! And the other parts of the palace, which was a very large one, were just as beautiful, and just as fabulously costly. The walls were faced with massive gold blocks which glittered so brightly with their own radiance that the house had a daylight of its own even when the sun refused to shine: every room and portico and doorway streamed with light, and the furniture matched the rooms. Indeed, it seemed the sort of palace that Jupiter himself might have built as his earthly residence. Psyche was entranced. She went timorously up the steps, and after a time dared to cross the threshold. The beauty of the hall lured her on; and every new sight added to her wonder and admiration. When well inside the palace she came on splendid treasure chambers stuffed with unbelievable riches; every wonderful thing that anyone could possibly imagine was there. But what amazed her even more than the stupendous wealth of this world treasury, was that no single chain, bar, lock or armed guard protected it.

'As she stood gazing in rapt delight, a voice suddenly spoke from nowhere: "Do these treasures astonish your Royal Highness? They are all yours. Why not go to your bedroom now, and rest your tired body. When you feel inclined for your bath, we will be there to help you—this is one of your maids speaking—and afterwards you will find your wedding banquet ready for you."

'Psyche was grateful to the unknown Providence that was taking such good care of her and did as the disembodied voice suggested. First she found her bedroom and dozed off again for awhile, then she went to the bath, where invisible hands undressed her, washed her, anointed her and dressed her again in her bridal costume. As she wandered out of the bathroom she noticed a semi-circular table with a comfortable chair in front of it; it was laid for a banquet, though there was nothing yet on it to eat or drink. She sat down expectantly—and at once nectarous wines and appetizing dishes appeared by magic, floating up to her of their own accord. She saw nobody at all; the waiters were mere voices, and when someone came in and sang and someone else accompanied him on the lyre, she saw neither of them, nor the lyre either. Then a whole invisible choir burst into song.

When this delightful banquet was over, Psyche thought it must
be about time to go to bed, so she went to her bedroom again
and undressed and lay awake for a long time.

'Towards midnight she heard a gentle whispering near her,
and began to feel lonely and scared. Anything might happen
in a vast uninhabited place like this, and she had fears for her
chastity. But no, it was the whisper of her unknown husband.

'Now he was climbing into bed with her. Now he was taking
her into his arms and making her his wife.

'He left her hastily just before daybreak, and almost at once she
heard the voices of her maids reassuring her that though she had
lost her virginity, her chastity was safe. So she went to sleep again.

'The next day she made herself more at home in her palace,
and on the following night her invisible husband paid her another
visit. The third day and night were spent in the same way until,
as one might expect, the novelty of having invisible servants wore
off and she settled down to what was a very enjoyable routine;
at any rate she could not feel lonely with so many voices about her.

'Meanwhile the old king and queen were doing exactly what
she had asked them not to do—wasting their time in unnecessary
grief and tears; and the news of Psyche's sad fate spread from
country to country until both her elder sisters heard all the details.
They left their palaces and hurried back in deep grief to their
native city to console their parents.

'On the night of their arrival Psyche's husband, whom she still
knew only by touch and hearing, warned her: "Lovely Psyche,
darling wife, the Fates are cruel: you are in deadly danger. Guard
against it vigilantly. Your elder sisters are alarmed at the report
of your death. They will soon be visiting the rock from which

the West Wind blew you down into this valley, to see whether they can find any trace of you there. If you happen to hear them mourning for you up there, pay no attention at all. You must not answer them, nor even look up to them; for that would cause me great unhappiness and bring utter ruin on yourself."

'Psyche promised to do as her husband asked; but when the darkness had vanished, and so had he, the poor girl spent the whole day in tears, complaining over and over again that not only was she a prisoner in this wonderful palace without a single human being to chat with, but her husband had now forbidden her to relieve the minds of her poor sisters, or even to look up at them without speaking. That night she went to bed without supper or bath or anything else to comfort her, and soaked her pillow with tears. Her husband came in earlier than usual, drew her to him, still weeping, and expostulated gently with her, "O Psyche, what did you promise me? What may I expect you to do next? You have cried all day and all evening and even now when I hold you close to me, you go on crying. Very well, then, do as you like, follow your own disastrous fancies; but I warn you solemnly that when you begin to wish you had listened to me, the harm will have been done."

'She pleaded earnestly with him, swearing she would die unless she were allowed to see her sisters and comfort them and have a short talk with them. In the end she forced him to consent. He even said that she might give them as much jewellery as she pleased; but he warned her with terrifying insistence that her sisters were evil-minded women and would try to make her discover what he looked like. If she listened to them, her sacrilegious curiosity would mean the end of all her present happiness and she would never lie in his arms again.

'She thanked him for his kindness and was quite herself again. "No, no," she protested, "I'd rather die a hundred times over than lose you. I have no idea who you are, but I love you. I love you desperately, I love you as I love my own soul; I wouldn't exchange your kisses for the kisses of the God Cupid himself. So please, please grant me one more favour! Tell your servant, the West Wind, to carry my sisters down here in the same delightful way that he carried me." She kissed him coaxingly, whispered love-words in his ear, wound her arms and legs more closely around him and called him: "My honey, my own husband, soul of my soul!" Overcome by the power of her love he was forced to yield, however reluctantly, and promised to give her what she asked. But he vanished again before daybreak.

8

Cupid and Psyche (II)

'MEANWHILE Psyche's sisters enquired their way to the rock where she had been abandoned. Hurrying there they wept and beat their breasts until the cliffs re-echoed. "Psyche! Psyche!" they screamed. The shrill cry reached the valley far below and Psyche ran out of her palace in feverish excitement, crying: "Sisters, dear sisters, why are you mourning for me? There's no need for that at all. Here am I, Psyche herself! Please, please stop that terrible noise and dry your tears. In a moment you'll be able to embrace me."

'Then she whistled up the West Wind, and gave him her husband's orders. He at once obliged with one of his gentle puffs, and wafted them safely down to her. The three sisters embraced and kissed rapturously. Soon they were shedding tears of joy, not of sorrow. "Come in now," said Psyche, "come in with me to see my new home. It will make you both very happy." She showed them her treasure chambers and they heard the voices of the big retinue of invisible slaves. She ordered a wonderful bath for them and feasted them splendidly at her magical table. But this revelation of Psyche's goddess-like prosperity made them both miserably jealous—particularly the younger one, who was always very inquisitive. She was dying to know who owned all this fabulous wealth; so she pressed Psyche to tell her what sort of a man her husband was, and how he treated her.

'Psyche was loyal to her promise and gave away nothing: but she made up a story for the occasion. She said lightly that, oh, her husband was a very handsome young man, with a little downy beard, and spent all his time hunting in the neighbouring hills and valleys. But when her sisters began to cross-examine her she grew afraid. Suppose she contradicted herself or made a slip or broke her promise? She loaded them both with jewelled pins and rings, festooned them with precious necklaces, then summoned the West Wind and asked him to fetch them away at once. He carried them up to the rock, and on their way back to the city the poison of envy began working again in their hearts.

'The elder said: "How blindly and cruelly and unjustly Fortune has treated us! Do *you* think it fair that we three sisters should be given such different destinies? You and I are the two eldest, yet we get exiled from our home and friends and married off to foreigners who treat us like slaves; while Psyche, the result of Mother's last feeble effort at child-bearing, is given the most marvellous palace in existence and a god for a husband, and doesn't even know how to make proper use of her tremendous wealth. Did you ever see such masses of amazing jewels, such cupboardsful of embroidered dresses? Why, the very floors were made of gems set in solid gold! If her husband is really as good-looking as she says, she is quite the luckiest woman in the whole world. The chances are that if he remains as fond of her as he is at present he will make her a goddess. And, my goodness, wasn't she behaving as if she were one already, with her proud looks and condescending airs? She's only flesh and blood after all, yet she orders the winds about and has a palaceful of invisible attendants. How I hate her! My husband's older than Father, balder than a pumpkin and as puny as a little boy; and he locks up everything in the house with bolts and chains."

' "*My* husband," said the younger sister, "is even worse than yours. He's doubled up with sciatica, which prevents him from sleeping with me more than once in a blue moon, and his fingers are so crooked and knobby with gout that I have to spend half my time massaging them. You remember what beautiful white hands I used to have? Well, look what a state they are in now from messing about with his stinking fomentations and disgusting salves and filthy plasters! I'm treated more like a surgeon's assistant than a queen. You're altogether too patient, my dear; in fact, if you will excuse my saying so, you're positively servile, the way you accept this monstrous state of affairs. Personally, I simply can't stand seeing my youngest sister living in such undeserved style. I'm glad you noticed how haughtily she treated us, how she bragged of her wealth and how stingy with her presents she was. Then, the moment she got bored with our visit, she whistled up the wind and had us blown off the premises. But I'll be ashamed to call myself a woman, if I don't see that she gets toppled down from her pinnacle before long and flung into the gutter. And if you feel as bitter as you ought to feel at the way she's insulted us both, what about joining forces and working out some plan for humbling her?"

' "I'm with you," said the elder sister. "And in the first place I suggest that we show nobody, not even Father and Mother, these presents of hers, and let nobody know that she's still alive. It's bad enough to have seen her revelling in her good luck, without having to bring the news home to be spread all over the place; and there's no pleasure in being rich unless people hear about it. Psyche must be made to realize that we're not her servants, but her elder sisters."

' "Good," said the younger one. "We'll go back to our shabby homes and our shabby old husbands without telling Father and Mother anything. But when either of us thinks of a good plan for humbling Psyche's pride, let's come here again and boldly put it into operation."

'The two bad sisters shook hands on this. They hid the valuable presents that Psyche had given them and, as they neared their father's palace, each began scratching her face and tearing out her hair in pretended grief at having found no trace of their sister; which made the king and queen sadder than ever. Then they separated: each went back full of malicious rage to her own adopted country, thinking of ways for ruining her innocent sister, even if it meant killing her.

'Meanwhile, Psyche's unseen husband gave her another warning. He asked her one night: "Do you realize that a dangerous storm is brewing in the far distance? It will soon be on you and unless you take the most careful precautions, it will sweep you away. These treacherous bitch-wolves are scheming for our destruction: they will urge you to look at my face, though as

I have often told you, once you see it, you lose me for ever. So if these hateful vampires come to visit you again—and I know very well that they will—you must refuse to speak to them. Or, if this is too difficult for a girl as open-hearted and simple as yourself, you must at least take care not to answer any questions about me. Pretend that you have not heard them. This is most important, because we have a family on the way: though you are still only a child, you will soon have a child of your own which shall be born divine if you keep our secret, but mortal if you divulge it."

'Psyche was exultant when she heard that she might have a god for a baby. She began excitedly counting the months and days that must pass before it was born. But she knew very few of the facts of life and could not make out why the mere breach of her maidenhead was having so odd an affect on her figure.

'The wicked sisters were now hurrying to Psyche's palace again, with the ruthless hate of Furies, and once more she was warned: "Today is the fatal day. Your enemies are near. They have struck camp, marshalled their forces and sounded the 'Charge'. They are enemies of your own sex and blood. They are your elder sisters, rushing at you with drawn swords aimed at your throat. O darling Psyche, what dangers surround us! Have pity on yourself and on me and on our unborn child! Keep my secret safe and so guard us all from the destruction that threatens us. Refuse to see those wicked women. They have forfeited the right to be called your sisters because of the deadly hate they bear you. Forbid them to come here, refuse to listen to them when, like Sirens leaning over the cliff, they make the rocks echo with their unlucky voices. Preserve absolute silence."

'Psyche, her voice broken with sobs, said: "Surely you can trust me? The last time my sisters came to visit me I gave you convincing proof of my loyalty and my power of keeping a secret; it will be the same again tomorrow. Only tell the West Wind to do his duty as before, and allow me to have a sight, at least, of my sisters; as a very poor consolation for never seeing you, my darling. These fragrant curls dangling all round your head; these cheeks as tender and smooth as my own; this breast which gives out such extraordinary heat; oh, how I look forward to finding out what you are really like by studying my baby's face! So please, be sweet and humour my craving—it will be bad for the baby if you refuse—and make your Psyche happy. You and I love each other so much. I promise that if you let me see them I won't be so frightened of the dark or so anxious to look at you when I have you safe in my arms, light of my life!" Her voice and sweet caresses broke down his resistance. He wiped her eyes dry with his hair, granted what she asked, and as usual disappeared again before the day broke.

'The wicked sisters landed together at the nearest port and, not even troubling to visit their parents, hurried stright to the rock above the valley and with extraordinary daring leaped down from it without waiting for the breeze to belly out their robes. However, the West Wind was bound to obey standing orders, reluctant though he might be: he caught them in his robe as they fell and brought them safely to the ground.

'They rushed into the palace crying: "Sister, dear sister, where are you?" and embraced their victim with what she took for deep affection. Then, with cheerful laughter masking their treachery, they cried: "Why, Psyche, you're not nearly so slim as you used to be. You'll be a mother before very long. We're dying to see what sort of a baby it's going to be, and Father and Mother will be absolutely delighted with the news. Oh, how we shall love to nurse your golden baby for you. If it takes after its parents, as it ought to, it will be a perfect little Cupid."

'They gradually wormed themselves into her confidence. Seeing that they were tired, she invited them to sit down and rest while water was heated for them; and when they had taken their baths, she gave them the most delicious supper they had ever tasted, course after course of tasty dishes, from spiced sausages to marzipan, while an unseen harpist played for them at her orders, and an unseen flautist, and a choir sang the most ravishing songs. But even such heavenly music as that failed to soften the hard hearts of the sisters. They insidiously brought the conversation round to her husband, asking her who he was, and from where his family came.

'Psyche was very simple-minded and, forgetting what story she had told them before, invented a new one. She said that he was a middle-aged merchant from the next province, very rich, with slightly grizzled hair. Then breaking the conversation off short, she loaded them with valuable presents and sent them away in their windy carriage.

'As they rode home the younger sister said: "Now, what do you make of the monstrous lies she tells us? First the silly creature says that her husband is a very young man with a downy beard, and then she says that he's middle-aged with grizzled hair! Quick work, eh? You may depend upon it that the beast is either hiding something from us, or else she doesn't know herself what her husband looks like."

' "Whatever the truth may be," said the elder sister, "we must ruin her as soon as possible. But if she really has never seen her husband, then he must be a god, and her baby will be a god too."

' "If anything like that happens, which Heaven forbid," said the younger, "I'll hang myself at once—I couldn't bear Psyche to mother an immortal. I think we have a clue now to the best way of tricking her. Meanwhile, what about calling on Father and Mother?"

'They went to the palace, where they gave their parents an off-hand greeting. The violence of their passions kept them awake all night. As soon as it was morning they hurried to the rock and floated down into the valley as usual with the help of the West Wind. Rubbing their eyelids hard until they managed to squeeze out a few tears, they went to Psyche and said: "Oh, sister, ignorance is indeed bliss! There you sit calmly and happily without the least suspicion of the terrible misfortune that has befallen you, while we are in absolute anguish about it. You see, we watch over your interests like true sisters, and since we three have always shared the same sorrows and joys it would be wrong for us to hide your danger from you. It is this, that the husband who comes secretly gliding into your bed at night is an enormous snake, with widely gaping jaws, a body that could coil around you a dozen times and a neck swollen with deadly poison. Remember what Apollo's oracle said: that you were destined to marry a savage wild beast. Several of the farmers who go hunting in the woods around this place have met him coming home at nightfall from his feeding ground, and ever so many of the people in the nearest village have seen him swimming across the ford there. They all say that he won't pamper you much longer, but that when your nine months are nearly up he will eat you alive; apparently his favourite food is a woman far gone in pregnancy. So you had better make up your mind whether you will come away and live with us—we would do anything in the world to save you—or whether you prefer to stay here with this fiendish reptile until you finish up in his guts. Perhaps you're fascinated by living here alone with your voices all day, and at night having secret and disgusting relations with a poisonous snake; if so, you are welcome to the life, but at all events we have done our duty as affectionate sisters by warning you how it must end."

'Poor silly Psyche was aghast at the dreadful news. She lost all control of herself, trembled, turned deathly pale, and forgetting all the warnings her husband had given her, and all her own promises, plunged headlong into the abyss of misfortune. She gasped out brokenly: "Dearest sisters, thank you for being so kind. You're quite right to warn me, and I believe that the people who told you were not making it up. The fact is, I have never seen my husband's face and haven't the least idea who he is or where he comes from. I only hear him speaking to me at night in whispers, and find it very hard to be married to someone who hates the light of day as much as he does. So I have every reason to suppose, as you do, that he must be some sort of monster. Besides, he is always giving me frightful warnings about what will happen if I try to see what he looks like. So please, if you can advise me what to do in this dreadful situation, tell me at once, like the dear sisters you are: otherwise, all the trouble you have been kind enough to take will be wasted."

'The wicked women saw that Psyche's defences were down, and her heart laid open to their attacks. They pressed their advantage savagely. The younger said: "Blood is thicker than water; the thought of your danger makes us forget our own. We two have talked the matter over countless times since yesterday and have come to the conclusion that you have only one chance of saving yourself. It is this. Get hold of a very sharp carving knife, make it sharper still by stropping it on your palm, then hide it somewhere on your side of the bed. Also, get hold of a lamp, have it filled full of oil, trim the wick carefully, light it and hide it behind the bedroom tapestry. Do all this with the greatest secrecy and when the monster visits you as usual, wait until he is stretched out at full length, and you know by his deep breathing that he's fast asleep. Then slip out of bed with the knife in your hand and tiptoe barefooted to the place where you have hidden the lamp. Finally, with its light to assist you, perform your noble deed, plunge the knife down with all your strength at the nape of the creature's poisonous neck, and cut off his head. We promise to stand close by and keep careful watch. The moment you have saved yourself by killing it, we shall come running in and help you to get away at once with all your treasure. After that, we'll marry you to a decent human being."

'When they saw that Psyche was now determined to follow their suggestion, they went quietly off, terrified to be anywhere near her when the catastrophe came; they were helped up to the rock by the West Wind, ran back to their ships as fast as they could and sailed off at once.

'Psyche was left alone, except in so far as a woman who had decided to kill her husband is haunted by the Furies. Her mind was as restless as a stormy sea. When she first began making preparations for her crime, her resolve was firm; but presently she wavered and started worrying about what would happen if she succeeded and what would happen if she failed. She hurried, then she dawdled, not feeling quite sure whether after all she was doing the right thing, then got furiously angry again. The strange part of the story is that though she loathed the idea of sleeping with a poisonous snake, she was still in love with her husband. However, as the evening drew on, she finally made up her mind and hurriedly got the lamp and carving knife ready.

'Night fell, and her husband came to bed, and as soon as they had finished kissing and embracing each other, he fell fast asleep. Psyche was not naturally either very strong or very brave, but the cruel power of fate made a virago of her. Holding the carving knife in a murderous grip, she uncovered the lamp and let its light shine on the bed.

'At once the secret was revealed. There lay the gentlest and sweetest of all wild creatures, Cupid himself, the beautiful Love-god, and at sight of him the flame of the lamp spurted joyfully up and the knife turned its edge for shame.

'Psyche was terrified. She lost all control of her senses, and pale as death, fell trembling to her knees, where she desperately tried to hide the knife by plunging it in her own heart. She would have succeeded, too, had the knife not shrunk from the crime and twisted itself out of her hand. Faint and unnerved though she was, she began to feel better as she stared at Cupid's divine beauty: his golden hair, washed in nectar and still scented with it, thick curls straying over white neck and flushed checks and falling prettily entangled on either side of his head—hair so bright that the flame of the lamp winked in the radiant light reflected from it. At his shoulders grew soft wings of the purest white, and though they were at rest, the tender down fringing the feathers quivered naughtily all the time. The rest of his body was so smooth and beautiful that Venus could never have been ashamed to acknowledge him as her son. At the foot of the bed lay this great god's bow, quiver and arrows.

'Psyche's curiosity could be satisfied only by a close examination of her husband's sacred weapons. She pulled an arrow out of the quiver and touched the point with the tip of her thumb to try its sharpness; but her hand was trembling and she pressed too hard. The skin was pierced and out came a drop or two of blood. So Psyche accidently fell in love with Love. Burning with greater passion for Cupid even than before, she flung herself panting upon him, desperate with desire, and smothered him with kisses; her one fear now being that he would wake too soon.

'While she clung to him, utterly bewildered with delight, the lamp which she was still holding, whether from treachery or from envy, or because it longed as it were to touch and kiss such a marvellously beautiful body, spurted a drop of scalding oil on the God's right shoulder. What a bold and impudent lamp, what a worthless vessel at the altar of Love—for the first lamp was surely invented by some lover who wished to prolong all night the passionate delights of his eye—so to scorch the God of all fire! Cupid sprang up in pain, and taking in the whole disgraceful scene at a glance, spread his wings and flew off without a word; but not before the poor girl had seized his right leg with both hands and clung to it. She looked very queer, carried up like that through the cloudy sky; but soon her strength failed her and she tumbled down to earth again.

'Cupid did not desert her immediately, but alighted on the top

118

of a cypress near by, where he stood reproaching her. "Oh, silly, foolish Psyche, it was for your sake that I disobeyed the orders of my mother Venus! She told me to inflame you with passion for some utterly worthless man, but I preferred to fly down from Heaven and become your lover myself. I know only too well that I acted thoughtlessly, and now look at the result! Cupid, the famous archer, wounds himself with one of his own arrows and marries a girl who mistakes him for a monster; she tries to chop off his head and darken the eyes that have beamed such love upon her. This was the danger of which I warned you again and again, gently begging you to be on your guard. As for those sisters of yours who turned you against me and gave you such damnable advice, I'll very soon be avenged on them. But your punishment will simply be that I'll fly away from you." He soared up into the air and was gone.

'Psyche lay motionless on the ground, following him with her eyes and moaning bitterly. When the steady beat of his wings had carried him clean out of her sight, she climbed up the bank of a river that flowed close by and flung herself into the water. But the kindly river, out of respect for the god whose warm power is felt as much by water-creatures as by beasts and birds, washed her ashore with a gentle wave and laid her high and dry on the flowery turf.

'Pan, the goat-legged country god, happened to be sitting near by, caressing the mountain nymph Echo and teaching her to repeat all sorts of pretty songs. A flock of she-goats roamed around, browsing greedily on the grass. Pan was already aware of Psyche's misfortune, so he gently beckoned to the desolate girl and did what he could to comfort her. "Pretty dear," he said soothingly.

"Though I'm only an old, old shepherd and very much of a countryman, I have picked up a good deal of experience in my time. So if I am right in my conjecture, or my divination as sensible people would call it—your unsteady walk, your pallor, your constant sighs, and your sad eyes show that you're desperately in love. Listen: make no further attempt at suicide by leaping from a precipice, or doing anything else violent. Stop crying, try to be cheerful, and open your heart to Cupid, the greatest of us gods; he's a thoroughly spoilt young fellow whom you must humour by praying to him only in the gentlest, sweetest language."

'It is very lucky to be addressed by Pan, but Psyche made no reply. She merely curtseyed dutifully and went on. She trudged along the road by the river for awhile, until for some reason or other she decided to follow a lane that led off it. Towards evening it brought her to a city of which she soon found out that her eldest sister was the queen. She announced her arrival at the palace and was at once admitted.

'After an exchange of embraces, the queen asked Psyche why she had come. Psyche answered: "You remember your advice about that carving knife and the monstrous snake who pretended to be my husband and was going to swallow me? Well, I took it, but no sooner had I shone my lamp on the bed than I saw a marvellous sight: Venus's divine son, Cupid himself, lying there in tranquil sleep. The joy and relief were too great for me. I quite lost my head and didn't know how to satisfy my longing for him; but then, by a dreadful accident, a drop of burning oil from the lamp spurted on his shoulder. The pain woke him at once. When he saw me holding the lamp and the knife, he shouted: 'Wicked woman, out of this bed at once! I divorce you here and now. I am going to marry your eldest sister instead.' Then he called for the West Wind, who blew me out of the palace and landed me here."

'Psyche had hardly finished her story before her sister, madly jealous of her for having been in bed with a god and burning with desire to have the same experience, rushed off to her husband with a story that her parents were dead, and that she must sail home at once. Off she went, and when at last she reached the rock, though another wind altogether was blowing, she shouted confidently: "Here I come, Cupid, a woman worthy of your love. West Wind, convey your mistress to the Palace at once!" Then she took a headlong leap; but she never reached the valley, either dead or alive, because the rocks cut her to pieces as she fell and scattered her flesh and guts all over the mountainside. So she got what she deserved, and the birds and beasts feasted on her remains.

'Psyche wandered on and on until she came to another city, where the other sister was queen, and told her the same story. The wicked woman wishing to supplant Psyche in Cupid's love, set sail at once, hurried to the rock, leaped off it and died in exactly the same way.'

9

Cupid and Psyche (III)

'Psyche continued on her travels through country after country, searching for Cupid; but he was in Heaven, lying in bed in his mother's royal suite, groaning for pain. Meanwhile a white gull, of the sort that skims the surface of the sea flapping the waves with its wings, dived down into the water; there it met Venus, who was enjoying a dip, and brought her the news that her son Cupid was confined to bed by a severe and painful burn, from which it was doubtful whether he would recover. It told her, too, that every sort of scandal about the Venus family was going around. People were saying that her son had flown down to some mountain or other for an indecent affair with a girl, and that she herself had abandoned her divine tasks and gone off for a seaside holiday. "The result is," screamed the gull, "that Pleasure, Grace and Wit have disappeared from the earth and everything there has become ugly, dull and slovenly. Nobody bothers any longer about his wife, his friends or his children; and the whole system of human love is in such complete disorder that it is now considered disgusting for anyone to show even natural affection."

'This talkative, meddlesome bird succeeded in setting Venus against her son. She grew very angry and cried: "So my promising lad has already taken a mistress, has he? Here, gull—you seem to be the only creature left with any true affection for me—tell me, do you know the name of the creature who has seduced my poor simple boy? Is she one of the Nymphs, or one of the Hours, or one of the Muses, or one of my own train of Graces?"

'The gull was very ready to spread the scandal it had picked up. "I cannot say for certain, Your Majesty, but unless my memory is playing me tricks, I think the story is that your son has fallen desperately in love with a human named Psyche."

'Venus was absolutely furious. "What! With her, of all women? With Psyche, the usurper of my beauty, the rival of my glory? This is worse and worse. It was through me that he got to know the girl. Does the impudent young wretch take me for a procuress?"

'She rose from the sea at once and hurried aloft to her golden room, where she found Cupid lying ill in bed, as the gull had told her. As she entered she bawled out at the top of her voice: "Now *is* this decent behaviour? A fine credit you are to your divine family and a fine reputation you're building up for yourself. You trample your mother's orders underfoot as though she had no authority over you whatsoever, and instead of tormenting her enemy with a dishonourable passion, as you were ordered to do, you have the impudence to sleep with the girl yourself. At your age, you lecherous little beast! I suppose you thought that I'd be delighted to have her for a daughter-in-law, eh? And I suppose, you also thought, you scamp, you debauched detestable brat, that you're my heir and that I'm past the age of child-bearing! Please understand that I'm quite capable of having another son, if I please, and a far better one than you, and quite prepared to disinherit you in his favour. However, to make you feel the disgrace still more keenly, I think I'll legally adopt the son of one of my slaves and hand over to him your wings, torch, bow and arrows, which you have been using in ways for which I never intended them. And I have every right to do that, because not one of them was supplied by your father Vulcan. The fact is, that you have been mischievous from your earliest years and always delighted in hurting people. You have often had the bad manners to shoot at your elders, and as for me, your mother, you shame me before the whole world day after day, you matricidal wretch, by sticking me full of your horrible little arrows. You sneer at me and call me 'the widow', I suppose because your father and I are no longer on speaking terms, and show not the slightest respect for your brave, invincible stepfather Mars; in fact, you do your best to annoy me by setting him after other women and making me madly jealous. But you'll soon be sorry that you played all those tricks; I warn you that this marriage of yours is going to leave a sour, bitter taste in your mouth."

'He did not answer, so she complained to herself in an undertone: "This is all very well, but everyone is laughing at me and I haven't the faintest idea what to do or where to go. How in the world am I to catch and cage the nasty little lizard? I suppose I'd better go for help to old Sobriety to whom I've always been so dreadfully rude for the sake of this spoilt son of mine. Must I really have anything to do with that dowdy, countrified old bore, my natural foe? The idea makes me shudder, yet revenge is sweet from whatever quarter it comes. Yes, I fear that she's the only person who can do anything for me. She'll give the little beast the thrashing of his life; confiscate his quiver, blunt his arrows, tear the string off his bow and quench his torch. Worse than that, she'll shave off his golden hair, which I used to curl so carefully with my own hands, and clip those lovely wings of his which I once whitened with the dazzling milk of my own breast. When that's been done, perhaps I'll feel a little better."

'She rushed off again and at once ran into her step-mother Juno and her aunt Ceres, who noticed how angry she looked and asked her why she was spoiling the beauty of her bright eyes with so sullen a frown. "Thank goodness I met you," she answered, "I needed you to calm me down. There is something you can do for me, if you'll be kind enough. Please make careful enquiries for the whereabouts of a runaway creature called Psyche—I'm sure you must have heard all about her and the family scandal she's caused by her affair with . . . with you know whom!"

'Of course, they knew all about it, and tried to soothe her fury. "Darling," Juno said, "you mustn't take this too much to heart. Why try to thwart his pleasures and kill the girl with whom he's fallen in love? What terrible sin has he committed? It is no crime, surely, to sleep with a pretty girl?"

'And Ceres said: "Darling, you imagine that he's still only a boy because he carries his years so gracefully, but you simply must realize that he's a young man now. Have you forgotten his age? And, really, Juno and I think it very strange that, as a mother and a woman of the world, you persist in poking your nose into what is really his own business, and that when you catch him out in a love affair you blame the poor darling for those very talents and inclinations that he inherits directly from yourself. What god or man will have any patience with you, you go about all the time waking sexual desire in people but at the same time try to repress similar feelings in your own son? Is it really your intention to close down the sole existing factory of woman's universal weakness?"

'The Goddesses were not quite honest in their defence of Cupid: they were afraid of his arrows and thought it wiser to speak well of him even when he was not about. Venus, seeing that they refused to take a serious view of her wrongs, indignantly turned her back on them and hurried off again to the sea.

'Meanwhile, Psyche was restlessly wandering about day and night in search for her husband. However angry he might be, she hoped to make him relent either by coaxing him in their own private love-language or by going down on her knees in abject repentance. One day she noticed a temple on the top of a steep hill. She said to herself: "I wonder if my husband is there?" So she walked quietly towards the hill, her heart full of love and hope, and reached the temple with some difficulty, after climbing ridge after ridge. But when she arrived at the sacred couch she found it heaped with votive gifts of wheat-sheaves, wheat-chaplets and ears of barley, also sickles and other harvest implements; but all scattered about untidily, as though flung down at the close of a hot summer day by careless reapers.

'She began to sort all these things carefully, and arrange them in their proper places, feeling that she must behave respectfully towards every deity whose temple she happened to visit and implore the help of the whole Heavenly family one by one. The temple belonged to the generous Goddess Ceres, who saw her busily at work and called out from afar: "Oh, you poor Psyche! Venus is furious and searching everywhere for you. She wants to be cruelly revenged on you. I am surprised that you can spare the time to look after my affairs for me, or think of anything at all but your own safety."

'Psyche's hair streamed across the temple floor as she prostrated herself at the Goddess's feet, which she wetted with her tears. She implored her protection: "I beseech you, Goddess, by the corn-stalks in your hand, by the happy ceremony of harvest-home, by the secret contents of the wicker baskets carried in your procession, by the winged dragons of your chariot, by the furrows of Sicily from which a cruel god once ravished your daughter Proserpine, by the wheels of his chariot, by the earth that closed upon her, by her dark descent and gloomy wedding, by her happy torch-lit return to earth, and by the other mysteries which Eleusis, your Attic sanctuary, silently conceals:—help me, oh please help your unhappy suppliant Psyche. Allow me, just for a few days, to hide myself under that stack of wheat-sheaves, until the great Goddess's rage has had time to cool down; or if not for so long as that, at least let me have a short rest, because, honestly, I am very, very tired, and haven't stopped travelling for a moment since I set out."

'Ceres answered: "Your tears and prayers go straight to my heart, and I would dearly love to help you; but the truth is that I can't afford to offend my niece. She has been one of my best friends for ages and ages and really has a very good heart when you get to know her. You'd better leave this temple at once and think yourself lucky that I don't have you placed under arrest."

'Psyche went away, twice as sad as she had come: she had never expected such a rebuff. But soon she saw below her in the valley another beautiful temple in the middle of a dark sacred grove. She feared to miss any chance, even a remote one, of putting things right for herself, so she went down to implore the protection of the deity of the place, whoever it might be. She saw various splendid offerings hanging from branches of the grove and from the temple door-posts; among them were rich garments embroidered with gold letters that spelt out the name of the goddess to whom all were dedicated, namely Juno, and recorded the particular favours which she had granted their donors.

'Psyche fell on her knees, wiped away her tears, and embracing the temple altar, still warm from a recent sacrifice, began to pray. "Sister and wife of great Jupiter, I cannot tell where you may be at the moment. You may be residing in one of your ancient temples on Samos—the Samians boast that you were born in their island and spent your whole impassioned childhood there. Or you may be visiting your happy city of Carthage on its high hill, where you are adored as a virgin travelling across Heaven in a lion-drawn chariot. Or you may be watching over the famous walls of Argos, past which the river Inachus flows, where you are adored as the Queen of Heaven, the Thunderer's bride. Wherever you are, you whom the whole East venerates as Zygia the Goddess of Marriage, and the whole West as Lucina, Goddess of Childbirth, I appeal to you now as Juno the Protectress: I beg you to watch over me in my overwhelming misfortune, and rescue me from the dangers that threaten me. You see, Goddess, I am very, very tired, and very, very frightened and I know that you're always ready to help women who are about to have babies, if they get into any sort of trouble."

'Juno appeared in all her august glory and said: "My dear, I should be only too pleased to help you, but unfortunately divine etiquette forbids. I can't possibly go against the wishes of Venus, who married my son Vulcan, you know, and whom I have always loved as though she were my own child. Besides, I am forbidden by law—one of the Fabian laws—to harbour any fugitive slave-girl without her owner's consent."

'Psyche was distressed by this second shipwreck of her hopes, and felt quite unable to go on looking for her winged husband. She gave up all hope of safety and said to herself: "Where in the world, or out of it, can I turn for help, now that even these powerful goddesses will do nothing for me but express their sympathy? My feet are so tangled in the snares of fate that it seems useless to ask them to take me anywhere else. Where is there a building in which I can hide myself from the watchful eyes of great Venus, even with all doors and windows locked? The fact is, my dear Psyche, that you must borrow a little male courage, you must boldly renounce all idle hopes of escape and make a voluntary surrender to your sovereign mistress. It may be too late, but you must at least try to calm her rage by submissive behaviour. Besides, after this long, useless search, you have quite a good chance of finding your husband at your mother-in-law's house."

'Psyche's decision to do her duty was risky and even suicidal, but she prepared herself for it by considering what sort of appeal she ought to make to her Mistress.

'Venus meanwhile had declined to use any human agencies in

her search for Psyche and returned to Heaven, where she ordered her chariot to be got ready. It was of burnished gold, with coachwork of such exquisite filigree that its intrinsic value was negligible compared with its value as a work of art. It had been her husband Vulcan's wedding present to her. Four white doves from the flock in constant attendance on her flew happily forward and offered their rainbow-coloured necks to the jewelled harness and, when Venus mounted, drew the chariot along at a spanking rate. Behind, flew a crowd of naughty sparrows and other little birds that sang very sweetly in announcement of the Goddess's arrival.

'Now the clouds vanished, the sky opened and the high upper air received her joyfully. Her singing retinue were not in the least afraid of swooping eagles or greedy hawks, and she drove straight to the royal citadel of Jupiter, where she demanded the immediate services of Mercury, the town-crier of Heaven, in a matter of great urgency. When Jupiter nodded his sapphire brow in assent, Venus was delighted; she retired from his presence and gave Mercury, who was now accompanying her, careful instructions. "Brother from Arcady, you know I have never in my life undertaken any business at all without your assistance, and you know how long I have been without news of my runaway slave girl. So you simply must make a public announcement offering a reward to the person who finds her, and insist on my orders being obeyed at once. Her person must be accurately described so that nobody will be able to plead ignorance as an excuse for harbouring her. Here is her dossier; Psyche is the name, and all particulars are included."

'She handed him a little book and immediately went home.

Mercury did as he was told. He went from country to country crying out: "Oyez, oyez! If any person can apprehend and seize the person of a runaway princess, one of the Lady Venus's slave-girls, by name PSYCHE, or give any information that will lead to her discovery, let such a person go to Mercury, Town-crier of Heaven, in his temple just outside the precincts of Our Lady of the Myrtles, Aventine Hill, Rome. The reward offered is as follows: seven sweet kisses from the mouth of the said Venus herself, and one exquisitely delicious thrust of her honeyed tongue between his pursed lips."

'A jealous competitive spirit naturally fired all mankind when they heard this reward announced, and it was this that put an immediate end to Psyche's hesitation. She was already near her mistress's gate when she was met by one of the household, named Old Habit, who screamed out at once at the top of her voice: "You wicked slut, you! So you've discovered at last that you have a mistress, eh? But don't pretend, you brazen-faced thing, that you haven't heard of the huge trouble that you've caused us in our search for you. Well, I'm glad you've fallen into my hands, not some other slave's, because you're safe here—safe in the jaws of Hell, and there won't be any delay in your punishment either, you obstinate, impertinent baggage!" She twisted her fingers in Psyche's hair and dragged her into Venus's presence, though she came along willingly enough.

'Venus burst into the hysterical laugh of a woman who is desperately angry. She shook her head menacingly and scratched her ear—the right ear, behind which the Throne of Vengeance is said to be situated. "Ah," she cried, "so you condescend to pay your respects to your mother-in-law, is that it? Or perhaps you have come to visit your husband's sick-bed, hearing that he's still dangerously ill from the burn you gave him? But make yourself at home. I promise you the sort of welcome that a good mother-in-law is bound to give her son's wife." She clapped her hands for her slaves, Anxiety and Grief, and when they ran up, gave Psyche over to them for punishment. They led her off, flogged her cruelly and tortured her in other ways besides, after which they brought her back to Venus's presence.

'Once more Venus yelled with laughter: "Just look at her!" she cried. "Look at the whore! That big belly of hers makes me feel quite sorry for her. By Heaven, it wrings my grandmotherly heart! Grandmother, indeed! How wonderful to be made a grandmother at my time of life! And to think that the son of this disgusting slave will be called Venus's own grandchild! No, but of course that is nonsense. A marriage between a god and a mortal, celebrated in the depth of the country without witnesses and lacking even the consent of the bride's father, can't possibly be recognized at Law; your child will be a bastard, my girl, even if I permit you to bring it into the world."

'With this, she flew at poor Psyche, tore her clothes to shreds, pulled out handfuls of her hair, then grabbed her by the shoulders and shook her until she nearly shook her head off, giving her a terrible time. Next she called for quantities of wheat, barley, millet, lentils, beans and the seeds of poppy and vetch, and mixed them all together into a huge heap. "You look such a dreadful sight, slave," she said, "that the only way that you are ever likely to get a lover is by hard work. So now I'll test you myself, to find out whether you're industrious. Do you see this pile of seeds all mixed together? Sort out the different kinds, stack them in separate little heaps, and prove that you're quick-fingered by getting every grain in its right place before nightfall." Without another word, she flew off to attend some wedding breakfast or other.

'Psyche made no attempt to set about her stupendous task, but sat gazing dumbly at it, until a very small ant, one of the country sort, happened to pass and realized what was going on. Pity for Psyche as wife of the mighty God of Love set the little thing shrieking wild curses at the cruel mother-in-law and scurrying about to round up every ant in the district. "Take pity on her, sisters, take pity on this pretty girl, you busy children of the generous Earth. She's the wife of Love himself and her life is in great danger. Quick, quick, to the rescue!"

'They came rushing up as fast as their six legs would carry them, wave upon wave of ants, and began working furiously to sort the pile out, grain by grain. Soon they had arranged it all tidily in separate heaps, and run off again at once.

'Venus returned that evening, a little drunk, smelling strongly of aphrodisiac ointments, and simply swathed in rose-wreaths. When she saw with what prodigious speed Psyche had finished the task, she said: "You didn't do a hand's stroke yourself, you wicked thing. This is the work of someone whom you have bewitched, poor fellow! but you'll be 'poor fellow' too, before I have done." She threw her part of a coarse loaf and went to bed.

'Meanwhile she had confined Cupid to his bedroom, partly to prevent him from playing his usual naughty tricks and so making his injury worse; partly to keep him away from his sweetheart. So the lovers spent a miserable night, unable to visit each other, although under the same roof.

'As soon as the Goddess of Dawn had set her team moving across the sky, Venus called Psyche and said: "Do you see the grove fringing the bank of that stream over there, with fruit bushes hanging low over the water? Shining golden sheep are wandering about in it, without a shepherd to look after them. I want you to fetch me a hank of their precious wool, and I don't care how you get it."

'Psyche rose willingly enough, but with no intention of obeying Venus's orders: she had made up her mind to throw herself in the stream and so end her sorrows. But a green reed, of the sort used in Pan's pipes, was blown upon by some divine breeze and whispered to her: "Wait, Psyche, wait! I know what dreadful sorrows you have suffered, but you must not pollute these sacred waters by a suicide. And, another thing, you must not go into the grove, to risk your life among those dangerous sheep; not yet. The heat of the sun so infuriates the beasts that they kill any human being who ventures among them. Either they gore them with their sharp horns, or butt them to death with their stony foreheads or bite them with their poisonous teeth. Wait, Psyche, wait until the afternoon wears to a close, and the serene whispers of these waters lull them asleep. Hide meanwhile under that tall plane-tree who drinks the same water as I do, and as soon as the sheep calm down, go into the grove and gather the wisps of golden wool that you'll find sticking on every briar there."

'It was a simple, kindly reed and Psyche took its advice, which proved to be sound: that evening she was able to return to Venus with a whole lapful of the delicate golden wool. Yet even her performance of this second dangerous task did not satisfy the Goddess, who frowned and told her with a cruel smile: "Someone·

has been helping you again, that's quite clear. But now I'll put your courage and prudence to a still severer test. Do you see the summit of that high mountain over there? You'll find that a dark-coloured stream cascades down its precipitous sides into a gorge below and then floods the Stygian marshes and feeds the hoarse River of Wailing. Here is a little jar. Go off at once and bring it back to me brimful of ice-cold water fetched from the very middle of the stream at the point where it bursts out of the rock."

'She gave Psyche a jar of polished crystal and packed her off with renewed threats of what would happen if she came back empty-handed.

'Psyche started at once for the top of the mountain, which was called Aroanius, thinking that there at least she would find a means of ending her wretched life. As she came near she saw what a stupendously dangerous and difficult task had been set her. The dreadful waters of the Styx burst out from half-way up an enormously tall, steep, slippery precipice; cascaded down into a narrow conduit which they had hollowed for themselves in the course of centuries, and flowed unseen into the gorge below. On both sides of their outlet she saw fierce dragons crawling, never asleep, always on guard with unwinking eyes, and stretching their long necks over the sacred water. And the waters sang as they rolled along, varying the words every now and then: "Be off! Be off!" and "What do you wish, wish, wish? Look! Look!" and "What are you at, are you at? Care, take care!". "Off with you, off with you, off with you! Death! Death!"

'Psyche stood still as stone, her mind far away: the utter impossibility of escaping alive from the trap that Venus had set for her was so overwhelming that she could no longer even relieve herself by tears—that last comfort of women when things go wrong with them. But the kind, sharp eyes of Providence notice when innocent souls are in trouble. At her suggestion Jupiter's royal bird, the rapacious eagle, suddenly sailed down to her from Heaven. He gratefully remembered the ancient debt that he owed to Cupid for having helped him to carry Ganymede, the beautiful Phrygian prince, up to Heaven to become Jupiter's cupbearer; and since Psyche was Cupid's wife he screamed down at her: "Silly, simple, inexperienced Psyche, how can you ever hope to steal one drop of this frightfully sacred stream? Surely you have heard that Jupiter himself fears the waters of Styx, and that just as you swear by the Blessed Gods, so they swear by the Sovereign Styx. But let me take that little jar." He quickly snatched it from her grasp and soared off on his strong wings, steering a zigzag course between the two rows of furious fangs and vibrating three-forked tongues, until he reached the required spot. The stream was reluctant to give up its water and warned him to escape while he still could, but he explained that the Goddess Venus wanted the water and that she had commissioned him to fetch it; a story which carried some weight with the stream. He filled the jar with the water and brought it safely back to the delighted Psyche.

'She returned with it to Venus but could not appease her fury even with this latest success. Venus was resolved to set a still more outrageous test, and said with a sweet smile that seemed to spell her complete ruin: "You must be a witch, a very clever, very wicked witch, else you could never have carried out my orders so exactly. But I have still one more task for you to perform, my dear girl. Please take this box and go down to the Underworld to the death-palace of Pluto. Hand it to Queen Prosperpine and say: 'The Lady Venus's compliments, and will you please send this box back to her with a little of your beauty in it, not very much but enough to last for at least one short day. She has had to make such a drain on her own store as a result of sitting up at night with her sick son, that she has none left.' Then come back with the box at once, because I must use her make-up before I appear at the Olympic Theatre tonight."

'This seemed the end of everything, since her orders were to go down to the Underworld of Tartarus. Psyche saw that she was openly and undisguisedly being sent to her death. She went at once to a high tower, deciding that her straightest and easiest way to the Underworld was to throw herself down from it. But the tower suddenly broke into human speech: "Poor child," it said, "do you really mean to commit suicide by jumping down from me? How rash of you to lose hope just before the end of your trials. Don't you realize that as soon as the breath is out of your body you will indeed go right down to the depths of Tartarus, but that once you take that way there's no hope of return? Listen to me. The famous Greek city of Lacedaemon is not far from here. Go there at once and ask to be directed to Taenarus, which is rather an out-of-the-way place to find. It's on a peninsula to the south. Once you get there you'll find one of the ventilation holes of the Underworld. Put your head through it and you'll see a road running downhill, but there'll be no traffic on it. Climb through at once and the road will lead you straight to Pluto's palace. But don't forget to take with you two pieces of barley

137

bread soaked in honey water, one in each hand, and two coins in your mouth.

' "When you have gone a good way along the road you'll meet a lame ass loaded with wood, and its lame driver will ask you to hand him some pieces of rope for tying up part of the load which the ass has dropped. Pass him by in silence. Then hurry forward until you reach the river of the dead, where Charon will at once ask you for his fee and ferry you across in his patched boat among crowds of ghosts. It seems that the God Avarice lives thereabouts, because neither Charon nor his great father Pluto does anything for nothing. (A poor man on the point of death is expected to have his passage-fee ready; but if he can't get hold of a coin, he isn't allowed to achieve true death, but must wander about disconsolately forever on this side of Styx.) Anyhow, give the dirty ruffian one of your coins, but let him take it from your mouth, not from your hand. While you are being ferried across the sluggish stream, the corpse of an old man will float by; he will raise a putrid hand and beg you to haul him into the boat. But you must be careful not to yield to any feeling of pity for him; that is forbidden. Once ashore, you will meet three women some distance away from the bank. They will be weaving cloth and will ask you to help them. To touch the cloth is also forbidden. All these apparitions, and others like them, are snares set for you by Venus; her object is to make you let go one of the sops you are carrying, and you must understand that the loss of even one of them would be fatal—it would prevent your return to this world. They are for you to give to Cerberus, the huge, fierce, formidable hound with three heads on three necks, all barking in unison, who terrifies the dead; though of course the dead have no need to be frightened by him because they are only shadows and he can't injure shadows.

' "Cerberus keeps perpetual guard at the threshold of Proserpine's dark palace, the desolate place where she lives with her husband Pluto. Throw him one of your sops and you'll find it easy to get past him into the presence of Proserpine herself. She'll give you a warm welcome, offer you a cushioned chair and have you brought a magnificent meal. But sit on the ground, ask for a piece of common bread and eat nothing else. Then deliver your message, and she'll give you what you came for.

' "As you go out, throw the cruel dog the remaining sop as a bribe to let you pass; then pay the greedy ferryman the remaining coin for your return fare across the river, and when you're safely on the other bank follow the road back until you see once again the familiar constellations of Heaven. One last, important warning; be careful not to open or even look at the box you carry back; that hidden receptacle of divine beauty is not for you to explore."

'It was a kind and divinely inspired tower and Psyche took its advice. She went at once to Taenarus where, armed with the coins and the two sops she ran down the road to the Underworld. She passed in silence by the lame man with the lame ass, paid Charon the first coin, stopped her ears to the entreaties of the floating corpse, refused to be taken in by the appeal of the spinning women, pacified the dreadful dog with the first sop and entered Proserpine's palace. There she refused the comfortable chair and the tempting meal, sat humbly at Proserpine's feet, content with a crust of common bread, and finally delivered her message. Proserpine secretively filled the box, shut it and returned it to her; then Psyche stopped the dog's barking with the second sop, paid Charon with the second coin and returned from the Underworld, feeling in far better health and spirits than while on her way down there. When she saw the daylight again she offered up a prayer of praise for its loveliness. Though she was in a hurry to complete her errand she foolishly allowed her curiosity to get the better of her. She said to herself: "I should be a fool to carry this little boxful of divine beauty without borrowing a tiny touch of it for my own use: I must do everything possible to please my beautiful lover."

'She opened the box, but it contained no beauty nor anything else, so far as she saw: but out crept a truly Stygian sleep which seized her, and wrapped her in a dense cloud of drowsiness. She fell prostrate and lay there like a corpse, the open box beside her.

'Cupid, now recovered from his injury and unable to bear Psyche's absence a moment longer, flew out through the narrow window of the bedroom where his mother had been holding him a prisoner. His wings, invigorated by their long rest, carried him faster than ever before. He hurried to Psyche, carefully brushed away the cloud of sleep from her body and shut it up again in its box, then roused her with a harmless prick of an arrow. "Poor girl," he said, "your curiosity has once more nearly ruined you. Hurry now and complete the task which my mother set you; and I'll see to everything else." He flew off, and she sprang up at once to deliver Proserpine's present to Venus.

'But Cupid, who had fallen more deeply in love with Psyche than ever and was alarmed by his mother's sudden conversion to respectability, returned to his naughty tricks. He flew at great speed to the very highest heaven and flung himself as a suppliant at Jupiter's feet, where he pleaded his case. Jupiter pinched his handsome cheeks and kissed his hand. Then he said: "My masterful child, you never pay me the respect which has been decreed me by the Council of Gods, and you're always shooting your arrows into my divine heart—the very seat of the laws that govern the four elements and all the constellations of the sky. Often you defile it with mortal love affairs, contrary to the Laws of Heaven, the Julian edict against adultery, and public peace, injuring my reputation and authority by involving me in sordid love intrigues and transmogrifying my serene appearance into that of serpent, fire, wild beast, bird or farmyard bull. Nevertheless, I can't forget how often I've nursed you on my knees and how soft-hearted I can be, so I'll do whatever you ask. But please realize that you must protect yourself against a Certain Person who might envy you your beautiful wife, and at the same time reward him for what he's going to do for you; so I advise you to introduce me to whatever other girl of really outstanding beauty happens to be about on the earth today."

'Then he ordered Mercury to call a Council of all Heavens, with a penalty of ten thousand drachmae for non-appearance. Everyone was afraid to be fined such a sum, so the Celestial Theatre filled up at once, and Almighty Jupiter from his sublime throne read the following address:

"Right honourable gods and goddesses whose names are registered in the White Roll of the Muses, you all know the young fellow over there whom I have brought up from boyhood and whose passionate nature must, in my opinion, be curbed in some way or other. It is enough to remind you of the daily complaints that come in of his

provoking someone or other to adultery or a similar crime. Well, I
have decided that we must stop the young rascal from doing anything
of the sort again by fastening the fetters of marriage securely upon
him. He has found and seduced a pretty girl called Psyche, and my
sentence is that he must have her, hold her, possess her and cherish her
from this time forth and for evermore."

'Then he turned to Venus: "My dear, you have no occasion to
be sad, or ashamed that your rank and station in Heaven has
been disgraced by your son's match; for I'll see that the marriage
is one between social equals, perfectly legitimate and in complete
accordance with civil law." He ordered Mercury to fetch Psyche
at once and escort her into his presence. When she arrived he
took a cup of nectar and handed it to her. "Drink, Psyche, and
become an immortal," he said. "Cupid will now never fly away
from your arms, but must remain your lawful husband for ever."

'Presently a great wedding breakfast was prepared. Cupid re-
clined in the place of honour with Psyche's head resting on his
breast; Jupiter was placed next, with Juno in the same comfortable position, and then all the other gods and goddesses in order
of seniority. Jupiter was served with nectar and ambrosia by
apple-cheeked Ganymede, his personal cup-bearer; Bacchus attended to everyone else. Vulcan was the chef; the Hours decorated
the palace with red roses and other bridal flowers; the Graces
sprinkled balsam water; the Muses chanted the marriage-hymn
to the accompaniment of flute and pipe-music from the godlings
Satyrus and Peniscus. Finally Apollo sang to his own lyre and
the music was so sweet that Venus came forward and performed a
lively step-dance in time to it. Psyche was properly married to

Cupid and in due time she bore him her child, a daughter whose name was Pleasure.'

*

I stood close by the girl prisoner listening to this beautiful story, and though it was told by a drunken and half-demented old woman, I regretted that I had no means of committing it to writing.

10

Defeat of the Bandits

THE BANDITS returned with a big haul of loot, but evidently at the expense of heavy fighting, because some of them were wounded. It was decided that these should have their wounds dressed and remain in the cave while the others went out again and fetched back some more sackfuls of loot which they had cached near the scene of their operations. After swallowing their dinner the un-wounded men drove my horse and myself out into the road, beating us with sticks, and took us uphill and downhill by a roundabout way until towards evening we reached the cache. We were very weary but they refused us a moment's rest: they loaded us up and hurried us back in such nervous haste that they drove me into a boulder that was lying on the road and capsized me. Then blows fell thick and fast and I had difficulty in rising because I had badly grazed my off hind-leg and bruised the near hoof. A bandit shouted: 'How long are we going to waste good fodder on this worn-out ass? Now he's gone lame as well.'

'Yes,' said another, 'he's brought us bad luck ever since we had him. Several of our brave comrades have been wounded and several more killed, and the loot hasn't been particularly good, either.'

Their leader agreed: 'Very well, as soon as he's carried this load back, which he seems most unwilling to do, I'll push him into the ravine as a present for the vultures.'

'No, no, that's too easy a death for the brute.'

They were still pleasantly arguing over the best way of killing me when we reached home again, for fear had winged my hooves. They quickly unloaded us and without giving us food or water, or even troubling to kill me, they called their wounded comrades out and returned with them at once to the cache to make up, they said, for the time lost by my laziness. They took my horse but decided to leave me behind.

The threat of death made me feel very uneasy. I said to myself: 'Lucius, why stand here tamely waiting for the last of this series of disastrous blows to fall and beat you to earth? These bandits have decided to put you to death, a very cruel death too, and they'll find little difficulty in carrying out their threat. You see that ravine with the sharp rocks jutting out from its sides? When you're pushed over, those spikes will catch you and tear you to pieces. The splendid magic which fascinated you so much has given you only the shape of an ass, and an ass's drudgery, not its thick hide; yours is as delicate as the skin of a horse-leech. Why not be a man in spirit at least and save yourself while you still have a chance? Now's the time; all the bandits are away. Are you afraid of an old woman with one foot in the grave, whom you can finish off with one kick of your lame hoof?'

'But where on earth can I go?' I continued. 'Who will give me hospitality? No, that's a stupid question; only an ass could have asked it. What traveller wouldn't be glad to mount on the back of any stray beast he met and ride off on it?' Exerting all my strength, I snapped the leather thong by which I was tied and was off as fast as my legs could carry me.

The old woman had eyes like a hawk; she snatched up the end of the thong as I charged by and with a courage that surprised me in a creature of her age tried to lead me back to the cave. But the bandits had threatened to kill me, so I could hardly afford to pity her. I flung out my hind hooves and knocked her down, but even when sprawling on the ground she clung grimly to the thong, so that for awhile I galloped along trailing her behind me. She yelled for someone to help, but that was wasting her breath. Nobody was about except Charitë, who ran out of the cave when she heard the old woman's cries. It was a remarkable scene: Dircë must have looked much the same when her stepsons Zethus and Amphion, in revenge for her cruelty, tied her by the hair to the tail of a mad bull. Charitë rose to the occasion courageously. She wrenched the thong out of the old woman's grasp, coaxed me to slacken my pace, mounted nimbly on my back and urged me on again. My own desire to escape was now reinforced by my determination to rescue the girl, as well as by the whacks which she gave me. My four feet beat the ground like a racehorse's, and I tried to answer the sweet words of encouragement she gave me by constant braying. Sometimes I turned my neck, pretending to be biting my flanks where they itched, and kissed her pretty feet.

She drew a deep breath and with an anxious upward glance began to pray: 'O blessed Gods, help me, please help me, now or never, in this time of greatest danger. And you, cruel Fortune, be kind to me for a change, please do! Surely you have vented your spite on me long enough? I swear to you, I have been in perfect torment.' Then she bent her head down and whispered in my ears: 'Ass, dearest ass, I'm relying on you for life and liberty. If you bring me safely home to my parents and my marvellous husband, how grateful we'll all be, how we'll honour you! The best food in the world will be yours for the asking. To begin with, I'll comb out your mane and braid it with my own hands; then I'll part and curl your forelocks and make them pretty; and then I'll spend hours teasing out and disentangling the matted hairs of your poor, long-neglected tail. I'll hang you all over with golden amulets, my saviour, until you twinkle like a starry sky, and I'll lead you in a triumphant procession with my slaves shouting your praises behind; and I'll make much of you all your life, bringing you nuts and titbits every day in my silk apron. But don't run away with the idea that good food, perfect leisure and a long, happy life will be all the reward you get from me; I'll have a memorial set up at home, a carved plaque picturing our flight, and I'll get some clever author to write the story out in a book for future generations to read. The title will be, let me see: "Flight on Ass-back: or, How a Young Lady of Royal Blood Escaped from Captivity." It's not a very learned subject, of course, but you'll have your niche in history: you'll be a modern instance to strengthen people's belief in mythology. I mean the stories of how Phrixus crossed the Dardanelles on the back of a ram, and how Arion piloted a dolphin, and how Europa rode across to Crete on the back of a swimming bull. And if it's really true that Jupiter was that bellowing bull, why shouldn't my braying ass be some god, or perhaps a man in transformation?'

She chattered on, sometimes sighing anxiously, sometimes hopefully praying, until we came to a fork in the road where she tugged at my halter and did her best to make me take the right-hand turning, which was her nearest way home. But I knew that this was the road that the bandits had taken when they went to recover what was left of the loot. I refused to do what she wanted and mentally expostulated with her: 'My poor girl, you're making very bad use of my services. What are you trying to do? Do you want to ride off to the other world? You'll bring both of us to our deaths, if you take that road.'

She insisted, I resisted, and while we were arguing the question like co-heirs in a law-suit about the division of landed property or, if you like, about a right of way, along came the bandits with the loot. The moon was full so they recognised us from some distance away and greeted us with shouts of ironical laughter. One of them cried: 'Whither away so fast by moonlight, my dear? Not afraid of ghosts and wandering spirits? No? What a good daughter you are, upon my word, stealing a surprise visit like this to your dear old parents. Well, it would be a shame to let you travel all alone, so we'll come with you as your escort and show you a short cut.' He caught hold of my bridle and turned me around, beating me mercilessly with a loaded stick. Naturally loth to face the death that threatened me as soon as I reached the cave again, I remembered my bad hoof and walked lame, bobbing my head up and down. The bandit jeered and gave me another whack with the stick. 'So you stumble and stagger again, do you? Your rotten hooves are good for galloping but not for walking, I suppose? A moment ago you were flying along like Pegasus.'

When we came to the hedged enclosure outside the cave we found the old woman hanging by the neck from the branch of a tall cypress-tree. The bandits cut her down, dragged her along at the end of the rope and pitched her into the ravine. Then they chained up the girl and began ravenously eating the supper which the wretched old woman had cooked for them 'with posthumous industry', as they joked. With hands and mouths full they discussed how to avenge the insult we had done them. As might have been expected in a rowdy mob like this all sorts of punishments were suggested, though everyone agreed on the death penalty.

'Burn her alive!'

'Tie her up for the wild beasts to finish off.'

'What about a crucifixion?'

'Put her through our regular series of tortures.'

At last one of them managed to calm the rest down and allow him a hearing. In a mild and pleasant voice he said: 'Comrades, the rules of our company and our reputation as humane soldiers of fortune forbid us to inflict any punishment which exceeds the crime. Personally, I should be ashamed in the circumstances if we had to fall back on wild beasts, or the cross, or the stake, or our regular tortures, or any instrument of sudden death as a means of avenging our insult. So listen to my suggestion, and let the girl live—the sort of life that she deserves. This morning, you remember, you decided to kill the ass. He was always a lazy beast and a proper glutton, and now he has shammed lame and aided and abetted our prisoner's attempt at escape. I suggest that tomorrow, instead of throwing him into the ravine, you cut his throat, gut him, and since he has preferred the girl to us, sew her up naked in his belly. Leave only her head sticking out from his rump; the rest of her body can be tucked inside. Then expose them together on a rock where the sun beats down hottest. The advantage of my suggestion is that both of them will suffer all the punishments you have rightly awarded them. The ass will die, as he has long deserved to do; the girl's head will be mauled by wild beasts and her body gnawed by worms; she'll be scorched as though at the stake, when the hot sun begins to cook up the ass's carcase; and when the dogs and vultures finally get at her guts she'll fancy herself on the cross. Yes, it's a pretty scheme when you begin reckoning out its minor advantages. In the first place, she'll be left alive in the belly of a dead beast; in the second, her nostrils will soon be filled with a disgusting stench; in the third, she'll suffer desperately from hunger and thirst; lastly, she'll not have the use of her hands to shorten her agonies by doing away with herself.'

The bandits agreed unanimously that this was the very thing. My long ears took in every word and I thought: 'O my poor body, tomorrow you'll be carrion!'

When the night drew to a close and the whole world was lit up by the splendid chariot of the Sun, a man arrived at the cave and sat down exhausted at the entrance. I could see from the greeting they gave him that he belonged to the company. After recovering his breath he said:

'It's all right about Milo's house; we have nothing to fear from the people of Hypata. You remember what my orders were after you'd robbed the place and started back here with the loot? I was to remain behind as a spy, mix with the crowd, pretend to be angry at what had happened, watch what steps were taken to investigate the robbery and identify the robbers, then return to you with a detailed report. Here it is then. A man who calls himself Lucius—his real name is unknown—is accused by everyone in Hypata of having organized the robbery: "a perfectly clear case, not mere guesswork," I was told.

'This Lucius had forged letters of introduction making him out to be a respectable person, and used them to ingratiate himself with Milo, who invited him to stay at his house and treated him like one of the family. He spent some little time there, made up to the slave-girl, with whom he pretended to be in love, took careful stock of all the bolts and fastenings of the house and found out where Milo stored his valuables. An important indication of his guilt, they told me, was that he disappeared at the very time of the robbery and had not been seen since. They said it was easy enough for him to get clear away on his white thoroughbred, which disappeared with him. His groom, who was still in the house when the constables arrived, was accused as accessory to the crime and his master's escape. The magistrates committed him to the town gaol and next day put him to the torture. They nearly killed him before they finished, and though as a matter of fact he confessed nothing that incriminated his master, a deputation was sent to Lucius's province with orders to search him out and bring him to book.'

I groaned inwardly during this report, to compare my past with my present—that happy Lord Lucius with this wretched doomed jackass. It occurred to me that the old sages had been right to speak of Fortune as blind and even eyeless, because of the way she rewards the unworthy or the positively wicked. She never shows the least sense in selecting her favourites: indeed, she even prefers men from whom, if she had any eyes in her head, she would feel bound to recoil in disgust. Her worst fault is encouraging people to form opinions about us that are

151

inconsistent with, and even plainly contradict, our true characters; so that the villain enjoys the reputation of the saint, and the completely innocent man gets the punishment earned by the wicked one. Take my case, for instance: she seemed to have done her very worst by changing me into an animal, a beast of burden, of the most ignoble sort, too. It was a misfortune that the most hardened criminal would consider a terrible one and deserving of his sincere sympathy; yet on the top of all, here I found myself accused not only of common housebreaking but of robbing my own generous host—a far worse crime and amounting almost to parricide. I had not even been allowed to defend myself or utter a single word of denial. And now that the charge was made in my presence, I could not bear anyone to think that my silence implied acquiescence or a guilty conscience. I was tormented with a desire to speak, if it were only to say *Non feci:* 'No, I didn't do it.'

I roared out *Non, Non* again and again, but I found *feci* impossible to pronounce though I made my loose lips quiver with the elocutory effort. So I went on with my *Non, Non!*

'But why do I go on and complain of Fortune?' I asked myself. 'Could anything have been more shameless than her first trick of making me a stable-mate and fellow-labourer with my own horse?' These reflections gave way to a more immediate one: namely that the robbers were about to sacrifice me and use my carcase as a prison for Charité in order to prevent her ghost from haunting them, as it would be bound to do if they killed her outright. I looked at my belly again and again and seemed to have the unfortunate girl already sewed up inside me.

The spy who had brought the news of my false accusation unstitched his clothes and took out a thousand gold pieces hidden in them which, he explained, he had robbed from different travellers whom he had met on his way home. He conscientiously put them into the common hoard. Then he asked anxiously after his comrades and when he was told that some of them, in fact all the bravest ones, had since been killed in one way or another, though all had died very gamely, he suggested that they should take a short vacation from banditry and spend the time in a recruiting campaign. Some of the local lads, he said, might have to be impressed and kept loyal by a sense of fear, some would be attracted by a prospect of loot and come forward as volunteers, others would be only too pleased to exchange a life of drudgery for membership of a company which exerted an almost sovereign power. He said he had come across a tall, powerfully built young beggar and told him that he ought to make better use of his hands than stretch them out for petty charity: why not help himself with them to gold? Lack of exercise was making him flabby, and it was a pity not to enjoy the advantages of health and strength while he still had them. After some argument the beggar had been persuaded to volunteer for service with the company; he was now waiting a little distance down the road.

The bandits all agreed to the proposed vacation and decided to accept the new recruit, who seemed to have the right qualifications, and afterwards look out for others like him to bring the company up to full strength again.

So the spy went out and soon returned with the beggar. He was extraordinarily broad-shouldered and a whole head taller than the biggest of the bandits, and though his beard was still mere down, he was incomparably the finest-looking man present.

His powerful chest and muscular stomach seemed to be bursting through the seams of the patched rags which served him for clothes.

His greeting as he came in was: 'Good morning, gentlemen. If you're as ready to accept me as I am to join your company, I'll be proud to be your comrade and serve with you under the patronage of the great god Mars. I'm a pretty bold fellow and always happier when blows are struck at me in battle than when gold coins are charitably pressed into my palm. Others fear death; I despise it. Don't judge me by these rags. I'm neither a pauper nor a tramp, but the former captain of a powerful bandit company which plundered and terrorized the whole of Macedonia. Haemus of Thrace is my name—one that has made whole provinces tremble—and my father was Thero, an equally famous bandit-captain. I was weaned on human blood, brought up in a bandit-cave, inherited my father's courage and followed in his footsteps. But I lost my entire band and all the huge treasures we had amassed. The trouble was that Mars grew angry with me because I attacked one of the Emperor's chief officers, a former provincial governor with an annual salary of two thousand gold pieces, who had lost his appointment by bad luck. Would you care to hear the story?'

'Yes, begin at the beginning, lad!'

'Very well, then. This officer, as I say, had an honourable career in the Imperial service and the Emperor himself thought highly of him. But he had jealous rivals who slandered him and got him sent into exile along with his wife the Lady Plotina—a very loyal, decent woman, with a contempt for city life, who had borne her husband ten children and now cheerfully shared his troubles. Before they went together under escort to the port of embarkation, she cut off her hair, tied strings of gold coin and her most valuable necklaces around her waist and put on man's clothes. The soldiers' drawn swords didn't frighten her and she took the greatest care of her husband; ran the same dangers, did all she could for him and behaved as courageously as the man she pretended to be. The worst part of the journey ended one evening when they sighted Zacynthus, where they were condemned to spend their exile, and sailed into the Bay of Actium. There they disembarked, because they found the swell disagreeable, and spent the night in a seaside cottage.

'We had left Macedonia and happened to be operating in that district, so we broke into the cottage, stripped it clean and got safely away. But it was a close shave, because Lady Plotina raised the alarm as soon as she heard the gate slam, running into the room where her husband was asleep and screaming: "Thieves! Thieves!" at the top of her voice. She not only roused her armed escort and all her slaves, calling on each one by name, but also shouted to the people in the neighbouring cottages to come to her help. We should never have got off without loss if her slaves hadn't panicked, every one of them scrambling off to a hiding-place.

'This wonderful woman—I won't apologize for calling her wonderful because it's the truth—then returned to Rome and appealed to the Emperor. She made out so strong a case for her husband that he consented not only to recall him from exile but to avenge the injuries he had suffered. In fact, he expressed the wish that Haemus's bandit company should cease to exist; and you know what authority Caesar's wishes carry. This wish was granted almost at once. Regular troops were sent against us and chased us night and day, until they ran us off our legs. The company was cut to pieces and only one man escaped: myself. I managed to creep out from the very jaws of death. Dressed in a woman's gaily coloured dress, with full skirts, a cloth cap pulled over my head and my feet squeezed into a pair of those thin white shoes that country girls wear, I jumped on the back of an ass loaded with barley-sheaves, and rode safely through the whole punitive force. Nobody saw through my disguise because I was still beardless at the time and my cheeks were as smooth and red as a boy's. Even after that I lived up to my father's reputation and my own, though I confess my experience of cold steel had made me a little nervous. Still disguised as a woman I made single-handed raids on country-houses and even fortified villages and built up this small stock of gold to help me along the road.'

He ripped open his rags and out tumbled two thousand gold pieces. 'Here,' he said, 'is my willing contribution to your funds— call it my dowry, if you like. And, if you'll accept me, I'm ready to captain your company and undertake in a short time to plate the walls of this rocky cave with pure gold.'

The bandits did not hesitate. They unanimously elected him captain and produced a tolerably clean tunic for him to wear. He discarded his rags, put it on, and embraced each of his new comrades in turn. Then he took his place on the couch at the head of the table, where his election was celebrated with a supper and a grand drinking bout. The bandits told him about the girl and how she had tried to escape on my back and about the monstrous death sentence that they had passed on us. He asked where the girl was and when they took him to her and he found her loaded with chains he turned away with a contemptuous curl of his

nostrils and said: 'Even if I dared quarrel with your decision, I'm
not so stupid as to do that. All the same, I should be ashamed not
to say what I feel about that girl and the ass. As your captain I'm
obliged to make your interests mine, so please allow me to tell
you frankly what I think; on the understanding, of course, that
if you disagree your decision stands. My view is that wise bandits
put profit before any other consideration whatsoever, even vengeance, which is a notoriously two-edged weapon. If you kill the
girl by sewing her up in the ass's belly you may soothe your feelings, but there's no profit in it for anyone, whereas if you take
her to some town or other and put her up for sale, a young pretty
girl like that with her maidenhead still intact ought to fetch a
high price. I used to do business with several big men in the
brothel-trade, one of whom, I know, will pay you a really large
sum for her and settle her in a suitably high-class establishment—
from which she won't be likely to run away. And you'll have
your revenge just the same; she certainly won't enjoy slaving in a
brothel. Now, you're at perfect liberty to decide what to do, and
I've offered you this advice merely because I think it will be to
your advantage.'

He had briefed himself to plead on behalf of the company's
funds; but he was also pleading for us, so the tedious deliberations
that followed were sheer torture to me. At last they agreed to
follow their new captain's advice, and at once unchained the girl.
Now, from the very moment that she saw this young blackguard
and heard him mention the brothel-trade and a high-class establishment her spirits had begun to rise and her face was wreathed
with smiles. I felt that this was really too much and almost turned
misogynist then and there: to see a young girl, still a virgin, who

pretended to be deeply in love with the man who was practically her husband and with whom she would have lived a most respectable life, suddenly entranced with the idea of working in a filthy brothel! The character of the whole female sex was on trial, and the judge was an ass!

The young captain said: 'I think we should invoke Mars and beg him to get us a good price for the girl and help us to pick up a few sound recruits. So far as I can see we have neither a suitable victim for the sacrifice nor enough wine for a proper drinking orgy. I need ten lads to come with me to the nearest town and fetch back the meat and wine we need as priests of our god.'

He and ten other bandits went off, and were soon back with skins full of wine and a small flock of sheep and goats. A large, shaggy he-goat was chosen for sacrifice to Mars, patron of gladiators and bandits; and the other beasts were for the banquet. Meanwhile the rest of the company had collected wood for a huge fire and cut green turfs for the altar. 'You'll find that I take the lead not only in your raids but in your entertainments,' said the new captain. He went briskly to work and showed his versatility by first sweeping the floor and smoothing the couches, then cooking and seasoning the meat and finally serving it out to his comrades on handsome dishes, and filling and re-filling their large wine cups. Now and then he found time to visit the girl, on the pretext of fetching something that he needed from her end of the cave, and brought her food stolen from the table and cups of wine. She accepted them gladly, and once or twice when he wanted to kiss her she was only too pleased and kissed him quite affectionately in return. I was shocked. I said to myself: 'You ought to be ashamed of yourself, my girl, to trample your old love underfoot and play the harlot in this robbers' den! Have you forgotten faithful Tlepolemus and your interrupted wedding? Do you really prefer this stranger, a bloodthirsty bandit at that, to the man whom you were to marry with your parents' approval? Doesn't your conscience stab you? And suppose that the other bandits happen to catch you kissing this fellow, what will you do then? Try again to escape on my back and so sentence me to death a second time? Really, you're risking my skin as well as your own in playing that little game.'

However, my indignation cooled when I found that I did the girl an injustice; for I gathered from something he said in my hearing, not of course caring whether I heard it or not—something indirect but clear enough for any intelligent ass to understand—that the new captain was not really Haemus the famous bandit, but her bridegroom Tlepolemus! What he said was this: 'Courage, dearest Charitë, your enemies will all soon be your prisoners.' And I noticed that though he refrained from drinking much himself he continued to treat the bandits to more and more wine, untempered now with water but well warmed, so that they were gradually falling into a drunken stupor. He may even—I don't know—have doctored their drink with some soporific drug. At last, when every single one of them lay dead drunk on the floor, Tlepolemus securely trussed them all up in turn with lengths of rope and lashed them together at his convenience; after which he mounted Charitë on my back and made off homewards with her.

As soon as we came within sight of his town everyone flocked out expectantly. Charitë's father, mother, relatives, freedmen, slaves and all ran delightedly towards us and formed up in procession behind us, followed by crowds of men, women and children of every age. It was indeed a memorable spectable: a virgin riding in triumph on an ass! As for myself, I rejoiced with my whole heart and decided to identify myself as closely as possible with the proceedings by pricking my ears, expanding my nostrils and braying strenuously; it was a thunderous noise I made. When we reached Charitë's house she ran upstairs to her room, where her parents hugged and kissed her, while Tlepolemus took me straight back to the cave. He had a large crowd of his fellow-townsmen with him, and a train of baggage animals. I was quite ready to go because, curious as ever, I wanted to see what sort of prisoners the robbers made. We found them still bound fast, with the bonds of sleep as well as with cord, and the former were the more powerful. So Tlepolemus and his friends ransacked the cave, loaded us with loot, then rolled some of the bandits over a near-by precipice without troubling to uncord them first; they beheaded the rest with their own swords and left their corpses lying in the cave.

We returned in triumph, exulting in the completeness of our vengeance, and handed in the loot at the public treasury, after which Charitë's interrupted wedding was duly concluded by her being escorted to Tlepolemus's house. She was a fine girl and put herself to the greatest trouble on my account. She called me her saviour, and on the wedding night ordered my manger to be filled with barley to the brim, and gave me hay enough to satisfy a Bactrian camel. But what sufficiently lurid curses could I heap on the head of Fotis, for having turned me into an ass rather than a hound, when I saw the dogs of the household gorged nearly to bursting on the meat left over from that princely wedding break-fast or stolen from the kitchen?

The next morning, after what I am sure was a wonderful initiation into the mysteries of sex, the radiant bride told her parents and husband how greatly indebted she was to me, and refused to change the subject until they promised to reward me with the highest possible honours. So they called a council of their wisest and most responsible friends to decide what form these honours should take. One suggested that I should be kept in a stable, excused from all work and fed continuously on the best barley, beans and vetch; but another had more consideration for my love of liberty and suggested that I should run wild in the meadows and father a set of fine mules for my mistress on her brood-mares that were pasturing there; and this was the decision that they finally adopted. So the bailiff of the stud-farm was sent for and I was handed to him with careful injunctions about my good treatment. I trotted gaily off with him, delighted at the prospect of being at last free from packs and bundles and at liberty to run about the meadows until spring came with its new crop of blossoms, when somewhere or other I would find roses growing. It occurred to me that if my master and mistress showed me such gratitude while I was still an ass, they would probably show me even more once I was restored to my proper shape.

11

At the Stud-Farm

THE BAILIFF took me to the stud-farm some miles out in the country, where I found that I was not to be given my liberty nor any of the other good things promised me. On the contrary, his stingy and evil-minded wife harnessed me to a mill and made me grind corn for the family by the sweat of my poor hide, which she beat with a leafy branch. Not content with using me as her household drudge, she put me to grind corn for her neighbours as well, and so made money out of me. She even withheld the barley that I had been promised and forced me to go round and round and round all day milling it, then sold it to the people at the next farm; and towards evening, when I was tired out, she brought me a supper of dirty, caked bran, full of grit.

This was bad enough, but Fortune cruelly exposed me to fresh trials—I suppose with the idea of allowing me to boast later on of 'distinguished conduct at home and in the field,' as the phrase is. The bailiff had remembered his instructions, none too soon, and turned me loose for awhile with the horses at pasture. Free at last, I frisked joyfully about and ambled up to the mares, reviewing them carefully to see which would be the most voluptuous to mount. But my hopes were utterly dashed when the stallions, who were in fine stud-condition from having been so long at grass and would in any case have been more than a match for a poor ass like myself, grew alarmed at the prospect of my tainting the purity of their stock. Disregarding the duty they owed their guest, they ran furiously at me and treated me like a hated rival. One reared up his huge forequarters and battered me with his hooves, another wheeled about and gave me a terrible kick with the full force of his hindquarters, a third let out a threatening whinny, laid back his ears and bit me all over with his sharp white teeth. I was reminded of the legend of King Diomede of Thrace, a powerful tyrant who, apparently in the cause of thrift, exposed his unfortunate guests to the rage of wild horses; he wanted to save barley by feeding the voracious creatures on raw meat. Yes, the stallions gave me such a rough time that I would have given a great deal to find myself safely back at the corn-mill, going giddily round and round.

Fortune seemed insatiable; now she thought out a new torment for me. I was detailed by the bailiff to fetch down wood from the top of a high mountain and the boy he put in charge of me must have been the wickedest ever born. He not only tired me out by making me sweat up and down that mountain and wear out my hooves on the sharp stones, but beat me cruelly and persistently until my bones ached to the marrow. He always hit me on the same spot, the off haunch, until he made the hide fester and break; a great gaping hole, or trench, appeared in it and though the blood ran down he continued to plant his blows there. He used to pile such a huge load on my back that anyone would have thought it

163

was intended for an elephant. It was badly balanced too and whenever it tipped over on one side, he trimmed it by piling stones on the lighter side instead of moving some of the faggots across from the heavier one. Even these miseries of mine did not satisfy him; when we had to cross a stream he kept his feet dry by jumping on my back, as if his weight were only a trifling addition to the dreadful load already piled on me. Then, if I happened to fall on the slippery bank, instead of helping me, as he ought to have done—either by pulling me up by my headstall or tail or by removing part of my load at least until I had regained my feet— this exemplary ass-boy did nothing at all, however weary I might be, but thrash the hair off my hide with a big stick, beginning with my eyes and working towards my tail, until the blows had the effect of a stimulating drug.

Another malicious trick that he used to play on me was to tie up a bunch of the sharpest and most poisonous thorns he could find and attach them to my tail; as I walked they swung against me and gave me almost unbearable torture. I was in a hideous dilemma: if I ran away to escape his beatings, I was pulled up short by the violent stabbing of the thorns; if I stood still to avoid the pain, his blows forced me mercilessly on once more. This detestable child seemed to think of nothing else except how to kill me in one way or another, and used to swear that in the end he really would. Then something happened that provoked his beastly mind to still greater beastliness: which was that one day I lost my temper, lifted up my heels and kicked him to some purpose. His retaliation was truly criminal; he took me out into the road with a heavy load of coarse flax, securely corded to my back, then as we passed through a shepherds' village he stole a live coal from the kitchen outside a cottage and put it in the middle of the flax. A fire soon broke out in the dry stalks, and blazed up dangerously, scorching my whole back. I saw no way to avoid being burned to death. To stand still and think out a plan for fighting the fire was impossible; but Fortune came to my rescue, if only to reserve me for greater dangers. I noticed a big, muddy puddle left over from the previous day's downpour, rushed towards it and rolled over. The flames were extinguished at once, and I got up again without my load and not seriously hurt. But the young fiend threw the whole blame for his own wickedness on me; he told the shepherds that I had purposely stumbled against one of their cooking fires to set the flax ablaze. Then he asked laughing: 'How long are we going to waste fodder on this fiery creature?'

A few days later he thought out a master scheme. He stopped at the first cottage he came to and sold the load of wood I was carrying; then led me home with nothing on my back, saying that he couldn't control my vicious ways and that he refused ever again to take me up the mountain for wood. 'Do you see this lazy, slow-footed beast? A real ass, he is! Besides all his other dirty tricks, he's now frightening the life out of me with newly invented ones. Whenever he sees a good-looking woman coming along the road, or a pretty girl—or a boy, it's all the same to him —he rushes madly at her, tossing off his load, saddle and all very often, and throws her down on the ground. Then he makes an indecent assault on her, panting lustfully and trying to force her to commit bestiality with him. He even puckers up his sinful old mouth into a kiss and gives her little love-bites. You may think that very amusing, but I get mixed up in all sorts of quarrels and fusses and one of these days I may find myself had up on a criminal charge. Half-an-hour ago we met a respectable young woman in the road, and this lecherous beast scattered his load of wood all over the place and knocked her down on the dirty ground. He would have raped her in public, if she hadn't shrieked for help from between his hooves and been rescued just in time by some passers-by. It would have been a hanging matter for me if the poor young woman had been smashed up and torn open and died of her injuries.'

He told several other lies of the same indecent sort, which offended me all the more because I had to keep silence. At last he worked the shepherds up into such excitement that they agreed I ought to be destroyed. One of them shouted: 'Yes, what about executing the promiscuous beast? He doesn't deserve to live. Hey, boy, cut off the head of this universal adulterer—that's what I call him—then throw his guts to our dogs. But keep the meat, it will do for supper. We can rub dust into his hide and take it back to the bailiff and say that the wolves got him. Simple, eh?'

The boy sharpened his knife on a whetstone, grinning evilly when he remembered the kick I had given him. But before he could carry out the sentence, another shepherd said: 'No, it would be a crime to kill so fine an ass and lose his services, just because he happens to be a bit frolicsome and randy. What's wrong with gelding him? That will cure the trouble and make him sweet-tempered and perfectly safe to handle. He'll grow fat and better-conditioned, too. I've known a great many cattle in my day, not only sulky asses but fiery horses, which were perfect rogues until the cause was removed. Then they became as mild and tractable as you please—warranted quiet to ride or drive. So if you don't object, I'll first go to the market (but that needn't take long) and then home to fetch my gelding irons, bring them straight back here and castrate this old satyr of yours in next to no time. I undertake to return him to you as gentle a beast as any wether in my flock.'

When I saw that I had been snatched from the jaws of death only to suffer the worst imaginable punishment, I began to weep silently. With that part of me removed, I might just as well be dead, I thought. Once more I contemplated suicide, either by starving myself to death or by throwing myself over some cliff; I was resolved that I would at least die unmutilated. But I had come to no practical decision by the next morning when the horrible boy took me out again for my usual trudge up the mountain. He tied me to the branch of a huge oak and went off with his axe for a little distance to chop my load of wood. Suddenly a she-bear popped her great head out of a near-by cave. The unexpected sight frightened me nearly out of my wits. I flung myself violently back on my haunches. The halter gave way, and I dashed off, not trusting to my hooves, but hurling myself bodily down the mountain slopes until I reached the plain at the foot; with no thought in my mind except how to escape from that frightful bear and from the still more frightful boy.

A traveller happened to be passing. He saw that I was a stray, caught me, jumped on my back and with the stick he was carrying whacked me along an unfamiliar lane. I carried him carefully in the hope of getting away from the gelders and cared little for his blows; I was used to blows by now. But Fortune, mischievous as ever, prevented me from escaping so easily and quickly caught me in a fresh trap; for our cattlemen who were out searching for a runaway cow happened to meet us. They caught me by my headstall, which they recognized at once, and began to drag me off.

My rider resisted boldly. 'Why are you pulling me about in this rude way?' he asked. 'Hands off, please! You seem to have no manners and no respect for the Law!'

'The Law!' shouted a cattleman scornfully. 'You're stealing our ass. Tell me where you have hidden the body of the boy who was driving him. You killed him, didn't you?'

They knocked him off the saddle and then kicked and punched him as he lay on the ground, though he protested with oaths that he had seen nobody with me. He said now that I had been straying and that he had caught me and ridden me off with the idea of restoring me to my owner and claiming a reward.

'By God,' he said, 'I wish that I'd never set eyes on this cursed ass! Or that he could speak and testify to my innocence. If he could tell you all he knows you'd be ashamed of the way you're treating me.'

The angry cattlemen paid no attention to his protests, but marched him along with a noose around his neck to the part of the mountain where the boy had been chopping wood. He was nowhere to be found, but at last they came across his remains, scraps of human flesh strewn all over the place. I knew that this was the bear's work and should certainly have said so, had I been able to speak; but all I could do was to rejoice in silence over my long-delayed revenge. They collected the pieces of boy and fitted them roughly together into a corpse, which they buried then and there. As for my gallant rider, they called him a bloody assassin, insisting that he had killed the boy and that they had caught him in the act of stealing me; they marched him to their hamlet and tied him up there, intending to hand him over to the magistrates next day on a charge of murder. Then the boy's parents appeared and started wailing and groaning, and the noise was at its height when up came the shepherd who had promised to geld me, eager to get the job done.

This was not at all a suitable moment for the operation. Someone told him: 'No, this wicked ass isn't responsible for today's tragedy; but come along tomorrow by all means and cut off his head or his privates, or whatever else you please. We'll be delighted to lend a hand.'

So disaster was again postponed and I felt grateful to the ass-boy whose timely death had won me a day's grace at least. But I was not allowed to spend even that short time in rest and gratitude. The boy's mother, in deep mourning, burst into my stable. She had been screaming and shrieking about her poor son's violent end, tearing out her white hair with both hands and sprinkling it with wood ash. Now she thumped her breast and howled out dismally: 'Look at him! Look at him, that heartless beast, that glutton, with his head stuck in the manger! Is it right that he should go on stuffing his guts with food and drink with never a thought for the awful fate that has overtaken his driver? He cares nothing at all for an old woman like me. He even has the audacity to think that he'll pass for innocent and escape being punished for all his sins. Criminals are like that; however deeply their consciences may reproach them, they never expect to be caught. Now in the name of the blessed gods, you vilest of four footed creatures —even if you could learn to talk, do you really think that you could persuade the biggest fool alive that you aren't responsible for my darling's murder? You could have fought for him with your teeth and hooves. You often used them to attack him; why couldn't you do the same in his defence? You should have galloped off with him on your back and saved him from that bandit's bloody hands. It was downright wicked of you to throw your rider—your fellow-servant, your guide, your comrade, the kind friend who fed you. Don't you know that it's against all moral principle and a punishable offence, too, to desert anyone who's in danger of death? All right, you murderer, you shan't stand there much longer, gloating on my grief. I'll show you on what reserves of strength people in grief can fall back.' She untied her apron and used the strings to knot my legs together, each to each, as tightly as she could to prevent me from retaliating. Next, she snatched up a great bar which was used to secure the stable door, and banged me with it until she had to let it drop in exhaustion. Then, complaining that her arms had got tired before she had fully avenged her son, she ran back into the house and took a burning faggot from the hearth, to thrust between my thighs. I had no means of defence but what I had used after my first attempt to escape: I squirted a volley of liquid excrement into her face and drove her off, blinded and stinking. If I had not done so, all would have been over with me, as it was with Meleager when his angry mother Althaea caught up the burning brand in revenge for the murder of her other sons.

•

About cockcrow, a household slave employed by my mistress and former fellow-sufferer, the Lady Charitë, arrived with the news that she and her husband Tlepolemus were both dead. It was a very strange and terrible tale that he declaimed there, by the fireside. 'Grooms, shepherds and herdsmen,' he said, 'our poor mistress Charitë has died in dreadful circumstances; but she did not go down to the Underworld without proper escort, as you shall hear. I'll tell you the whole story from the beginning; it really deserves to be recorded by someone more gifted than I am, some great historian with the happy knack of writing easy and elegant prose.'

This was his version:

'In the next town from ours lived a wealthy knight named Thrasyllus, a debauched young fellow who was always drinking and whoring in the public brothels; you may have heard of him. He was on terms of friendship with a company of bandits and sometimes even took part in their murders. Yes, that was the sort of man he was; and everyone knew it. When our mistress was old enough to be married, Thrasyllus was one of her most persistent suitors, and set his heart on winning her. But though he was better bred than any of his rivals and brought her parents magnificent presents, he was turned down ignominiously because of his bad reputation. As you know, the Lady Charitë then married Tlepolemus, a very worthy young gentleman; but Thrasyllus, furious at having been rejected and more in love with Charitë than ever, refused to abandon all hope of winning her, and waited for the opportunity of committing a bloody crime. He thought of nothing else, but it was some time before he had the chance of putting his plans into action. On the day that Tlepolemus had managed, by courage and cunning, to rescue our mistress Charitë from that robbers' den, Thrasyllus was spokesman for the crowd of people who offered their congratulations. He said that he had come to express the joy of his fellow-townsmen that the young pair were safely re-united, and their hope that the marriage would

171

be blessed with children. My master and mistress admitted him to the house and showed him the hospitality that his rank demanded; and he hid his wicked designs so cleverly that he passed for the most loyal of friends, worming himself into their intimacy by frequent calls. He was often asked to dinner, with the result that he fell more deeply in love with our poor mistress than ever. There's nothing so remarkable in that, because the fire of love burns small at first and gives out a pleasant warmth; but fan it with the wind of the loved one's presence and the flames shoot up and scorch you cruelly. Thrasyllus spent a long time wondering how to begin a secret love affair with our mistress. He found that too many eyes were on the watch to make adultery practicable; that even if he could persuade her to give him what he wanted, she knew nothing of the art of deceiving a husband; and that Tlepolemus and she were so deeply and increasingly devoted to each other that it would be impossible to separate them. He could achieve nothing. But he was desperate to possess her and refused to regard the case as hopeless, despite these apparently insurmountable obstacles. You know that what looks difficult when one first falls in love, after a time looks easy enough. This, by the way, is a most instructive story, all about the lengths to which a man's violent passion can drive him.

'One day Tlepolemus rode out with Thrasyllus to hunt wild beasts—that is, if you can call a doe a wild beast—because the Lady Charité refused to let him hunt anything that had either tusks or horns. Hunting nets were spread around a thickly wooded hill and pedigree hounds put in to dislodge the quarry. Anyone could have seen that it was a well-trained pack because they fanned out at once and allowed no creature any chance to slip past them. For a time they followed the scent silently until at last one of them gave tongue and then the music broke out excitedly, making the whole wood ring. But it was no sort of gentle doe they had started, neither roe, nor red, nor fallow—but an enormous wild boar, the biggest ever seen, a brawny, thick-skinned, filthy beast with bristles like a hedgehog's and fiery eyes. Out he came like a thunderbolt, foaming at the mouth and gnashing his tusks. The leading hounds tried to get a grip on him but were torn open and tossed aside; then he broke the nets at his first rush and got clear away.

'We beaters were unused to such dangerous sport, and having no weapons or other means of defence, we scattered in panic and hid ourselves in thick bushes or behind trees. Here was Thrasyllus's chance for playing his treacherous trick. He said to Tlepolemus: "Why are we standing here and letting that wonderful beast escape? Is it just surprise? Or are we as frightened as those wretched slaves who have run off trembling like a lot of old women? Why not mount and go after him? You take a javelin; I'll take a boar-spear."

'So off they galloped in pursuit; but the boar was confident that he was a match for them both. He wheeled round and stood glaring at them, with a horribly ferocious look, making up his mind which of them to charge first. Tlepolemus let fly his javelin, which lodged in the boar's back; but Thrasyllus, instead of following up this advantage, charged Tlepolemus's horse with his lance and hamstrung it. The horse sank in a pool of its own blood, rolled over and threw Tlepolemus. The boar attacked him at once, ripping off his clothes and wounding him in several places as he tried to rise. Thrasyllus—what a fiend!—so far from feeling re-

morse for what he had just done, ran at Tlepolemus who was
shouting for help and trying to protect his gored legs, and drove
his lance into him. He aimed at the right thigh, which was the
safest place to choose, because the thrust would be indistinguishable, he knew, from a tusk-wound. Only then did he run the boar
through, and killed him without difficulty.

'When all was over, Thrasyllus called us from our hiding places
and we ran up, to find that our master was already lifeless.
Thrasyllus was elated at the death of the man he loathed: but he
disguised his feelings and taking his cue from us—we were all
lamenting in deep and genuine grief—hugged and kissed his victim's corpse and played the part of mourner in realistic detail, except that he couldn't squeeze out a single tear.

'The news of Tlepolemus's death spread quickly and reached
his own family first. The moment the Lady Charitë heard of it—
she will never hear bad news again, poor woman—she went frantic. She ran through the crowded streets of the town and across
the fields, like a Bacchanal, shrieking out her dead husband's
name. Everyone she met turned and followed her with cries of
sympathy, and soon the whole town was streaming after her to
the scene of the murder. At last she reached the spot, fell prostrate
on his dead body and then and there all but gasped out the life
that she had made one with his. However, her friends succeeded
in dragging her away and, greatly against her will, she remained
alive.

'Well, the corpse was carried to the tomb and the whole town
formed the funeral procession. Thrasyllus was there. He wailed
aloud, roared, beat his breast and even managed to weep; you see,
the tears that he had been unable to force out in the first pretence

of grief were now supplied by the joy of the occasion. He hid his true feelings with all sorts of affectionate phrases, pitifully apostrophizing Tlepolemus as "My friend, my dear old playmate, my comrade, my brother . . . alas, my poor brother Tlepolemus!" Every now and then he caught at the Lady Charitë's hands to prevent her from beating her breast, and tried to blunt her distress with vibrating words of sympathy, quoting numerous historical instances of the uncertainty of fate. But of course this was only an excuse for laying his murderous hands on our poor mistress and titillating his odious lust.

'As soon as the funeral was over she tried to follow Tlepolemus to the grave. She did not care how, so she fixed on the easiest and least violent way, the one that comes closest to quiet sleep; that is to say, refusing to eat, neglecting herself, hiding herself away in a dark room and leaving the light of day for good and all. Thrasyllus would have none of this, and by pleading with her himself and then persuading her friends and servants, and lastly her parents to plead in the same sense, forced her to refresh her poor body, now nearly wasted away by the ill-usage she had given it, with a bath and a little food. She would have refused even this but for the respect she felt for her parents, and though her looks were calmer now, they were still very sorrowful, and she went through the daily round of her life in inward torment. Day and night, longing for Tlepolemus ate at her heart; she ordered an image of the God Dionysus to be carved with his features, and paid it divine honours, so that even the comforts of religion became pure misery to her.

'The impatient Thrasyllus, true to his name—it means "rashness"—couldn't bear to wait until the madness of her grief had

gradually dulled into resignation, and her tears had stopped flowing. She was still at the stage of tearing her clothes and pulling
out strands of her hair, when he began to discuss marriage with
her; his indecent haste was almost a blurted confession of his unspeakable treachery. The Lady Charitë was so shocked by his
proposal, which came on her like a thunderclap, that she fell down
in a faint, as though lightning-struck or blasted by the rays of
some malignant star. When she came to herself and remembered
what had happened, she screamed aloud; but refrained from giving the villain his answer until she had time to consider carefully.
Meanwhile the ghost of the murdered man visited her lonely bed
as she slept and displayed its ghastly blood-stained face. It said:
"My own wife—nobody else will ever call you that, unless the
bonds that united us have been severed by my terrible death, and
my image is gradually dimming in your memory—ah, if this is so,
marry again by all means, be happy, take any husband you please,
but only not that traitor Thrasyllus. Have nothing to do with
him: do not eat at the same table with him, do not even talk to
him, let alone share one bed with him. His hands are stained with
my blood, the blood of the man he called his best friend. These
gory wounds that you have bathed with your tears were not all of
them made by the boar's tusks; the deepest and most mortal one
came from the lance of Thrasyllus!" The ghost then explained in
detail what had happened. When she had first gone to sleep the
tears had been trickling down her beautiful cheeks, wetting the
pillow; now, roused from this nightmare as though by the wrench
of the rack, she broke again into a loud wail of grief, ripped open
her nightgown and tore her pretty arms with her nails until they
bled.

'Well, at the time she told nobody about the apparition and pretended to have no knowledge of the murder; but she decided in secret to punish the odious Thrasyllus before finally freeing herself from the intolerable burden of life. He came again to renew his pleas, and though her ears were deaf to them, she was a far finer actress than he had given her credit for being and let him go on and on unchecked, until at last she gently begged him to say no more. "Please, Thrasyllus!" she said. "You must remember that the face of my dear husband, who was like a brother to you, is still vivid in my mind; I seem to smell the lovely scent of his body; he is alive in my heart. It would be a kindness if you gave me time to recover from the shock of his death, letting the remaining months of the year run out before you say anything more. You see, if we married too soon, that would damage my reputation and also be dangerous for you: my husband's ghost would have the right to feel resentful and might bring about your death."

'She undertook to marry him when the time of mourning was over; but even this was not enough to check his greed and impatience. He began to make indecent proposals and would not be refused. At last she pretended to give in and said: "At any rate, there's one thing upon which I must insist: that if we sleep together before our marriage, nobody in this household must know anything about it."

'She completely deceived him. He agreed at once to the secret love affair, but said that he could hardly wait until darkness fell; nothing in the world mattered more to him now than possessing her.

' "Listen," she said, "you must come to my suite about midnight alone, well muffled up. Make no noise at all until you are outside the door, then give a single low whistle, and wait. My old nurse will be sitting just inside to let you in. She'll guide you through the darkness to my bedroom."

'How long the day seemed to Thrasyllus, who was greatly intrigued by this combination of mourning and secret passion! But the sun went down at last and he came to her suite as she had instructed him and stumbled expectantly towards her bedroom. "Hush," said the old woman, who had been ordered to treat him with obsequious politeness. "Hush, my Lord!" She noiselessly produced wine cups and a flagon of wine doctored with a sleeping draught. "Your Lordship must please wait a little while," she said. "My mistress has been called to her father, who is ill. She won't keep you waiting long. Drink this, and be ready for her when she comes." He suspected nothing, drank cup after cup and was soon fast asleep.

'As soon as he was lying helplessly on his back, the nurse ran for the Lady Charitë, who came quickly in with a determined step and bent quivering with rage over him. "Look at him," she said, "Look at him, my husband's faithful comrade, this bold hunter who thinks he's going to marry me! Look at his hand, the hand that shed my blood; look at his breast, in which so many stratagems were hatched to my ruin; look at his eyes, which I have been unfortunate enough to please. It seems he had some intuition of the fate prepared for him when he said that he was impatient for darkness to fall. Sleep soundly, murderer, sleep without fear! I have not come with a sword or a lance: do you think I would honour you with a death like my husband's? No, your eyes shall die in your living head, you will never see me again ex-

cept in dreams. Oh, I'll make you envy Tlepolemus in his death!
You shall never look at the sun again; you shall need a hand to
guide you wherever you go. You shall never put your arms around
me, nor consummate the marriage which you have promised
yourself. You shall experience neither the restfulness of death nor
the pleasure of being alive, but wander like a lost ghost between
the Underworld and the Upper. And you'll search for the hand
that blinded you, but never know—this you'll find the hardest
thing of all to bear—whom to accuse of the deed. For now I owe
my noble husband's ghost a drink-offering of the blood that flows
from your eyes. That will satisfy his vengeance."

'After a pause she began again: "Why do I delay, I wonder?
Why allow you this short grace before the torture begins? Perhaps you are dreaming that you are in bed with me? That is
dangerous; my name is Poison. Come, it is time to wake from the
darkness of sleep to a worse darkness; to lift up your blind face
and know that I am avenged, to realize your misfortune and reck-
on up the full sum of your afflictions.

' "A bashful bride, am I? Your eyes charm me, eh? How prettily the wedding torches flare! The Furies shall be your brides-
maids; and your best man shall be Blindness, the dark keeper of
your unquiet conscience."

'After this burst of eloquence, she pulled a bronze pin from her
hair and plunged it again and again into Thrasyllus's eyes. Then,
leaving him there to awake in pain and blindness from his
drugged sleep, she caught up a sword which had been Tlepolemus's and rushed madly off with it through the town towards his
tomb. We slaves streamed out after her, shouting for her to stop,
because we were certain that she was about to perform some

desperate act. We cried to one another: "She's mad, she's mad! Disarm her, for God's sake!" A great crowd of townspeople tumbled out of their beds and joined us. But she stood by her dead husband's tomb and kept us off with the naked sword.

'We were all weeping and lamenting, but she reproved us. "This is not the time for tears or mourning. Why mourn when I have just done a great deed? I have avenged my husband's death; I have punished the man who destroyed our marriage, punished him as he deserved. Now I must find my way back with this sword to my darling Tlepolemus."

'She told us all about her husband's apparition, and how she had deceived Thrasyllus; then plunged the sword in beneath her right breast. She fell spouting blood, babbled a few incoherent words and died as nobly as she had lived. Her relatives at once took up the corpse, washed it carefully and laid it by the side of her beloved Tlepolemus; so the two are now reunited for all time.

'When the news of her death came to Thrasyllus he could think of no form of suicide dismal enough to atone for the catastrophe he had caused; his guilty heart told him that merely to die by the sword would be to clean a way out. So he asked to be carried to the tomb, where he stood crying repeatedly: "Here I am, ghosts whom I wronged! I have come, unsummoned, to await your vengeance."

'He allowed himself to die there of starvation.'

12

With the Eunuch Priests

SIGHS AND TEARS from the listening countrymen interrupted this tragic account of the calamity that had overtaken their master and mistress, but these were largely expressive of self-pity: they feared that when the estate changed hands it would be the worse for them. They all decided to run away. The bailiff, into whose charge I had been given with such careful orders to treat me well, stripped the house of everything valuable, loaded me and his other pack animals with the loot and left in a hurry. Women, children, cocks, hens, geese, kids and puppies—in short, whatever livestock could not keep the pace of the convoy—travelled on our legs. But heavy as was my load, I did not mind in the least, so relieved I felt to escape the knife of that horrible gelder.

We crossed the wooded mountain and the plain on the other side, and as the evening shadows lengthened on our road we reached a thriving town. The authorities requested us not to continue our journey that night, or even the following morning, because the district was overrun by packs of enormous wolves, grown so bold that they even turned highwaymen and pulled down travellers on the roads or stormed farm-buildings, showing as little respect for the armed occupants as for their defenceless flocks. We were warned that the road we wished to take was strewn with half-eaten corpses and clean-picked skeletons and that we ought to proceed with all possible caution, travelling only in broad daylight—the higher the sun, the milder the wolves—and in a compact body, not straggling along anyhow.

However, in their blind haste to shake off possible pursuers our rascally people disregarded this warning, loaded us up again without waiting for dawn, and drove us onward. Well aware of the danger, and not wanting to feel wolf-fangs in my rump, I worked my way into the middle of the herd of pack-animals. Everyone was surprised to see me outpace several horses, but this was due to my terror, not my natural fleetness of foot. It occurred to me that the famous Pegasus must have had a similar experience: the reason they called him 'the winged horse' was doubtless that he was so terrified of being bitten by the fire-breathing Chimaera that he buck-jumped right up to the sky.

Our people had armed themselves as if for a pitched battle, with lances, spears, javelins and clubs. Some picked up stones from the rough road, a few carried sharp stakes, and most of them waved blazing torches to frighten the wolves away. It only needed trumpet music to give the impression that we were an army on the march. Whether because of our numbers and the great noise we raised, or because of the torches, we did not see a single wolf even in the distance; of course, they may all have cleared off beforehand to some other district. So we made this dangerous passage—if it really was as dangerous as it seemed, and certainly we were all terrified—in perfect safety as regards wolves.

But when we reached a small village, the inhabitants very natural-ly mistook us for a brigade of bandits. They were in such alarm that they unchained a pack of large mastiffs which they kept as watch-dogs, very savage beasts, worse than any wolf or bear, and set them at us with shouts, halloos and discordant cries.

The mastiffs rushed forward and attacked us from all sides, mauling us indiscriminately and pulling several beasts and men to the ground. It was certainly a remarkable, though a very piti-able sight: how they worked their way through the whole crowd of us, snapping and biting as they went, rounded up stampeding beasts, savaged men who stood their ground and mounted menac-ingly on the bodies of the fallen.

Worse followed. Posted on their roofs and on a small hill close by, the villagers pelted us with stones, until we could not decide which we liked least: the attack from close quarters or the sup-porting bombardment. A stone hit the head of a woman seated on my back, who began to scream and bellow for her husband. He ran to her and wiped the blood from her wound, shouting up at the houses: 'In the name of Heaven, what is all this about? Why attack poor, hard-working travellers who have never harmed you? What sort of people are you, anyhow? You don't live in dens like wild animals, or in caves like savages. Then why do you en-joy shedding innocent blood? Do you take us for bandits?'

Almost immediately the shower of stones ceased, the mastiffs were called off and one of the villagers shouted from his perch on the top of a cypress: 'All right. We aren't bandits, either. We want nothing from you. We were only afraid that you were at-tacking the village, that was all. Go ahead now, and good luck to you! The battle is over.'

183

So on we went, some of us bitten, some bruised by stones, all of us more or less damaged, until we reached a wood with pleasant green glades and tall trees, where the bailiff called a halt for rest and refreshment. Our people threw themselves down wherever they happened to be standing and lay motionless for awhile until they felt a little rested, then they began to attend to their wounds, every man for himself, washing off the blood in a brook that ran through the wood, applying various remedies, then bandaging themselves; the bruises they sponged with water.

An old man appeared at the top of the hill with goats feeding around him. One of our people hailed him and asked whether he had any milk or fresh cheese for sale. He shook his head two or three times before answering: 'How can you think of food or drink or anything else of the sort? Don't you know in what sort of a place you are camping?' He turned his back and went off with his goats.

His question and the abrupt way he left us alarmed our people. They all began wondering what was wrong with the place. But there was nobody to enlighten them until another old man appeared, a tall, bent old man, dragging his feet wearily towards us and leaning heavily on a stick. When he reached the glade where we had halted, he fell down on his knees, his eyes streaming with tears, embraced our people one after the other and groaned out: 'I appeal to you, my lucky gentlemen, as you hope to live strong and hearty until you reach my age, help a poor old man, who has lost his only comfort in life: save my little grandson from the jaws of death! He is such a dear little boy. We were travelling along the road together when he heard a sparrow twittering on a hedge and tried to catch it. But he fell into a deep ditch hidden by rank undergrowth and there he is stuck. I know by his cries that he is still alive, but as you see I am old and shaky and haven't the strength to pull him out. You strong young gentlemen could easily help me. Pity a poor unhappy old man! The child is the last survivor of my family.'

He tore at his white hair, and naturally we were all touched by his appeal. One of the cattlemen—the youngest, boldest and strongest of the whole company—the only one, too, who had escaped without a scratch from our one-sided battle, sprang up and asked where the boy was. The old man pointed at a clump of bushes a little way off and eagerly led him towards them. When we animals had grazed and our drivers had finished eating and dressing their wounds, it was time to pack up and continue our journey. Loud cries were raised for the young cattleman, who had been away a surprisingly long time, and when he did not reappear a friend was sent to warn him that we were on the move again. The friend returned almost at once, pale and trembling, with an extraordinary story: he had found the body of the young cattleman lying on its back, half-eaten, with a monstrous snake coiled over it. The unhappy old man was nowhere to be seen.

So that was evidently what the man with the goats had meant: he had been warning us against the dreadful creature that haunted the glade. Our people hurried as fast as they could from the deadly place, whacking us hard with their sticks. The next stage of the journey was covered in double quick time.

We spent that night at a village, where the people told us a dreadful story. I feel impelled to include it in this book because it concerned a gruesome relic still to be seen on the farm where we were quartered.

The previous farm-bailiff, who was married to a fellow-slave, had fallen in love with a free woman, not of his master's household, and made her his mistress. When his wife came to hear of it she was so vexed that she burned his account-books and all the contents of his store-room. Even this did not satisfy her: she tied one end of a rope around her neck and the other around the neck of her little child, but then instead of committing suicide by hanging, plunged into a well and dragged the poor child after her. Her death so shocked the owner of the farm that he seized the bailiff whose infidelity had provoked it and ordered him to be stripped naked, smeared all over with honey and bound fast to a rotten fig-tree which was swarming with ants inside and out. As soon as the ants smelt the honey they began running over him and with minute but innumerable and incessant bites gradually ate him up, flesh, guts and all. He survived the torture for some time, but in the end there was nothing left of him but his skeleton, picked clean; which we saw, all white and dry, still tied to the fig-tree.

The people who told us the story were still heavy-hearted about the bailiff, and were glad to leave the unlucky place. We travelled all day over level country and that night reached a fine, handsome town which our weary people decided to make their permanent home. It was a good place for eluding pursuers who came from some distance away, and also well stocked with food. There the bailiff allowed us pack-animals three days to recover our condition, after which he led us out for sale.

The auctioneer shouted our prices at the top of his voice, and though all the horses and all my fellow-asses soon found prosperous-looking buyers I was passed over contemptuously. The rude way that people handled me and examined my teeth to see

how old I was outraged me; one man poked his nasty, dirty
fingers into my gums again and again until I caught his hand
between my teeth and nearly bit it in two. This discouraged
people from making an offer: they took me for a real rogue. Then
the auctioneer, shouting till he almost cracked his throat, made
all sorts of stupid jokes about me. 'Look at this screw, gentlemen!'
he cried. 'What's the sense in asking you to bid for this dirty-
coloured, hoofless old cuddy, guaranteed lazy in everything but
vice, with a hide like a sieve? What about making a present of
the brute to anyone who won't mind wasting hay on him?' The
bystanders roared with laughter.

But merciless Fortune, whom I had failed either to shake off
or appease, however deeply I suffered, now again loured at me
and, of course, found me a buyer whom she could depend upon
to prolong my agonies. He was an old eunuch, nearly bald, with
what greyish hair he still had left dangling in long curls on his
neck: one of the scum that turns the Great Goddess of Syria into a
beggar-woman, hawking her along the roads from town to town
to the accompaniment of cymbals and castanets. This odious creature was set on buying me and asked the auctioneer my history.
The auctioneer joked: 'We got him from the Cappadocian slave-
market; he's a fine strong fellow, too.'

'His age?'

'Five years, according to the astrologer who cast his nativity;
but he may have more accurate information himself from the
public registrar, if you care to press him on the point. No, sir,
at the risk of falling foul of the Cornelian Law by selling you a
slave known to be a Roman citizen, I don't mind parting with

him. You'll find him a good worker, useful both on the road and in the bedroom. Why not make an offer?'

The eunuch asked question after question and at last came to the important point: was I quiet to ride or drive?

'Quiet, is it?' said the auctioneer. 'This isn't an ass, it's a bell-wether, so gentle that you can do anything you like with him. None of your biters and kickers, but the sort of animal that makes you ready to swear he's really a decent, honest man bound up in ass-hide. You can prove it easily. Lift up his tail, shove your nose in, and see how he takes it.'

The old rascal saw that he was being laughed at and lost his temper. 'Damn you,' he cried, 'you lunatic auctioneer, you sense-less lump of stinking meat! May the almighty and all-creative Queen of Heaven, with the blessed Sabazius, and Bellona, and the Idaean Mother too, and Venus with her Adonis—and all the rest of them—knock out both your eyes! That will teach you to make stupid jokes at my expense. Do you think that I can trust my Goddess to the back of any restive beast? Suppose he were to pitch her to the ground? What would happen to poor me? I should have to run about with my hair streaming in the wind in search of a doctor to attend to her bruises.'

I had a sudden impulse to rear up as though I were mad, so as to discourage him from buying me; but he forestalled me by making an offer of seventeen drachmae and counting them out at once. The bailiff was as delighted as I was vexed; and glad to be rid of me. He picked up the coins and handed me over to my new master, rush-halter and all.

The eunuch, whose name was Philebus, led me off to his lodgings. When he reached the door he called out: 'Look, girls, look!

188

I have bought you a lovely new man-servant!' The girls were a set of disgusting young eunuch priests who broke into falsetto screams and hysterical giggles of joy, thinking that Philebus really meant what he said, and that they would now have a fine time with me. When they discovered that I was an ass, not a man, they were as surprised as the Achaeans were at Aulis when a doe was miraculously substituted for Agamemnon's daughter Iphigeneia; and in their disappointment they began making nasty, sarcastic remarks. 'A man-servant for us? No, darling Philebus. A husband for yourself, you mean! But you mustn't be a greedy old pig. You must let us have a share of him now and then, because we *are* your little lovey-doveys, aren't we? Promise you will!' Then they took me and tied me to the manger.

This queer family included one real man, a great big slave, whom they had bought with money collected by begging. When they went out, leading the Goddess in procession, he would walk in front playing the horn—he played extremely well—and at home they used him in all sorts of ways, especially in bed. When he saw me arrive he was delighted and heaped my manger with fodder. He cried out happily: 'Thank Heavens, you are here at last to help me with my terrible work. Long life to you, friend! If only you can please your masters and give me a chance to recover my strength! I'm utterly worn out!'

This set me worrying again.

The next morning the eunuch priests prepared to go out on their rounds, all dressed in different colours and looking absolutely hideous, their faces daubed with rouge and their eye-sockets painted to bring out the brightness of their eyes. They wore mitre-shaped birettas, saffron-coloured chasubles, silk surplices, girdles and yellow shoes. Some of them sported white tunics with an irregular criss-cross of narrow purple stripes. They covered the Goddess with a silk mantle and set her on my back, the horn-player struck up and they started brandishing enormous swords and maces, and leaping about like maniacs, with their arms bared to the shoulders.

After passing through several hamlets we reached a large country-house where, raising a yell at the gate, they rushed frantically in and danced again. They would throw their heads forward so that their long hair fell down over their faces, then rotate them so rapidly that it wheeled around in a circle. Every now and then they would bite themselves savagely and as a climax cut their arms with the sharp knives that they carried. One of them let himself go more ecstatically than the rest. Heaving deep sighs from the very bottom of his lungs, as if filled with the spirit of the Goddess, he pretended to go stark-mad. (A strange notion, this, that divine immanency, instead of doing men good, enfeebles or disorders their senses; but if you read on you will see how Providence eventually intervened to punish these charlatans.) He began by making a bogus confession of guilt, crying out in prophetic tones that he had in some way offended against the holy laws of his religion. Then he called on his own hands to inflict the necessary punishment and snatching up one of the whips that these half-men always carry, the sort with several long lashes of woollen yarn strung with sheep's knuckle-bones, gave himself a terrific flogging. The ground was slippery with the blood that oozed from the knife-cuts and the wounds made by the flying bones, but he bore the pain with amazing fortitude. The sight made me uneasy. Suppose this Syrian Goddess might have a craving for ass's blood, as some people have for ass's milk!

At last they grew tired, or thought that they had cut themselves about enough for the day; so they stopped. The crowd that had gathered competed for the pleasure of dropping money into the open pockets of their robes, and not only small change, but silver, too. They also gave them a barrel of wine, cheese, milk, barley and wheat flour, not to mention a present of barley for myself as the Goddess's own beast. All this was stuffed into the offertory bags which we carried and I went off doubly laden: I was at once a walking temple and a walking larder.

We worked the whole district in this way until one day, after taking an unusually large collection in one of the towns, my masters (or mistresses) decided to give themselves a really good time. First they got a fine, plump ram from a farmer, by telling him some prophetic nonsense or other, and undertook to sacrifice it to appease the Goddess's hunger, Then they got everything ready for the banquet, paid a visit to the public baths, and came back with a hefty-loking young labourer.

They all sat down to table together, but the priests had eaten only a few mouthfuls of the first course before they jumped up, crowded round their guest's couch, pushed him down on his back, pulled off his clothes and made such loathsome suggestions that I could stand it no longer. I tried to shout: 'Help, help! Rape! Rape! Arrest these he-whores!' But all that came out was 'He-whore', He-whore,' in fine ringing tones that would have done credit to any ass alive.

The timing was lucky, because a party of young men were out looking for an ass that had been stolen the night before, and going from inn to inn, searching the stables. One of them happened to hear me bray and thinking that I might be the stolen beast, hidden somewhere inside the house, they rushed in unexpectedly and interrupted the fun. They roused the neighbourhood and told everyone about their disgusting find, while ironically complimenting the priests on their truly religious chastity. The news ran from mouth to mouth, and everyone's feelings were outraged; my masters panicked, packed up everything, and left the town hurriedly about midnight.

We covered a good deal of ground before dawn and when the sun was up found ourselves in a lonely spot where the priests consulted together for a long time and finally decided to show me no mercy. They lifted the Goddess off my back and laid her on the ground, then took off my gear, tied me to a tree, and flogged me with the knuckle-bone whip until I was nearly dead. One of them wanted to hamstring me with an axe, in revenge for the scandal that I had spread about his chastity; but the others voted him down, not because they felt any mercy for me, but because if they killed me, where would they find another mount for the recumbent Goddess? So they loaded me up again and drove me forward, beating me with the flat of their swords until we reached the next large town. One of the leading citizens, a very religious-minded man, heard the tinkle of our cymbals, the banging of our tambourines and the melancholy Phrygian music of the horn. He came out to meet us and devoutly offered to lodge the Goddess in his mansion. We all entered with her and he tried to win her favour by offering her the deepest possible veneration and the finest victims he could procure. But it was there that I had the closest shave of my life.

This is what happened. One of our host's country tenants had presented him with a haunch of venison from a tall, plump stag that he had killed himself. Hephaestion the cook carelessly hung it rather too low on the kitchen door and a stray hound was able to pull it down and carry it off. When Hephaestion discovered his loss, for which he had only himself to blame, he began to cry miserably. There seemed to be nothing he could do, and what would happen when his master called for his supper he dared not imagine. He worked himself up into such a state of terror that he called his little son to him, kissed him a tender goodbye, picked up a rope and went off to hang himself. His wife, who loved him dearly, heard the dreadful news just in time. She wrenched the rope from his hands and asked him: 'Are you blind, my sweet Hephaestion? Has this accident so unbalanced you that you can't see the door that Providence has kept open for your escape? If you still have any sense left after your awful discovery, please, please use it and listen to me! You know the priests' ass which was brought in today? Take it to some lonely spot and cut its throat. Then carve off a haunch, like the one you have lost, stew it till tender, disguise the flavour with the most savoury sauce you can invent, and serve it up as venison at the master's table.'

The rogue of a cook, overjoyed at the prospect of saving his life at the price of mine, called his wife the cleverest woman in the world and began sharpening his kitchen knives.

Time pressed. I could not afford to stay where I was and concoct a plan for saving myself. I decided to escape from the knife which I felt so close to my throat, by running away at once. I broke my halter and galloped off as fast as my legs would carry me, not forgetting to kick out my heels as I went. I shot across the first portico and, without hesitating for a moment, dashed into the dining-room where the master of the house was banqueting with the priests on sacrificial meats. I knocked down and smashed a great part of the dinner service and some of the tables, too. He was greatly annoyed by my irreverent entry and the damage I had caused. 'Take away this frisky brute,' he told one of his slaves. 'Shut him up in a safe place where his pranks won't disturb the peace of my guests.' Rescued from the knife by my own cleverness, I was glad indeed to be locked up securely in my cell.

But no one can prosper, however wise he may be, if Fortune should rule otherwise: he can never cancel or modify the fate predestined for him by Providence. My stratagem, which seemed to have saved me from immediate death, had landed me in another danger which nearly ruined me. As I afterwards learned, one of the house-slaves rushed terror-stricken into the supper-room, with the news that a mad dog had just entered the house through a back door which opened on a lane. First he had made a furious attack on the hounds, then broken into the stables to vent his rage on the horses, and lastly gone for the slaves as well. He had bitten Myrtilus the muleteer, Hephaestion the cook, Hypatarius the butler, Apollonius the house-physician and several other members of the staff who had tried to expel him from the house. Some of the animals that he had bitten were already showing clear signs of rabies.

The news struck everyone present with dismay, and guessing from my wild behaviour that I had also become infected, my masters caught up whatever weapons lay at hand and began appealing frantically to one another: 'Kill him, do kill him, for everyone's sake!' Really, it was they who were mad, not I. They would almost certainly have butchered me with the lances, spears and axes which the slaves eagerly pushed into their hands, if I had not got wind of the danger and fled before the storm. I escaped from the cell where I was confined and rushed into the bedroom assigned to my masters. They were afraid to follow me in, so they shut and bolted the door after me and kept a guard all night outside, hoping that when morning came, instead of having to fight me they would find me dead of my terrible disease. Well, there I was locked in, but all alone and at liberty to be myself at last. I took full advantage of this blessed gift of Fortune: I lay down on the bed and enjoyed what I had missed for so long, a good sleep in human style.

It was broad daylight when I awoke. I jumped up refreshed after my wonderful night and heard my masters discussing me outside. One of them was saying: 'But darling, the poor beast can't still be mad, surely? I'm certain the virus must have worked itself out by now and left him all right again.'

'Oh, but darling, I couldn't disagree with you more.'

They decided to peep at me through a crack in the door, and there they saw me standing at my ease, apparently as quiet and well as ever I had been. They ventured to open the door and make a closer examination. One of them, appointed by Heaven to be my saviour, suggested a simple way of discovering whether I were mad or not; to put a basin full of fresh water before me. If I drank it without hesitation, as usual, this would be a sure proof that I was in perfect health; but if I backed away in obvious terror, that would mean that I was still in the grip of rabies. The standard medical text-books, he said, all prescribed this test, and he had often seen it confirmed in practice.

They all agreed, and at once fetched me a large basinful of fine clear water from the nearest fountain and placed it before me, still tightly grasping their weapons. Feeling very thirsty, I went straight up to it, plunged my muzzle in and drank every drop of water; which did me good in more ways than one. Then I stood still and allowed them to pat me, stroke my ears, lead me about by the head-stall and do anything else they pleased, to convince them that it was all a mistake: that I was a gentle beast and perfectly right in the head.

Next day, with these two great dangers behind me, I was loaded again with the Goddess's baggage and we marched off to the sound of cymbals and castanets, on our usual begging rounds. We passed through a few hamlets and military posts and came to a village said by the inhabitants to have been built on the ruins of a famous ancient city. We put up at the first inn we came to, where we heard a good story about one of the villagers, a poor man grossly deceived by his wife, and I should like you to hear it too.

Well:—

This man depended for his livelihood on his small earnings as a jobbing smith, and his wife had no property either but was famous for her sexual appetite. One morning early, as soon as he had gone off to work, an impudent lover of his wife's slipped into the house and was soon tucked up in bed with her. The unsuspecting smith happened to return while they were still hard at work. Finding the door locked and barred, he nodded approval—how chaste his wife must be to take such careful precautions against any intrusions on her privacy! Then he whistled under the window, in his usual way, to announce his return. She was a resourceful woman and, disengaging her lover from a particularly tight embrace, hid him in a big tub that stood in a corner of the room. It was dirty and rotten, but quite empty. Then she opened the door and began scolding: 'You lazy fellow, strolling back as usual with folded arms and nothing in your pockets! When are you going to start working for your living and bring us home something to eat? What about me, eh? Here I sit every day from dawn to dusk at my spinning wheel, working my fingers to the bone and earning only just enough to keep oil in the lamp. What a miserable hole this is, too! I only wish I were my friend Daphne: she can eat and drink all day long and take as many lovers as she pleases.'

'Hey, what's all this?' cried the smith, his feelings injured. 'What fault of mine is it if the contractor has to spend the day in court and lays us off until tomorrow? And it isn't as though I hadn't thought about our dinner: you see that useless old tub cluttering up our little place? I have just sold it to a man for five drachmae. He'll be here soon to put down the money and carry it away. So lend me a hand, will you? I want to move it outside for him.'

She was not in the least disconcerted, and quickly thought of a plan for lulling any suspicions he might have. She laughed rudely: 'What a wonderful husband I have, to be sure! And what a good nose he has for a bargain! He goes out and sells our tub for five drachmae. I'm only a woman, but I have already sold it for seven without even setting foot outside the house.'

He was delighted. 'Who on earth gave you such a good price?'

'Hush, you idiot,' she said. 'He's still down inside the thing, having a good look to see whether it's sound.'

The lover took his cue from her at once. He bobbed up and said: 'I'll tell you what, ma'am, your tub is very old and seems to be cracked in scores of places.' Then he turned to the smith: 'I don't know who you are, little man, but I should be much obliged for a candle. I must scrape the inside and see whether it's the sort of article I need. I haven't any money to throw away; it doesn't grow on apple-trees these days, does it?'

So the simple-minded smith lighted a candle without delay and said: 'No, no, mate, don't put yourself to so much trouble. You stand by while I give the tub a good clean-up for you.'

He peeled off his tunic, took the candle, lifted up the tub, turned it bottom upwards, then got inside and began working away busily.

The eager lover at once lifted up the smith's wife, laid her on the tub bottom upwards above her husband's head and followed his example. She greatly enjoyed the situation, like the whore she was. With her head hanging back over the side of the tub she directed the work by laying her finger on various spots in turn with: 'Here, darling, here! ... Now there ...' until both jobs were finished to her satisfaction. The smith was paid his seven drachmae, but had to carry the tub on his own back to the lover's lodgings.

My masters stayed a few days at this place, where the public were very kind to them: in particular they made a good deal of money by professing to tell fortunes. Between them these pious frauds composed an all-purpose oracle for the Goddess to deliver by their mouths, and used it to cheat a great many people who came to consult her on all sorts of questions.

It ran:

> *Yoke the oxen, plough the land;*
> *High the golden grain will stand.*

Suppose that a man came to ask the Goddess whether he ought to marry. The answer was plain: he ought to take on the yoke of matrimony and raise a fine crop of children. Or suppose that he wanted to know whether he ought to buy land: the yoked oxen and the good harvests were quite to the point. Or suppose it was about going on a business trip: the oxen, the least restless of all beasts, were to be yoked and the golden grain spelt a prosperous return. Or suppose a soldier was warned for active service, or a constable ordered to join in the pursuit of bandits: the priests explained the oracle as meaning that he should put the necks of his enemies under the yoke and reap a rich harvest when the time came for the loot, or booty, to be divided among the victors.

They certainly reaped a rich harvest by this dishonest way of foretelling the future, but one day they grew tired of perpetual enquiries for which they had only one stock answer, and we went on again at nightfall. It was a worse journey by far than the one on which the bailiff had taken me, because the road was full of deep holes and ruts brimful of water, and covered in places with thick, very slippery mud. I had at last reached a firm stretch of country lane, exhausted and with my legs bruised by frequent falls, when a body of armed horsemen suddenly charged down on us. Reining in with difficulty, they seized Philebus and the others by the throats and pummelled them with their fists. 'Take that,

that, and that,' they shouted, 'you sacrilegious wretches!' Then
they hand-cuffed them and asked: 'Where's the golden chalice
that you dared to steal from the temple of Juno with the excuse
of conducting a solemn service there behind closed doors? You
hoped to escape punishment for your sin, did you, by sneaking
out of town before daylight?'

Presently one of the horsemen came up to me and putting his
hand into the pocket of the Goddess's robe produced the lost cup
and held it up for everyone to see. But even this glaring proof
of theft caused these nasty creatures no embarrassment. They
turned the whole affair into a joke. 'What bad luck!' they cried.
'Isn't that just the sort of accident that would happen to honest
men like ourselves? For the sake of one miserable little chalice,
which Juno gave as a keepsake to her sister the Syrian Goddess,
we ministers of religion find ourselves threatened with death!'

However, for all their lies and frivolous excuses, they were
marched back and put into the town gaol. The chalice and the
sacred image I had carried were solemnly laid up in the temple
of Juno and next day I was led out and put up for auction again.

13

At the Mill-House

A BAKER from the next town bought me for seven drachmae more than Philebus had paid and, loading me up with a heavy sack of corn which he had just bought, took me by a rough road, all loose stones and tree roots, to his bakery which was also a mill-house.

A good many other beasts were kept there to turn his mills—he had several of them—all day and all night too, for the mill-stones never stood still. He treated me with the consideration due to a new arrival by giving me a well-filled manger and a holiday; I suppose he did not want me to be discouraged by realizing at once what my prospects were. The joy of having nothing to do and plenty to eat did not last beyond the first day. The next morning I was harnessed to what seemed to me the largest mill of all, my eyes were blindfolded and I was put into a little circular track, along which I was supposed to go round and round without stopping. Not having yet taken leave of my wits I did not accept this discipline without protest, and though when I was a man I had often seen machines of this sort at work, and had even turned

201

a smaller one for the bailiff's wife when I was an ass, I pretended complete ignorance of my duties and stood stock-still, as if dazed. I fondly imagined that when they saw I was unfit for the mill they would put me to some other less exacting work, or even send me out to pasture. But my cleverness overreached itself. I was still blindfolded and not expecting any trouble, when several men with sticks came up, and at a given signal all shouted together and began whacking me. The sudden attack and noise startled me. Instead of stopping to think what I must do next, I heaved hard on my rush rope and started briskly along the track. All the men burst out laughing at my sudden change of behaviour.

When the day was nearly over and I was too tired to take another step forward, they unharnessed me and let me retire to my manger. Although I was nearly fainting with hunger and weariness, and in great need of refreshment, fear and my old curiosity made me neglect the food they gave me—there was no lack of it—to observe the life at that detestable mill with fascinated horror. Ye gods, what a pack of runts the poor creatures were who looked after us! Their skins were seamed all over with the marks of old floggings, as you could easily see through the holes in their ragged shirts that shaded rather than covered their scarred backs; but some wore only loin-cloths. They had letters branded on their foreheads, and half-shaved heads and irons on their legs. Their complexions were frightfully yellow, their eyelids caked with the smoke of the baking ovens, their eyes so bleary and inflamed that they could hardly see out of them, and they were powdered like athletes in the arena, but with dirty flour, not dust.

As for my fellow animals, what a string of worn-out old mules and geldings, and how they drooped their heads over their piles of straw! Their necks were covered with running sores, they coughed ceaselessly and wheezed through their nostrils. Their chests were raw from the galling of the breast ropes, their ribs showed through their broken hides from the continual beating and their hooves had lengthened into something like slippers from the everlasting march round and round the mill. Every one of them had the mange.

The dreadful condition of these poor beasts, whom I might soon be brought to resemble, so depressed me that I drooped my head like them and grieved for the degradation into which I had fallen since those far-off days when I was Lord Lucius. My only consolation was the unique opportunity I had of observing all that was said and done around me; because nobody showed any reserve in my presence. Homer was quite right to characterize Odysseus, whom he offered as an example of the highest wisdom and prudence, as one who had 'visited many cities and come to know many different peoples.' I am grateful now whenever I recall those days: my many adventures in ass-disguise enormously enlarged my experience, even if they have not taught me wisdom. It was at this mill that I picked up a story which I hope will amuse you as much as it amused me.

The baker who had bought me was a decent enough fellow, but was unhappily married. His wife was the wickedest woman I met in all my travels and treated him so badly that I used often to groan in secret pity for him. There was no single vice which she did not possess: her heart was a regular cesspool into which every sort of filthy sewer emptied. She was malicious, cruel, spiteful, lecherous, drunken, selfish, obstinate, as mean in her petty thefts as she was wasteful in her grand orgies, and an enemy of all that was honest and clean. She also professed perfect scorn for the Immortals and rejected all true religion in favour of a fantastic and blasphemous cult of an 'Only God.' In his honour she practised various absurd ceremonies which gave her the excuse of getting drunk quite early in the day and playing the whore at all hours; most people, including her husband, were quite deceived by her.

This bitch took an unexplained dislike to me and persecuted me with amazing rancour. She used to call out from her bed before dawn: 'Hey, men, lead out the new ass and harness him to the mill!' And as soon as she was up she made them give me an almighty beating under her personal supervision and at breakfast time, when we were unharnessed, kept me from the manger until long after my companions had been fed and rested.

Her cruelty sharpened my natural curiosity about her goings-on. I knew that a young fellow was always visiting her bedroom and I longed to catch a glimpse of his features; unfortunately, the blinkers that I wore for my work at the mill prevented this. But for them, I felt sure that I should have been able to catch the whore at her tricks. A nasty old woman acted as her confidante and go-between and the two were inseparable. As soon as breakfast was over they would drink flagons of untempered wine, as if for a bet, and their one topic of conversation was how to cheat the poor baker. Though I had never forgiven Fotis for her frightful blunder of transforming me into an ass instead of a bird, I had one compensation at least: that my long ears could pick up conversations at a great distance.

One day I heard the old confidante squeak: 'Mistress, you ought never to have chosen that lover of yours without consulting me.

I can see that his feeble love-making falls so far short of your own passion that you suffer tortures. The truth is that he's a born coward and your horrible husband's scowl frightens him out of his senses. Only compare him with young Philesietaerus: now there's a man for you! Handsome, generous, strong and always to be relied on to trick the most suspicious husband. My word, he deserves to enjoy the favours of every lady in the land; yes, if any man in all Greece is worthy to wear a gold crown it's Philesietaerus—if only for the trick he played the other day on a jealous husband. That was a beautiful illustration of the difference between a real lover and your own young man.'

'Out with the story,' said the baker's wife.

'You know Barbarus, don't you? I mean the municipal councillor, nicknamed "Scorpion" because of his nasty nature. Well, he married a beautiful girl of good family and now keeps her locked up in his house with every imaginable precaution against the risk that any one may become too friendly with her.'

'Why, of course: I know Aretë very well. We were at school together.'

'In that case I may as well stop talking, because you'll have heard the story.'

'I haven't heard a word of it and I'm dying to know what happened. Start from the beginning, Auntie, and go straight on to the end.' So the old woman, who had a wonderful fund of stories, began:

'Barbarus had to go on a journey. It was one of those unavoidable calls and he wanted to do everything possible to keep Aretë faithful to him in his absence. So he sent for a slave of his called Myrmex, the most trustworthy member of his household, and secretly ordered him to keep an eye on her. "If anything goes wrong, Myrmex," he said, "if any man as much as touches her with the tip of his finger as he passes her in the street, I'll chain you up in a dark dungeon, and starve you to death."

'He confirmed this threat with such solemn oaths that Myrmex was terribly frightened and made up his mind to watch Aretë with the utmost vigilance. Then Barbarus set out on his journey with his mind at rest. Myrmex, on the other hand, was so nervous and so meticulous about obeying orders that he wouldn't let Aretë out of his sight for a moment. He kept her shut indoors all day spinning wool, and when she had to go out in the evening to the baths he went with her, clinging tight to a corner of her skirt and sticking to her like glue. But her beauty couldn't escape the keen eyes of such a connoisseur of beauty as Philesietaerus, who felt not only challenged by her reputation for impregnable virtue but piqued by the extraordinary precautions taken to guard it; and fell so violently in love that he was prepared to run any risk to win her. He swore he would lay siege to the castle in which she was imprisoned and take it by storm, despite the garrison commander's disciplined defence.

'He knew the frailty of human nature: he knew that gold can smooth every rough path and break down gates of steel. So catching Myrmex alone for a moment he confessed that he loved Aretë pasionately, and implored him to find some way of easing his torment. "If you don't come quickly to my rescue," he swore, "I'll be dead before Barbarus returns." He added: "Besides, you have nothing to fear. It's a very simple business. All I have to do is to steal into the house by night, alone, and come out again almost at once."

'He reinforced his gentle pleas with a wedge that he reckoned would soon split this tough log wide open: he showed Myrmex a handful of shining gold coins straight from the mint. "Of these thirty," he said, "twenty are for your mistress, ten for yourself."

'The proposal so staggered Myrmex that he rushed away in terror without listening to another word. But he couldn't rid his mind of the glitter of the gold, and though he'd left it all behind and never stopped running until he reached home, he still seemed to have the beautiful coins with him and clutched them tightly in his imagination. The poor fellow spent the rest of the day miserably. He was torn by contradictory feelings; on one hand, a sense of the duty he owed Barbarus, and terror of the ghastly punishment that threatened him if he were discovered; on the other, a sense of the duty he owed himself and the bewitching thought of possessing the coins if all went well. His hunger for those beautiful golden things grew stronger every hour; it gnawed at him all night and prevented him from sleeping. "Stay!" cried Prudence; "Come, fetch us," the coins beckoned. By dawn, cupidity had cast out fear. He rose, and gulping down his shame ran to his mistress's bedroom and delivered Philesietaerus's message.

'Aretë is not the sort of woman who falls in love easily, but being a born prostitute she sold her virtue for the filthy lucre without the least hesitation. Myrmex was overjoyed at the catastrophe which had ended his long record of faithful service, and was so eager not merely to claim the money but actually to handle and possess it, that he ran straight to Philesietaerus's house and told him that Aretë would take pity on him. Philesietaerus paid him his ten gold pieces on the spot. Imagine how Myrmex felt! He had never before had so much as two copper farthings to rub together.

'That night he brought Philesietaerus muffled and disguised into Aretë's bedroom, but about midnight while the naked recruits in the service of the Love-goddess were undergoing their preliminary training, or to put it more bluntly while they were happily accommodating themselves to each other's sexual proclivities, a loud knock sounded on the door: Barbarus had unexpectedly returned. When nobody came to let him in, he began shouting and pounding the door with a stone. The long delay made him more and more suspicious and he threatened at the top of his voice to put Myrmex to the torture. The suddenness of the disaster put Myrmex into a state of mortal terror, but he quavered back that he had hidden the key so carefully that he couldn't find it again in the dark.

'The commotion gave Philesietaerus the alarm; he dressed in a hurry and ran out of the room, unfortunately forgetting his shoes. Myrmex then put the key in the lock and admitted the bawling, swearing Barbarus, who hurried to Aretë's bedroom while Philesietaerus slipped out unnoticed and Myrmex locked the door behind him.

Myrmex went back to bed in great relief. But Barbarus when he got up next morning found a strange pair of shoes under his bed, and at once put two and two together. However, he didn't reveal his suspicions to Aretë, or to any of the servants; he quietly picked up the shoes, slipped them into his pocket and ordered Myrmex's hands to be chained behind him. Then he strode along Market Street, groaning for rage, his eyebrows drawn down in the grimmest sort of scowl and his face distorted with fury. He had sworn to himself to trace the adulterer by means of the shoes. Myrmax followed under escort, his manacles jingling, and though he hadn't been caught red-handed in any crime, his conscience tortured him. He wept and howled, trying to excite the pity of passers-by, though what good that would have done, I'm sure I don't know.

'By a great stroke of luck Philesietaerus happened to come along and, though he had a pressing engagement elsewhere, the sight of the angry master and the terrified slave pulled him up at once. It was a forcible reminder of the slip he had made in his hurry to escape from the bedroom. He guessed what had happened, but instead of losing his head he reacted with his usual presence of mind. Pushing the escort aside he rushed at Myrmex, shouting at the top of his voice and knocking his face about with his fists—though careful to pull his punches. "You lying black-guard," he yelled, "I hope your master, not to mention all the gods whose names you took in vain yesterday afternoon, will punish you as you deserve. I know you all right, you're the sneak-thief who walked off with my shoes at the baths. By God, you deserve to have those manacles left on your wrists until they rust through; you deserve to be shut up in a dark dungeon for the rest of your life."

'Now wasn't that brilliant of Philesietaerus? And on the spur of the moment, too! Barbarus was completely taken in. He turned around and went straight home, released Myrmex, handed him the slippers and "take these back to their rightful owner, you thief," he said, "if you wish to earn my forgiveness." '

The story was hardly done before the baker's wife broke in: 'Yes, indeed, Aretë was a lucky, lucky woman to get a lover like that. Unfortunately, mine is such a coward that he trembles at every creak of the mill; even the blinkered face of that mangy old ass over there scares him.'

'Never mind, dear. He's a smart lad and I undertake to bring him along presently as fresh as paint and as bold as brass, ready to die in your service. We'll be seeing each other again tonight, eh?'

So she went off and the baker's wife prepared a supper grand enough for a priests' banquet, carefully decanting vintage wine, cooking up a delicious ragout of tender meat and thick gravy and waiting for her lover's arrival as if for the advent of some god; luckily her husband had been invited to supper at the laundryman's, next door. When evening came I was unharnessed from the mill and allowed to go to my manger, at the other end of the big room where the supper party was to take place. It was splendid to be released from drudgery and have my blinkers removed; now I had free use of my eyes and could watch all that the wicked woman was doing.

Darkness gathered; the sun sank behind the ocean to give its light to the other side of the earth and presently the old woman brought the lover in. He was only a boy, with no hair on his cheeks, but healthy-looking and very handsome. The baker's wife kissed him passionately again and again and sat him down to table. But he had hardly put his lips to the first glass that she handed him as an appetizer when the baker was heard returning, hours before he was expected. 'God damn the man!' cried the devoted wife. 'I hope he trips over the doorstep and breaks a leg.'

The boy sat there, pale with fright, but the bin into which she used to bolt the flour was not far off, between my manger and the door, and she shoved him under it. As the baker came in she said with perfect composure: 'My dear, how nice to see you! But why have you come back so soon? Surely your old friend the laundry-man . . .?'

'I could bear it no longer,' he broke in with a deep sigh. 'That dreadful wife of his! Heavens, I could never have believed it. She seemed so respectable, so well-behaved. Upon my word, it was a revelation; I swear to you, by that image of the Corn-goddess over there, I could hardly believe the evidence of my own eyes.'

'Tell me what happened.'

'No, no, I'd be ashamed.'

'O, please do. You must tell me what happened. I shall never be satisfied until I hear all about it.'

He yielded in the end and began telling her the story of the disgraceful goings-on at his neighbour's house; quite unaware that there was anything wrong at his own.

'Well,' he said, 'you know that the laundryman is one of my oldest friends, and his wife has always seemed a thoroughly honest woman, looked up to by the neighbourhood, and has managed her husband's affairs decently enough. But not long ago she fell in love with a man, and they began to have secret meetings, and tonight when the laundryman and I came back to supper from the baths, it seems we interrupted them in the middle of their fun. Startled and confused by our sudden arrival, she could find no better hiding-place for her lover than a high wicker cage, with cloths hung over it to bleach in the fumes of the sulphur fire inside. It seemed a safe enough place, so she came and sat down to supper with us. But the lover was forced to breathe in the suffocating sulphur fumes, and you know how it is with sulphur: the smell is so acrid and penetrating that it makes one sneeze and sneeze. The laundryman, who was on his couch at the other side of the table from his wife, heard the first sneeze from immediately behind her. "Bless you, my dear!" he said, and "bless you, bless you!" at the second and third sneeze. But the noise went on and on, and at last he began to take notice and suspect that something was wrong. He pushed the table aside, got up, turned the cage over, and there he found his rival panting for breath, nearly at his last gasp.

'My kind host went mad with rage and shouted for a slave to fetch him his cutlass. He was on the point of cutting the poor wretch's throat, when I managed to restrain him, though with great difficulty. I pointed out that if left to himself, his rival would soon die from sulphur poisoning, but if he were found with his throat cut everyone would get into trouble, myself included.

'My appeals to our old friendship carried little weight with him because he was boiling with rage; however, he saw the force of my argument and dragged the unconscious man out into the lane to die. Then I managed to persuade his wife to leave home at once and take refuge with friends until he had time to cool down slightly. I was pretty sure by the look of him that if she stayed he'd do something desperate: he'd probably kill her and himself, too. Well, all this was quite enough entertainment for one night, so I came home, and here I am.'

The story was punctuated by virtuous exclamations of horror and indignant curses from the baker's wife, who brazened out her own guilt pretty well. She called her neighbour a snake in the grass, a shameless whore, a disgrace to her whole sex, a woman without a rag of decency left or any sense of what she owed her husband. 'Imagine her turning his house into a brothel!' she cried. 'A respectable married woman, too, behaving like the lowest sort of tart. Such women deserve to be burned alive.' Still, she was not altogether at her ease. She wanted to free her lover from his unhappy confinement as soon as she could, and tried to make the baker go to bed early.

'No, wife,' said the baker. 'I missed my supper at the laundry-man's and I'm hungry. Let's eat.'

She quickly and very crossly served him up the supper that she had intended for the boy under the bin. Meanwhile my feelings were so outraged by her behaviour that I felt quite a pain in my stomach: first those lecherous kisses and now this impudent pretence at virtue. I was anxious to find some way of helping my master by exposing her wickedness: for example, by kicking the bin over and revealing her lover squatting underneath it like a tortoise in its shell.

'How scandalously she treats the poor man,' I thought. At this moment Providence came to my aid. It was our watering time and the lame old man who was in charge of us came to drive us to the near-by pond. This gave me the very chance I needed for getting my own back on the baker's wife. I noticed as I passed the bin that the boy's fingers were sticking out from underneath. I planted the edge of my hoof on them and squashed them flat. The pain was excruciating. He could not help crying aloud and pushing the bin over as he jumped up. There he stood for everyone to see, and the baker's wife was unmasked.

The baker did not seem so shocked by his discovery as I had

expected. He began mildly and quietly to reassure the trembling boy, who had the fear of death in his eyes, begging him not to be afraid. 'Don't take me for a barbarian or a savage,' he said. 'I don't intend to suffocate you with sulphur fumes and you're too pretty a boy, too pretty by far, to take into court. It would be a shame if the death penalty exacted by the Adultery Law were passed on you. And I don't intend to bring a divorce case against my wife or sue for a division of property: this business can be settled out of court by a simple deed of partnership and we can all three snuggle down happily in the same bed. My wife and I have never quarrelled about anything: we have been sensible enough to live together on such good terms that what pleases one of us has always pleased the other. But it's only justice that the wife should not have more authority than her husband.'

He went on joking quietly as he made the unwilling boy come along to the bedroom with him. Not to outrage his wife's modesty he locked her in another room, then climbed into bed with the boy and enjoyed a wonderful revenge for the wrong she had done him. The next morning at the first sign of dawn he called the two toughest of his mill-hands who hoisted the boy up for him to thrash on the bare backside with a stick. After giving him a dozen or two of the best, he said: 'Such a nice little boy, too! You ought to be ashamed of turning down lovers of your own age and trying to break up respectable homes. You'll be getting yourself a bad name, my son, and adultery is a very, very serious crime, don't you forget that!'

He gave him another half-dozen for good luck and chased him out of the house. So this most enterprising adulterer got away with his life, which was better luck than he had hoped for, but with sobs and cries for his pretty white backside, which was aching terribly after all that it had been through.

The baker divorced his wife by proxy soon afterwards. Naturally a very wicked woman, she was exasperated by this public affront, and took refuge in the magical arts with which women of her sort usually defend themselves. She visited a witch, who had the reputation of being able to do whatever she liked with the help of charms and drugs, offered her valuable presents, and implored her either to soften the baker's heart and make him relent towards her or, if that was impossible, to send some spectre or frightful demonic power to frighten the soul out of his body.

The witch, who was able to exert a certain pressure on the gods, then set to work. She began with fairly mild experiments in the black art, trying to influence the heart of the aggrieved baker and return it to its usual affectionate feelings for his wife. But when she found herself unable to make any impression on it she flew in a temper with the gods. She said that by treating her conjurations with contempt they were cheating her of the reward that had been promised her if she succeeded; so she threatened to kill the poor baker by setting on him the ghost of a woman who had died by violence.

(I hear some smart reader objecting: 'Look here, Lucius, you were an ass, tied up in the mill-house. How were you clever enough to find out the secrets of these women?' Read on, sir, and you will soon see how I found out all about my master's death. I was an ass, I agree; but I still kept my human intelligence.)

About noon a hideous-looking woman entered the mill-house.

She was dressed in dirty rags and evinced great grief; I took her for someone accused of a capital crime. She had a patched mourning mantle loosely thrown about her; her feet were naked; her thin face was the colour of boxwood under its coat of filth, and her grey hair, patched with white and daubed with dirty ashes, tumbled down over it. She came up to the baker, took him gently by the hand and pretending that she had something private to tell him, led him aside into the bedroom. She shut the door and they remained together in conference for a long time.

When all the wheat which he had given the men to grind had gone through the mill, and more was needed, they knocked at the bedroom door and called out: 'More wheat, Master, more wheat!'

No answer.

They knocked more loudly than before, shouting: 'More wheat Master, MORE WHEAT!' at the top of their voices.

Silence.

The door had been carefully bolted inside, so suspecting foul play they decided to break it open. One, two, three! With a concerted heave they burst the hinges and toppled into the room.

The woman was nowhere to be seen, but the baker was dangling from a rafter with a rope around his neck. He was quite dead when they cut him down.

They raised the customary howl of mourning and all sobbed for grief; and the funeral took place the same evening, a very large crowd gathering at the grave-side. The next morning the baker's daughter, who had recently married a man from a neighbouring village, came running to the mill-house with her hair disordered, weeping and beating her breast; which was remarkable, because no message about her stepmother's divorce and her father's suicide had yet reached her. But her father's pitiful ghost had appeared to her in the night, with the noose around his neck, telling her exactly all that had happened, beginning with the stepmother's adultery and ending with her resort to black magic: how his soul had been bewitched out of his body and forced to descend to the world of shadows. After a time the servants managed to quiet her, and eight days later, when the required sacrifices at the tomb had been completed, she auctioned the millhouse and all its contents—she was the sole heiress—including the slaves and us animals. Strange, how a home suddenly disintegrates at a sale, and its components are scattered in all directions haphazardly!

14

With the Market-Gardener and the Centurion

AMONG THE BIDDERS was a market-gardener to whom I was knocked down for the sum of fifty drachmae. That seemed a great deal of money to the poor man, but he hoped to get it back by working hard and making me do the same. I must describe the life I led while in his service. He used to drive me to the nearest market every day with a load of green-stuff and after selling it to the dealers there would climb on my back and return to his holding. Then he dug his trenches or watered his plants or stooped over them, at one job or another, his hands never idle; while I rested contentedly all day. It was by no means a bad life until the circling year brought us from the vintage season, always a pleasant time, into the wintry sign of Capricorn with its torrential rains and nightly ground frosts. My stable had no door or roof and I nearly died of cold, because my poor master could not afford to provide me, or himself even, with either straw or blankets. His only protection against the weather was the thatch of the small tool shed which served him for a home.

Going to market those days was not a pleasant experience. I had no shoes to protect my hooves from the hard edges of the frozen ruts or projecting pieces of broken ice, and always went breakfastless. My master and I shared our meals, and very frugal they were: mainly old tough lettuces that had run to seed and looked more like brooms, frost-bitten, stinking, and full of a bitter juice.

One moonless night a farmer from the next village lost his way in the dark, got drenched to the skin and turned his exhausted horse into our holding. My master received him hospitably and made him as comfortable as possible, considering the badness of the weather and the poverty in which we lived; at least he managed to get some much needed sleep and showed his gratitude next day by inviting my master to visit him, and promising him a present of corn, oil, and a couple of wine-kegs. He jumped at the offer, and taking with him a sack for the corn, and some empty leather bottles for the oil, rode me along to the farm, which was some seven miles away.

The farmer had gone ahead and on our arrival generously invited my master to join him in a good square meal. They were busily drinking each other's health and chatting jovially when a very startling thing happened. A hen ran cackling around the farmyard as though she badly wanted to lay an egg. The farmer saw her and said: 'You're a good girl, you lay more eggs than any other hen in the run. There's been one a day from you for the last month or more, and now I see you're anxious to contribute something to our dinner . . . Hey, boy!' he called to one of his slaves—'put the basket in the corner where she always lays.'

The basket was fetched but the hen refused to go into it.

Instead, she ran up to her master and laid something at his feet. It was not an egg but an ominous anachronism: a fully fledged chicken, with claws, eyes and all complete, which immediately ran cheeping after its mother.

This was followed by another prodigy, startling enough to make the bravest man sweat with fear: the stone floor under the table seemed suddenly to split open and a gaping chasm appeared, filled with a bubbling fountain of blood, drops of which flew up and bespattered the cups and dishes. While everyone sat staring in horror and dismay at this monstrous apparition, wondering what it portended, a slave ran in from the cellar, to report that the wine, which had been racked-off some time before, was working again in the jars and spilling over on the cellar floor, as though a big fire had been lighted underneath. Next, a pack of weasels approached the house and dragged a dead snake inside. Finally, a small green frog jumped out of the sheep-dog's mouth, and an old ram which was standing close by leaped at the dog and severed its windpipe with a single bite. This horrible sequence of wonders so dumbfounded the farmer and his family that they had no notion how they stood or what they ought to do. Clearly, the anger of the gods must be averted with sacrifices, but with what sort of sacrifices? Which of all these prodigies was the most serious? Which had the first claim on their attention, and which could safely be left to be dealt with later? They sat at a loss, goggling and gaping, ready for the worst.

At last another slave ran in with news of a terrible visitation. It should be explained that the farmer was the proud father of three sons, now grown-up, well-educated and highly respectable. They had long been friendly with a poor neighbour whose cottage stood next to the estate of a young nobleman, one who made very bad use of the power that his wealth and family connexions gave him. He employed an army of retainers and slaves, kept the whole district under his thumb, and had lately been treating his poor neighbour very high-handedly: slaughtering his sheep, driving off his oxen, and trampling down his green corn. He was now trying to dispossess him of his land as well, by a fictitious claim that it fell wholly within the boundaries of his own estate.

The poor man, though mild and inoffensive, did not enjoy being robbed by his rich, greedy neighbour and asked a number of his friends to help him determine what exactly were the limits of his family property; he told them that he hoped to keep enough of it at least to dig himself a grave. Among these friends were the three brothers, who saw that he was in great distress and determined to give him whatever help they could. But the nobleman was so madly resolved on crushing the poor man that, far from being alarmed or even impressed by the arrival of so many of his fellow-citizens, he refused to relinquish his thieving claims. He would not even keep a civil tongue in his head. They offered themselves as arbitrators, courteously pointing out the impropriety of trying to gain possession of what was not legally his; but for all their sweet reasonableness he continued insolent as ever and at last solemnly swore that he and his family would rather die than submit to any such interference—so to hell with arbitration and the whole pack of busybodies!

'Hey, slaves,' he shouted, 'take the fellow by the ears, haul him away from here and make sure he's never seen around these parts again.'

Everyone was scandalized, and one of the brothers spoke out at once, telling the nobleman that rich though he was, his threats carried no weight. He was wasting his words: the Law was so humane that even the poorest man could always get redress for the encroachments of an arrogant neighbour.

This retort was like oil to a lighted wick, or sulphur to a bonfire, or a cat-o'-nine-tails to a Fury: it roused him to a perfect frenzy of rage. 'Be damned to you, and be damned to the Law!' he yelled, and ordered his men to let loose all the dogs on the estate, watch-dogs, sheep-dogs and all—blood-thirsty beasts, trained to worry the carcases of animals that had fallen dead in the fields and to fasten their teeth in the legs of casual trespassers and hold on tight.

'At 'em, boys!' shouted the shepherds, and the dogs rushed, barking horribly, at the poor man's supporters and began mauling them. They tried to escape but the dogs pursued them, and the faster they ran, the more furiously they were attacked. The youngest of the three brothers happened to stumble as he ran and stubbed his toes against a stone. Down he fell, and the dogs leaped on him and savaged him, ripping great pieces of flesh off his bones and swallowing them. The others heard his screams and turned back to his rescue, muffling their left arms with their cloaks and picking up large stones to drive off the dogs. But nothing could be done. The brutes had tasted blood and would not let go, so he was torn to pieces before their very eyes. His dying words were: 'Avenge me, brothers!'

With a complete disregard of the consequences they rushed at the dastardly nobleman and pelted him with stones. But he had played this game of forcible enclosure several times before and was too old a hand to be taken by surprise. He hurled a javelin at one of them and drove it through his body; yet, though it wounded him mortally, he did not fall. The point lodged in the earth on the other side and the greater part of the haft followed it, leaving him writhing transfixed, with his body off the ground. Then a big, tall fellow, one of the murderer's retainers, let fly with a stone at the remaining brother from some way off, trying to put his arm out of action. It grazed his fingers and glanced off, but everyone thought it had injured him seriously, which gave the quick-witted young fellow the chance of avenging his brothers. Pretending that his hand was disabled, he shouted at the nobleman: 'Very well, then, enjoy your glorious triumph over our whole family, glut your vindictive heart with the blood of my two brothers and me! And finish your unholy task while you are about it: look, one or two of your fellow-citizens are still lying insensible on the ground over there. But remember this: that when you have thrown my poor friend out of his cottage, however far you push the boundaries of your estate, you'll always have neighbours of one sort or another. Meanwhile, consider yourself lucky that a cursèd stone has left my hand hanging numb and powerless: I should certainly have used it to cut off your head.'

The exasperated nobleman drew his sword and rushed forward, intending to finish him off with a single blow. What followed was quite unexpected. He had picked a quarrel with a better man than himself. His sword hand was caught in a powerful grip, the weapon wrested from him, and he was struck on the head with it again and again until his wicked spirit was parted from his body.

223

The retainers came rushing to the rescue, but the victor was too quick for them. The sword, still dripping with the nobleman's blood, served to cut his own throat.

*

This was the news that the prodigies had foreshadowed. The farmer, his heart broken by the weight of his misfortunes, could not utter so much as a single word, nor shed a tear. He picked up the knife with which he had just been cutting cheese for his guests, and used it on his own throat, just as his son had used the nobleman's sword. Then he fell face forward on the table and the stream of blood from his severed arteries washed away the visionary stains that had fallen on it from the fountain under the floor.

My master condoled with everyone present on the sudden violent extinction of his host's family. He was deeply disappointed at having to go away with nothing in his sacks or bottles, but showed his gratitude for the meal by bursting into tears and wringing his empty hands. Then he mounted on my back and rode home again by the same road we had taken.

It was an unlucky journey. We were stopped by a tall Roman soldier, a centurion, who asked my master in haughty tones: 'Where are you riding that pack-ass?' My master was still a little dazed and confused by the prodigies he had just witnessed and, knowing no Latin, disregarded the question and rode on. His silence offended the centurion, who could not refrain from striking him on the head with his vine-rod and hauling him off my back. My master then replied meekly: 'I'm sorry, Sir. I don't understand your language, so I didn't know what you said just now.'

The centurion spoke in Greek this time: 'Where are you riding that ass?'

'To the nearest village.'

'Well, I need him. The Colonel's baggage has to be carried from the fort and we're short of pack animals.' He caught hold of my halter and began leading me back along the road.

Wiping away the blood that trickled down his face from the cut made by the vine-rod, my master begged the centurion to treat him in a more comradely way. 'And if you do so, Sir,' he said, 'I'm sure that it will bring you good luck. Anyhow, this is a very lazy ass, and has that cursed disease, Sir, that's called the falling sickness. It's as much as he can do to carry a few bundles of green-stuff to market from my little holding: he's all blown at the finish. Load him up with a real burden and you'll break his heart.'

But the cruel soldier would not listen to a word of all this. When my master realized that he was resolved to steal me and that he had shifted his grip on the vine-rod and was about to bash in his head with the knobbed end, he took desperate action. Pretending to clasp the soldier's knees in suppliant style he tackled him low, pulled both legs from under him, and brought him down with a crash on the back of his head. Then he jumped on him, hit him, pounded him all over—face, arms and ribs—first with his fists and elbows and then with a stone he grabbed from the road. Once he was down, the centurion could offer no resistance; all he could do was to gasp out threats of how he would punish my master as soon as he was on his legs again. He swore he would make mincemeat of him with his sword.

This gave my master timely warning: he snatched the sword

out of the scabbard, threw it as far away as he could and gave
the centurion an even harder pounding than before. He lay on
his back so bruised and wounded that he was incapable of rising
and his only hope of escaping with his life was to sham dead.
My master then retrieved the sword, mounted me again, and
galloped me straight back to the village. Not caring to go home,
for the time being at least, he rode me up to the house of a close
friend of his, a shopkeeper, where he made a clean breast of
what he had done to the centurion and implored his protection.
'Hide me and my ass somewhere safe for a couple of days until
this trouble blows over. If they catch me they'll kill me.'

The shopkeeper at once undertook to help him for the sake of
old times. They tied my legs together and dragged me upstairs
into the attic, but my master stayed in the shop on the ground
floor, where he climbed into a chest and pulled down the lid.

Meanwhile, as I heard later, the centurion tottered into the
village like a man trying to walk off a drunken stupor, dazed
with the pain of his injuries and leaning heavily on his rod. Pride
kept him from telling any of the villagers the story of his igno-
minious defeat at my master's hands, so he silently swallowed the
disgrace. Presently he met some of his comrades, who advised
him to lie low for awhile in the barracks. Not only would he
forfeit his honour as a soldier if it were known that a market-
gardener had given him such a knocking-about, but the loss of his
sword was equivalent in military law to desertion, a breaking
of the oath of loyalty he had sworn to the Emperor. They undertook to search for my master and me, if he gave them a description of us, and avenge the regimental honour.

As might have been expected, a cruel neighbour betrayed us;

so they went to the civil magistrate and told him that they had dropped a valuable silver cup on the road, the property of their commanding officer, and that a market-gardener had found it, refused to give it up and was now hiding in a neighbour's house. The magistrate noted the officer's name, and other particulars, then came to the door of the shop, where he announced loudly that he had good reason to believe that we were concealed about the premises, and that if the owner failed to deliver my master to justice he might find himself sentenced to death on the charge of harbouring a felon.

The shopkeeper was a brave fellow and a true friend: he replied that he knew nothing at all about us and that he had not seen my master for some days. But the soldiers, swearing in the Emperor's own name, insisted that he was somewhere in that house and nowhere else. The magistrate then consented to make a close search of the premises, to find out how much truth there was in the shopkeeper's obstinate denial. He sent in the constables and other local officials with an order to search the house from top to bottom; but they came out with the report that they could find neither ass nor man, either upstairs or down. The dispute grew hot on both sides, the soldiers swearing in the Emperor's name that they knew for certain we were there, the shopkeeper swearing by all the gods of Olympus that they were telling lies.

I was an inquisitive and restless ass, as you know, and when I heard angry voices raised outside, I craned my neck a little way out of the attic window to discover, if I could, what all the fuss was about. One of the soldiers happened to be looking up at the time. He was not standing where he could see me but his eye was caught by the shadow of my head and ears which was thrown on the wall of the next house. 'Look, look!' he said. All the soldiers shouted, burst into the shop, rushed upstairs to my hiding place and hauled me down. Then they made a thorough search of the shop itself, and when they opened the chest, there was my poor master. They dragged him out for the magistrate's inspection, and he was taken to gaol on the capital charge of robbing a Roman officer.

The notion of my peering out of the window so tickled the soldiers that they joked about it for days; and someone combined two well-known proverbs * into the catchword: 'All because of a peeping ass's shadow', which is now current all over the country. What became of my master next day, or his friend the shopkeeper, I have no notion, but the centurion who had been so well punished for his haughtiness led me away from the manger where I had been tied up. There was nobody to prevent him. He took me to what I suppose was his billet, where he loaded me up and made quite a military figure of me. On the top of his towering pile of baggage and equipment he had placed a twinkling brass helmet, a shield so highly polished that it hurt

* 'Because an ass peeped' and 'All because of an ass's shadow'. The first, found in the corresponding passage of Lucian's *Ass*, is based on a long and ruinous law-suit brought by a potter against a man whose ass peeped in at his shop-window and broke some pots; the second, quoted by Plato and Menander, on the story of a dispute that broke out in a treeless desert between a traveller riding on an ass, and the driver from whom he had hired it. The traveller wished to take a siesta in the ass's shadow, but the driver refused on the ground that he had hired only the ass, not its shadow as well. Both men were eventually found dying from injuries that they had given each other, and the ass was nowhere to be seen.

one's eyes to look at it, and a javelin with a remarkably long haft. This arrangement, which made us look rather like a miniature army coming down the road, was not prescribed in regimental orders but intended to overawe civilians. We went across a plain by a good road and finally came to a small town where we put up, not at an inn but at the house of a municipal councillor. The centurion left me there in charge of a slave and reported at once to his colonel.

15

At the Councillor's House

NOTHING OF IMPORTANCE happened to me for the next few days, but I must record a sensational murder trial that took place during my stay here; because the chief characters concerned were the owners of my billet, the councillor, his wife and his two sons, and the drama had been going on around me. The son had done very well at school and was, in fact, a paragon of all the virtues; any father would have been proud of him. His mother had died some years before and his father had married again, so that the other son, now twelve years old, was only his half-brother. The councillor allowed the new wife, whose looks were a good deal better than her character, a free hand in the house; and whether she was naturally vicious, or whether it was fate and she could not help herself, I am not prepared to say, but at any rate she fell madly in love with her stepson. Readers are warned that what follows is tragedy not comedy, and that they must read it in a suitably grave frame of mind.

Well, so long as the little Love-god was only an infant, the stepmother found it easy to disguise her guilty blushes and say

nothing about the affair. But when he grew up and began playing his mad tricks, setting her whole soul in a cruel blaze with
his arrows of fire, she had to sham ill as the only possible means
of hiding her torment. Now, everyone knows that the physical
symptoms of love are not readily distinguishable from those of
ordinary illness: for example, an unhealthy pallor, dull eyes,
weakness of the knees, insomnia and fits of sighing which increase in intensity the longer the crisis is protracted. Her complaint might, in fact, have been fairly diagnosed as influenza but
for the complication of her continual bursts of weeping. 'Alas,
when prophets are such fools', as Virgil says somewhere, and
'Alas, when doctors are such fools', as I say here. Those who
attended her were puzzled by her rapid pulse, her irregular temperature, the difficulty she seemed to have in breathing, her
frequent tossing and turning in bed, and had no notion what to
prescribe. Good God, any simple student of love could have
diagnosed the fever at once!

Her condition got worse and worse until she could bear the
pain no longer and broke her silence by sending for her elder
son. *Son!* oh, if only she had never been obliged to call him that,
or if only she could cease using the word, which was a perpetual
reproach to her feelings.

He went to her bedroom at once, with anxiety puckering his
forehead like an old man's. He had no notion what she wanted
of him, but since she was his father's wife and his brother's
mother, he felt that he ought to go. When he entered the room,
though the effort of keeping silence so long had nearly killed her,
somehow she could not say what she wanted. She went aground
on the sands of doubt, so to speak, and felt too deeply ashamed

231

to use any of the conversational openings which she had carefully thought out for this embarrassing interview. Presently the
unsuspecting stepson asked her without any prompting and
very sympathetically: 'Mother, what is really wrong with you?'

She burst into tears, hid her face in a corner of her nightdress
and managed to sob out: 'You. It's you who are making me ill.
And what's more you're the only remedy for my fever. I'll die
unless you cure me.'

'I,' he cried aghast. 'What have *I* done to make you ill?'

'You looked at me. You looked into my eyes and set something inside me on fire. I'm being slowly burned to death. Don't
let any silly scruples about your father's rights prevent you from
taking pity on me. It's all your fault that I'm lying here in such
agony, and if you do as I ask you'll act in his best interests:
you'll be saving his wife from death. You can't blame me for
loving you: you're a younger edition of your dear father. Come,
darling, nobody is about, there's nothing to fear; it's a wonderful chance for you to enjoy yourself. You may call it incest, but
it's something that you simply must do, and you know the
proverb: "No crime discovered, no crime committed".'

The suddenness of this disastrous revelation so confused him
that, though he shuddered at the very idea of consenting to her
request, he thought it best not to upset her by too blunt a refusal. He played for safety by asking her to wait a little longer,
meanwhile promising her all she wanted. 'Now, Mother,' he
said, 'take proper care of your health and be easy in your mind.
I'll soon find an opportunity to be with you, but we must wait
until father has gone out riding!' Then he left the room in a
hurry. Even to look at her now made him feel ill. Realizing that

the whole family would be ruined unless he did the right thing, and that he must confide in someone really wise and sensible, he hurried at once to his old schoolmaster and explained what had happened.

The old man thought for a long time before telling him that the best advice he could give was to fly before the storm of fate by leaving home immediately. But while he was making the necessary arrangements, his stepmother, who could not bear to wait even a day or two longer, found a pretext for sending her husband off in a hurry to inspect one of his distant farms. No sooner was he out of the house than, in a state of frantic passion, she sent her stepson a note holding him to his word.

His loathing for her was so strong that he could not face a fresh interview. He sent back a message excusing himself and when she twice repeated her demand made a different excuse on each occasion. She understood in the end that he had no intention of keeping his promise. At once her mood changed, and her incestuous passion turned to diabolical hatred. She called one of her slaves, who had formed part of her dowry and who held emancipated views on the dignity of crime, and disclosed all her guilty secrets to him. They put their heads together and decided that the best thing to do in the circumstances was to poison the stepson. She sent the scoundrel out at once to buy a packet of the deadliest poison on sale. When he came back with it she dissolved it in a cupful of wine which she put aside for the innocent stepson to drink.

About midday, while they were still busily discussing the best means of administering the poison, this wicked woman's own son came home from school, ate his lunch, felt thirsty, found the

233

cup of poisoned wine, and of course without suspecting that it contained poison for his elder brother, drank it off at a gulp. He fell senseless to the ground. The slave whose task was to take him to and from school was horrified by the catastrophe and shouted at the top of his voice for the mother and the house-slaves. When it became known that the boy had just drunk a cup of wine it was agreed that he must have been poisoned, but the question was, by whom; and on that there was no agreement at all.

Stepmothers have a reputation for maliciousness which was perfectly justified in this case. She was by no means dismayed by the dreadful death of her own son, or by the guilt of being his murderess, or by the prospect of her husband's grief when he returned home. All that occurred to her was a splendid opportunity for revenge. She sent a messenger at once to recall her husband with news of the disaster and, when he hurried home, she had the audacity to tell him that her son had been poisoned by his stepbrother. This was true in a figurative sense: it was his brother's poison which had killed him. But her version was that the stepson had made incestuous proposals to her and that when she had refused to listen he had retaliated by poisoning her son. She embroidered this terrible lie by saying that when she accused him of the murder he had drawn his sword and threatened to kill her.

The councillor was in a dreadful state of mind. One son was awaiting burial; the other was bound to be condemned to death for incest and fratricide, and he could feel no pity for him either, but only hatred, when the wife whom he loved and trusted came weeping to him with this shocking story. After making arrangements for the child's funeral, the unhappy old man with tears still running down his cheeks and ashes on his white hair, which he tore out by the handful, went straight to the market place from the yet unlighted pyre. There, in a passionate address to the magistrates, he did all he could to make them condemn his surviving son to death, pleading, sobbing and going so far as to embrace the knees of his fellow-councillors.

The magistrates were moved to indignant sympathy, and so were the townspeople, who wished to waive the formalities of a trial, with its routine of tedious depositions by witnesses for the prosecution and long-winded arguments for the defence. They shouted: 'Stone him! Stone him!' and 'A crime against public morality should be publicly avenged.' However, the magistrates feared that to condone an act of rough justice would weaken the popular respect for law and order and encourage mass-rioting. They asked the councillors' support for their decision to hold a properly conducted trial, with witnesses called on both sides and carefully examined, and a verdict authoritatively delivered. 'No man,' they said, 'should be condemned without a hearing, as if this were a barbarous or tyrannical community; especially in such peaceful times as the present. That would constitute a dreadful precedent.'

Their sound decision was accepted unanimously, and the town clerk was sent at once to convene a meeting of the judicial council. The members were soon assembled in court, seated in order of rank and seniority. Then the town clerk summoned the prosecution to prepare their case, ordered the accused to be brought in, and finally announced that in conformity with Attic Law and the procedure adopted by the Areopagus, counsel on

235

both sides must plead without preamble or any unnecessary appeal to the emotions of the court. Since I was not present at the trial myself, but tied up to my manger, my story is necessarily derived at second hand from the casual conversation of various visitors to the stable; but I will be careful to record only what I found, after checking the accounts, to be the exact truth.

When both barristers had finished their pleas, counsel for the defence being content with a general denial of all the charges, the court ruled that they could not give their verdict in a case of such importance merely on circumstantial evidence and called the stepmother's slave, who was quoted by the prosecution as the only witness who knew all the facts of the case. That gallows bird showed no nervousness when he stepped up to give his evidence: although it was a very serious case and the court was packed, he had no doubt about the verdict and no qualms of conscience. He made a long statement on oath, improving his mistress's story with inventions of his own. His version was that the stepson, mortified by the repulse of his incestuous advances, had bought a packet of poison, then sent for him and, bribing him with a large sum of money to keep his mouth shut, had ordered him to administer it to the child.

'At that, your worships, though I assure the accused that I'll never do so wicked a thing and that he can keep his money, the accused gives me the poisoned cup—he mixes it before my eyes —and says I must give it to the young gentleman to drink, and if I don't, why, then he'll kill me instead. Well, I take the cup off with me but I don't give it to the young gentleman, and then the accused comes after me and suspects that I'm keeping it to show his father as evidence against him, so he gets it back from me and hands it to the young gentleman himself, and the young gentleman drinks it off.'

The witness was a good actor and when he had concluded his speech, with a convincing show of respectful agitation, the case was declared closed, counsel for defence being given no opportunity to call the evidence of the schoolmaster in whom the stepson had confided, or of the slave who had been present when the child had picked up the cup and drunk it, or even of the innocent defendant himself. The court, with one sole dissentient, was convinced of his guilt and however tender-hearted they might be, saw no alternative but to sentence him, as the Law provided, to be sewn up in a leather sack with four living creatures, a dog, a cock, a viper and an ape, emblems of the four deadly sins, and cast into a river. It now remained to drop their ballots into the brass urn; if this registered a sentence of death the proceedings would be at an end and the condemned man would be handed over to the public executioner.

At the last moment, the single dissentient—an old doctor, widely respected and of unquestioned integrity—came forward, and putting one hand over the mouth of the urn to prevent anyone from dropping his ballot in prematurely, addressed the court:

'My lords and gentlemen. I am proud to think that I have never in all my life forfeited your good opinion, and hope not to do so today by my refusal to acquiesce in the judicial murder of an innocent man—my refusal to let you be deceived by the eloquent lies of a slave into breaking the oath you have all sworn, to deliver a fair and impartial verdict. It would be easy enough to pretend I concur with you, but I will not trick my own conscience or smother the reverence which I owe the gods by voting for the death sentence. Listen attentively and I will give you the true facts of the case.

'The criminal who has just been giving evidence came to me two days ago and offered me two hundred gold pieces for a quick and deadly poison. He said he needed it for a friend suffering from an incurable disease who wanted to free himself by suicide from the misery of life. His story was glib but unconvincing, and I suspected foul play; so though I gave him his packet, I was careful not to become a party to whatever crime he had in mind, by accepting immediate payment of the fee. I asked him to leave the money-bag at my pharmacy and to come with me to the goldsmith's on the following day, which was yesterday, to have the coins weighed in case any of them were counterfeit or of light weight. Meanwhile, at my request, he sealed the string at the neck with his thumb-ring.

'When he did not come as we had arranged, and when I heard in court just now that he was to be called as a witness, I hastily sent a slave back to my house to fetch the bag. Here it is. Will you show him the impression of his seal and ask him whether he acknowledges it? If it proves to be his, you will wonder how he dares accuse the prisoner of buying the poison which he bought himself.'

The slave began to tremble violently, his face turned ashen and he burst into a cold sweat. Shifting his weight from one foot to another, he gaped and scratched his head, stammering out such wild nonsense that no reasonable person could possibly have believed him innocent. However, he presently recovered his self-composure, denied ever having visited the doctor and accused him of lying. Not only was the doctor on oath to deliver a just verdict in this case but his professional honour was now impugned. He redoubled his efforts to bring the slave to book, and at last the magistrates ordered the court officials to seize the fellow's hand and compare the seal on the ring with the wax-impression at the neck of the bag. They corresponded exactly.

According to Greek custom an attempt was then made to extort a confession from the slave by racking him on the wheel, making him ride the wooden horse with weights tied to his feet and flogging him; but he was remarkably tough and would not recant even when they burned his soles in the brazier. At last the doctor exclaimed: 'Upon my word, I refuse either to let the young man in the dock be punished by you for a crime of which he is not guilty, or to let this slave make fools of the Court and escape punishment for his wickedness. Allow me to give you clear proof of the truth of my statements. When this shameless rogue came to me for a quick and deadly poison, I remembered that the art of medicine was invented for the saving, not the taking, of human life and decided that it would be a breach of my professional principles if I sold poison to a potential murderer. But I feared that, if I refused to sell, he might go elsewhere for poison or commit the murder which he had in mind by some other means—a sword, for instance, or the first weapon that lay handy. So what I gave him was not really a poison: it was a soporific called mandragora, which is of such powerful action that the trance it induces is practically indistinguishable from death. You need not be surprised that this slave has been prepared, in his desperation, to face the traditional tortures to which he has been condemned; after all, they are nothing in comparison with the punishment to which an immediate confession of his guilt would have subjected him. But if the boy really did take the drug I prepared, then he must still be alive, though in a coma; as soon as the effect has worn off, he will wake up and this murder trial will automatically come to an end. But if he is really dead, then a further investigation will be needed; his death will be due to causes of which I am ignorant.'

This was fair enough, and the trial was adjourned at once. Excitement ran so high that everyone set off at a run for the pyre, the magistrates and other members of the court as well as the general public. The father won the race and lifted the coffin-lid himself, just as the child, coming out of his death-like trance, was trying to sit up. He hugged him close but, finding no words wonderful enough to express his joy and relief, carried him down in silence for everyone to see, and presently brought him into Court still swathed in his grave-clothes.

The facts of the case were no longer in dispute: the wickedness of the slave, and the still greater wickedness of the stepmother were finally exposed. She was condemned to perpetual exile, he was crucified; and, by a unanimous vote, the bag and its contents were presented to the good old doctor as a reward for the coma which he had induced with such happy results. So the story came to an extraordinarily dramatic end, almost as if a god had stepped down from his heavenly car; for the councillor, who a moment before had believed himself childless, was once more the father of two sons.

16

Under the Trainer

A SUDDEN CHANGE of fortune was awaiting me, too. The centurion who had commandeered me from the market-gardener was sent to Rome by his regimental commander with despatches for the Emperor. He sold me for eleven drachmae to two brothers, kitchen slaves to a wealthy nobleman named Thyasus who was staying in the neighbourhood. One was a confectioner, the other a cook famous for his ragouts and sauces. They bought me as a pack-beast for carrying the many kitchen utensils that Thyasus needed while he was traveling abroad. I was accepted as a third partner in their firm and during the whole period of my transformation never had such a good time as with them. Every evening after Thyasus had dined—and he always dined in grand style—my masters used to carry back the left-over to our little room: one brought generous helpings of roast pork, chicken, fish and similar delicacies: the other brought bread, tarts, puff-pastry, twisted cheese-straws, marzipan lizards and many varieties of honey-cake. But when they had locked the door and gone off to the baths to refresh themselves, I used to cram myself with the splendid food the gods had graciously put at my disposal, not being such a fool, such a complete ass, as to turn it down in favour of the coarse hay in my manger.

For a long time I was wonderfully successful in my pilfering: my technique was to take only a little from each of the many dishes on the table, knowing that my masters would never suspect an ass of playing such tricks on them. But gradually I grew overconfident and ate whatever I fancied: in fact, I picked out the best dishes and licked them clean. My masters, who began to notice their daily losses, were surprised and perplexed, and though even then it did not occur to them to fix their suspicions on me, each privately determined to find out who was the thief. They now kept a jealous watch on the dishes and counted every cake and cutlet, each eyeing the other as reproachfully as if he were a pickpocket.

Finally, the cook spoke frankly and to the point. 'Really Brother, I call this pretty shabby behaviour. Every day, for a long time now, you have been stealing left-overs, always the best ones, too, selling them behind my back and then expecting me to go halves with you in what's left. If you are tired of our business partnership let us dissolve it by all means, but continue to live together affectionately like the brothers we are. Otherwise, the friction between us will increase daily and end in a violent quarrel.'

'I like that!' retorted the confectioner. 'By God, I like that! First you steal the stuff and then, to forestall the complaints which I have been holding back patiently all this time—I was determined to put up with it as long as I could, rather than accuse my own brother of being a sneak thief—you have the impertinence to accuse *me*! However, I'm glad that this dirty business has come into the open; we can settle it somehow at last instead of smothering our feelings until they finally blaze up and destroy us . . . You remember that play we saw about the two brothers, Eteocles and Polynices, who killed each other after a quarrel about fair shares in the government of Thebes?'

These exchanges ended only when each of them had taken a solemn oath that he had not been guilty of the slightest dishonesty or taken more than his fair share of the food. They agreed to form a united front and use every possible means to discover who was robbing them. 'It is out of the question, of course,' one of them said, 'that the ass could be the culprit. Asses don't like our sort of food.'

'Still, evening after evening, all the best left-overs have disappeared, and only the ass has been in the room.'

'It can't be the flies.'

'They would have to be gigantic flies with as wide a wingspread as the harpies had—the creatures that used to rob King Phineus of his supper in the days of the Argonauts.'

The welcome change in my diet from fodder to human food, plenty of it, too, had the effect of plumping me up, softening my tanned hide and giving my coat a handsome silky nap. It was this that gave me away, because my masters realized that I was twice as stout as when they had bought me, though I was leaving my daily feed of hay untouched. 'Handsome is as handsome does!' they thought. One day they pretended to go off to the baths as usual and locked the door behind them, but peeped in through a crack and watched me making short work of the delicacies left within my reach.

243

Forgetting all about their losses, they burst into a sudden roar of laughter at this extraordinary sight: the ass who was a gourmet! They called a number of other slaves to take turns at the crack and watch me at my feast: had anyone ever seen anything like it before in all his life? Their laughter was so loud and prolonged that when their master Thyasus happened to come by he wanted to know what the joke was. They asked him to peep through the crack and see for himself.

He laughed until his stomach ached, then opened the door and observed me closely. When I realized that my luck had not only held but showed signs of improvement, I went on eating quite at my ease, and the louder he laughed, the greater my self-possession. At last, fascinated by the novelty of the sight, he ordered me to be led to the supper-room—no, when I come to think of it, he led me there himself. The table was already laid and he ordered every sort of food to be put in front of me, including dishes that had not yet been touched. Although feeling pretty full already I was anxious to oblige him in any way I could, and ate everything he gave me as if I still had a keen appetite.

Thyasus and his friends were curious to find out exactly what I would eat. They thought of all the things that an ass would be most likely to loathe and offered them to me as a test of my politeness. For instance, meat seasoned with asafoetida, devilled chicken and some exotic sort of pickled fish. How the rafters of the room shook with laughter when I cleared every dish!

At last the licensed buffoon of the party asked: 'Now what about a drop of wine for our guest, eh?'

'Not at all a bad idea, you scoundrel,' said Thyasus. 'I dare say he wouldn't say no to a cup of honeyed wine—here, boy, give that gold cup a good rinsing and offer it to my guest! And tell him that I drink his very good health.'

Everyone awaited the result with intense curiosity. The huge cup was handed to me, and without pausing to consider whether it would be wise to drink, I screwed up my mouth, pretending to lick my lips in anticipation, and drained the cup at one gulp, though in the leisurely style of an experienced drinker.

A storm of applause, and a general toast to my health. My enraptured host sent for the two brothers and undertook to pay them four times the price they had given for me; after which he put me in the charge of a well-to-do freedman of his, to whom he was greatly attached, and begged him to treat me with all possible care. This freedman showed me tenderness and humanity and did his best to improve the good opinion that Thyasus already had of him by teaching me tricks. First, he taught me how to recline at table, leaning on one elbow; next, how to wrestle and even how to dance on my hind legs; finally—and this won me peculiar admiration—how to use sign language. I learned to nod my head as a sign of approval, and to toss it back as a sign of rejection, also to turn towards the wine-waiter when I was thirsty and show that I needed a drink by winking first one eye and then the other. I was a quick and docile pupil; which was not really very remarkable, because I could have performed all my tricks without any training at all. But I had been afraid of behaving like a human being without previous instruction: most people would have taken it as a portent of sinister events, and I should probably have found myself certified as a monster. Then they would have beheaded me and thrown my fat carcase to the vultures.

The tale of my wonderful talents spread in all directions, so that my master became famous on my account. People said: 'Think of it! He has an ass whom he treats like a friend and invites to dinner with him. Believe it or not, that ass can wrestle, and actually dance, and understands what people say to him, and uses a language of signs!'

Here I must tell you, rather late in the day, who Thyasus was. He came from Corinth, the capital of the province of Achaia, and having been successively raised to all the junior offices to which his rank and position entitled him he was now to be Lord Chief Justice of Corinth for the next five years. Since convention required him to live up to the dignity of this appointment by staging a public entertainment, he had undertaken to provide a three-day gladiatorial show in evidence of his open-handedness. It was this, indeed, that accounted for his presence in the north: he was trying to please his fellow-citizens by buying up the finest wild animals and hiring the most famous gladiators in all Thessaly. Now, having found all that he needed, he was on the point of returning to Corinth, quite satisfied with his purchases; but instead of riding in one of his own splendid gigs, some covered and some open, which formed the tail of his long retinue, or on one of his valuable Thessalian thoroughbred hunters or pedigreed Gallic cobs, preferred to mount lovingly on my back; saying that he had come to despise all other forms of conveyance. I now sported gilt harness, a red morocco saddle, a purple ass-cloth, a silver bit and little bells that tinkled as I went along. He used to talk to me in the kindest way, telling me for example how delighted he was to own a charger whom he could count as his friend. When we reached the port of Iolcos we embarked with our menagerie and finished our journey by sea, sailing along the coast of Boeotia and Attica until we arrived at Corinth, where a vast crowd poured out to greet us. I think, though, that more people were there to see me than to welcome Thyasus.

So many visitors wanted to watch my performances that my trainer decided to make money out of me. He kept the stable doors shut and charged a high price for admittance, one person at a time. His daily takings were considerable.

Among these visitors was a rich noblewoman. My various tricks enchanted her and at last she conceived the odd desire of getting to know me intimately. In fact, she grew so passionately fond of me that, like Pasiphaë in the legend who fell in love with a bull, she bribed my trainer with a large sum of money to let her spend a night in my company. I am sorry to record that the rascal agreed with no thought for anything but his own pocket.

When I had dined with Thyasus and come back to my stable, I found the noblewoman waiting for me. She had been there some time already. Heavens, what magnificent preparations she had made for her love-affair! Four eunuchs had spread the floor with several plump feather-beds, covered them with a Tyrian purple cloth embroidered in gold, and laid a heap of little pillows at the head end, of the downy sort used by women of fashion. Then, not wishing to postpone their mistress's enjoyment by staying a moment longer than necessary, out they trooped, but left fine, white candles burning to light up the shadowy corners.

She undressed at once, taking everything off, even to the gauze scarf tied across her beautiful breasts, then stood close to the lamp

and rubbed her body all over with oil of balsam from a pewter
pot. She then did the same to mine, most generously, but concen-
trating mostly on my nose. After this she gave me a lingering
kiss—not of the mercenary sort that one expects in a brothel, or
from a whore picked up in the street or sent along by an agency,
but a pure, sincere, really loving kiss. 'Darling,' she cried, 'I love
you. You are all I want in this world. I could never live without you.' She added all the other pretty things that women say
when they want men to share their own passionate feelings. Then
she took me by my head-band and had no difficulty in making me
lie down on the bed, reclining on one elbow, because that was one
of the tricks I had learned, and she evidently was not expecting me
to do anything that I had not done before.

You must understand that she was a beautiful woman and
desperately eager for my embraces. Besides, I had been continent
for several months and now, with all this fragrant scent in my
nostrils and a kegful of Thyasus's best wine inside me, I felt fit
for anything. All the same, I was worried, very worried indeed, at
the thought of sleeping with so lovely a woman: my great hairy legs
and hard hooves pressed against her milk-and-honey skin—her
dewy red lips kissed by my huge mouth with its ugly great teeth.
Worst of all, how could any woman alive, though exuding lust
from her very finger nails, accept the formidable challenge of my
thighs? If I proved too much for her, if I seriously injured her—
think of it, a noblewoman too—my master would be forced to use
me in his promised entertainment as food for his wild beasts. But
her burning eyes devoured mine, as she cooed sweetly at me
between kisses and finally gasped: 'Ah, ah, I have you safe now,
my little dove, my little birdie.' Then I realized how foolish my

fears had been. She pressed me closer and closer to her and met my challenge to the full. I tried to back away, but she resisted every attempt to spare her, twining her arms tight around my back, until I wondered whether after all I was capable of serving her as she wished. I began to appreciate the story of Pasiphaë: if she was anything like this woman she had every reason to fix her affections on the bull who fathered the Minotaur on her. My new mistress did not allow me to sleep a wink that night, but as soon as the embarrassing daylight crept into the room she crept out, first pleading with my keeper to let her spend another night with me for the same fee. He was willing enough to agree, partly because she paid handsomely, partly because he wished to give Thyasus a novel peep-show.

He went off at once to Thyasus with a detailed account of the night's events, and was rewarded with a large tip. 'Splendid, splendid!' cried Thyasus. 'That's the very act we need to liven up our show. But what a pity that his sweetheart is a noblewoman: her family would never allow her to perform in public.'

Advertisements circulated in the brothel districts of Corinth failed to find any volunteer to take her place: apparently no woman was abandoned enough to sell what remained of her reputation even for the generous fee that was offered. In the end Thyasus did not have to pay anything: he got hold of a woman who had been sentenced to be thrown to the wild beasts but would, he thought, make a suitable mistress for me. We were to be caged up together in the centre of the packed amphitheatre.

*

I had already heard the woman's story. Many years before this, the father of the little boy who afterwards became her husband had set out on a long journey, ordering his wife, who was expecting another baby, to kill it as soon as born, but only if it turned out to be a girl. It was a girl, and not having the heart to obey orders, she asked a neighbour to bring the child up for her and on her husband's return, told him it was dead. When the girl grew to marriageable age, the mother could not give her the dowry to which she was entitled by birth, or not without the father's knowledge: so she decided to take her son into the secret. She had another reason for doing so: the girl did not know whose daughter she really was, and what if her brother, by bad luck, fell in love with her and tried to seduce her!

The brother, a good-natured man, felt obliged to obey his mother and behave as a kind brother should. He kept the family secret dark and to all appearances what he did for his sister was merely an act of common charity: he gave her a home in his own house and let it be thought that she was an orphan, without a legal guardian, whom he had decided to marry off to his best friend. He undertook to find her dowry himself.

This admirable, innocent arrangement somehow provoked Fortune to behave with more than her usual spitefulness. The brother was already married to the woman whose story I am telling, and her bitter jealousy of the supposed orphan led her in the end to commit the series of crimes for which she was now condemned to be thrown to the wild beasts. She suspected her husband of having already made the girl his mistress, and of intending to make her his wife. When suspicion turned to hate, she thought of a very cruel plan for ridding herself of her rival.

She would steal her husband's signet ring, go for a visit to their country house; and from there send a slave to tell the girl that the husband wanted her to visit him there as soon as possible and without any escort. The slave who, though faithful to his mistress, was otherwise an absolute rogue, would show the girl the signet ring as a proof that the message was urgent and authentic.

The girl was anxious enough to obey her brother—for she knew now that he was her brother, as nobody else did—and the signet ring had the required effect. She hurried out all alone to the country house and there ran into the trap laid for her: she was set upon with sadistic fury, stripped naked and flogged till she was nearly dead. The poor girl was forced by the pain to reveal the secret. 'He's my brother, he's my brother,' she kept on sobbing: but she was wasting her words. The sister-in-law paid no attention to her, dismissing the story as an invention, and finally snatched up a blazing torch which she thrust between her thighs, so that she died in agony.

The brother and the friend whom the girl was to have married, heard the terrible news of her death and fetched the corpse home for burial, each lamenting over it in his own way. The brother took the news hardest, for his wife was the last person in the world whom he could have wished to be the murderess. He took to his bed in such anguish of mind that brain-fever set in and his temperature rose so high that nobody expected him to recover unless with the help of some very powerful drug.

His wife, who had long since forfeited the right to be so called, then went to a doctor well known for his gross lack of professional principles—he had already murdered several patients at the request of their relatives and privately boasted of his successes—offering him six hundred gold pieces for an instantaneous poison. When he consented, she came back and told her husband that he must drink a medicine known to eminent physicians as 'the sacred potion', the effect of which is to ease gastric pain and carry off bilious secretions. Really, of course, the potion mixed for him was sacred not to Apollo the god of healing but to Proserpine the goddess of death.

The whole family was present, and several friends and relatives as well, when the doctor came in with the potion, stirred it well in its cup, and offered it to the sick man. But the murderess boldly decided to get rid of her accomplice in this new crime and at the same time save herself the expense of paying him. As the sick man was about to accept the cup, she restrained him. 'Doctor,' she said, 'I feel it my duty as a wife to insist on your having a good taste of this medicine yourself before giving it to my dear husband. I want to make certain that it contains no poison. I'm sure that so learned and so careful a man as you are won't be offended by my request. I make it only as a matter of form.'

The doctor was so surprised by this bloody-minded woman's self-assurance, that on the spur of the moment he could think of no excuse for refusing. If he showed the least fear or hesitation everyone present would suspect him of poisoning the cup, so he was forced to take a good swig. The husband confidently followed his example and drank what was left.

That was all for the moment, and the doctor wanted to hurry home before it was too late for an antidote that would counteract the effects of the poison he had taken. But she was bent on completing her infernal work and would not let him out of her sight. 'You must stay here until the potion has begun to work,' she said, 'and we can judge of its effect on my husband's health'. He begged to be excused, he protested against his unwarrantable

252

detention, but by the time she had agreed to let him go the poison was already playing havoc with his intestines. He managed to struggle home in excruciating pain and had only just enough time before he died to tell his wife what had happened and ask her at least to collect the stipulated fee for the poisoning. And that was the end of this celebrated doctor.

His patient succumbed soon afterwards and the murderess wept long and deceitfully over the corpse. A few days later when the funeral rites at his tomb had been completed, the doctor's widow came and asked for her fee, pointing out that two murders had been provided at the price of one. The murderess remained true to character. In the friendliest tones and with a convincing show of good faith she answered that of course she would pay the money—if only she could have a little more of the same mixture to complete the business she had begun.

The doctor's widow was taken in, declared that she would be delighted to oblige, and knowing that the murderess was a wealthy woman, tried to get into her good books by running home at once and fetching her the whole case of poisons that had belonged to the late doctor. With this perfect armoury of crime in her possession, she prepared to go in for murder on a large scale. She had a little daughter by the husband whom she had just killed, and felt piqued that the child, as next-of-kin to her father, would inherit all his property. She wanted it all for herself, now that she had taken legal advice and discovered that, whatever their moral character, mothers always come in for the reversion of legacies bequeathed to their children. In fact, she showed herself as bad a mother as she had been a wife: when she invited the doctor's widow to breakfast, and slipped the poison into the food she was about to eat, she also gave a dose to her own little girl. The child choked and died almost at once; and the doctor's widow, when she felt the dreadful poison working in her intestines, and began to feel difficulty in breathing, realized at once what had happened. She rushed off to the home of the Governor, calling aloud for justice and declaring that she had some terrible crimes to reveal. A big crowd supported her and the Governor granted her an immediate interview. She told him the whole story from beginning to end; then her head dizzied, her mouth closed convulsively, she ground her teeth and fell dead at his feet.

He was an able and experienced officer and decided to allow no delay in bringing this hateful woman, who was accused of killing five people, to summary justice. He sent for her female slaves at once, tortured the truth out of them, and on the strength of their depositions sentenced her to death. Doubtless she deserved a still worse fate than merely to be thrown to the wild beasts; still, this was the most appropriate sentence that occurred to the Governor at the time.

~~17~~

The Goddess Isis Intervenes

THIS was the woman with whom it had been decided that I should have public connexion, a performance which almost amounted to a legal marriage. It was with extreme anguish that I waited for the day of the show. I was tempted to commit suicide rather than defile myself and be put to everlasting shame by bedding down with this wicked creature before the eyes of the entire amphitheatre.

Alas, I had no fingers or palms: how could I draw a sword with the round stump of my off fore-hoof? Only one slender hope remained to console me in my desperation: that the new year was here at last and wild flowers would soon be springing up all over the countryside, spreading a bright sheen of colour across the pastures. And in the gardens the imprisoned rose-buds would break out from their thorny stocks, and open, and exhale their delicate scents. One taste of rose-leaves, and I should be Lucius again.

The fateful day came at last, and I was escorted towards the amphitheatre through cheering crowds at the head of a long

255

procession. During the first part of the performance, which was devoted to ballet, I was placed just outside the entrance, where I was glad to crop some tender young grass which I found growing there, raising my eyes curiously every now and then to watch the performance through the open gate.

By way of prelude a number of beautiful boys and girls in rich costumes were moving with dignity through the graceful mazes of the Greek Pyrrhic dance. Sometimes different streams of dancers would weave in and out of the same circle, sometimes all would join hands and dance sideways across the stage, then separate into four wedge-shaped groups with the blunt ends enclosing a square space; sometimes there would be a sudden divorce of the sexes, the boys and the girls separating from each other.

Presently the trumpet blew the Retreat, to signal the end of these complicated dance-movements, and the backdrops were removed to disclose a far more elaborate performance.

The scene was an artificial wooden mountain, supposed to represent Homer's famous Mount Ida, an imposing piece of stage-architecture, quite high, turfed all over and planted with scores of trees. The designer had contrived that a stream should break out at the top of the mountain and tumble down the side. A herd of she-goats were cropping the grass, and a young man strolled about, supposedly in charge of them, dressed in flowing Asiatic robes with a gold tiara on his head. He represented Paris the Phrygian shepherd. Then a handsome boy came forward, naked except for a rich cloak worn over his left shoulder, and between the strands of his long yellow hair one could see two little golden wings; these wings, with the serpent-rod and the herald's wand that he carried, showed him to be the God Mercury. He came dancing towards Paris and after presenting him with a golden apple explained Jupiter's orders in sign language, then retired gracefully. The next character to appear was Juno, played by a girl with very fine features, a white diadem on her head and a sceptre in her hand. Then Minerva came running in; easily recognised by her shining helmet with its mantling of olive-leaves, her high-lifted shield and the spear that she was brandishing as if about to fight someone. She was followed by another girl of extraordinary beauty and such an ambrosial complexion that she could only be Venus—Venus before marriage. To show her perfect figure to fullest advantage she wore nothing at all except a thin gauze apron which inquisitive little winds kept blowing aside for an amorous peep at her downy young thighs, or pressing tight against them so as to reveal their voluptuous contours. Her body was dazzlingly white, to show that she had descended from heaven, and her gauze apron was blue to show that she would shortly return to her home in the sea.

Each of the girls who played the parts of these goddesses was escorted by her own attendants. Juno had two young actors with her, representing Castor and Pollux; I guessed who they were by their helmets, shaped like the halves of the egg-shell in which they were born to their mother Leda, and with spiky stars painted on them—the constellation of the Twins. Juno advanced calmly towards Paris, to the sound of gentle flute-music in the Ionian mode; her short, confident nods were an assurance that if he judged her to be the most beautiful of the three she would make him Emperor of all Asia.

Minerva's attendants were two young men, representing Terror and Fear, who danced a fling before her with drawn swords, and a bagpiper who followed behind, playing a battle march in the Dorian mode. The deep braying drones contrasted with the shrill screech of the chaunter which stirred the dancers to ecstasy, like the trumpet's call to battle. Minerva herself joined in the fling, tossing her head from side to side, her eyes gleaming like daggers, and her quick, excited writhings promised Paris that if he gave the verdict in her favour she would help him to become the bravest and most successful soldier the world had ever known.

Then in came Venus, smiling sweetly and greeted with a roar of welcome by the audience. She advanced to the centre of the stage, with a whole school of happy little boys crowding around her, so chubby and white-skinned that you might have taken them to be real cupids flown down from Heaven or in from the sea. They had little wings and little archery sets and (this was a nice touch) all carried lighted torches as if they were conducting their mistress to her wedding breakfast. In came a great crowd of beautiful girls: the most graceful Graces, the loveliest Seasons, who strewed the path before Venus with bouquets and loose flowers, propitiating her, as Queen of all pleasures, with the shorn locks of spring.

Presently the flutes broke into sentimental Lydian airs. The audience was charmed when Venus began dancing to the music with slow, lingering steps and gentle swaying of her hips and head, and hardly perceptible motions of her arms to match the flautist's delicate modulations. Her eyelids fluttered luxuriously or opened wide to let fly passionate glances, so that at times she seemed to be dancing with her eyes alone. As soon as she came before the judge she promised with tense gestures that if she were preferred to her rivals she would marry him to the most beautiful

258

woman in the world, her own human counterpart. Young Paris gladly handed her the golden apple in token of her victory.

Well, then, you lowest of the low, yes, I am referring to the whole legal profession, all you cattle-like law-clerks and vulture-like barristers—are you really surprised that modern judges are corrupt, when here you have proof that in the earliest ages of man-kind, in this first court-of-law ever convened, the simple shepherd, who had been appointed by Jupiter himself to give judgement in a question that was troubling heaven and earth, succumbed to a barefaced sexual bribe (which was to prove the ruin of his entire family) and sold his verdict in open court? No, sirs! And you will recall a later precedent when Agamemnon, the illustrious commander-in-chief of the Greek armies before Troy, condemned the wise and learned Palamedes to death as a traitor, though fully aware that the charges against him were false. You will also recall his judgement in the dispute between Odysseus and Ajax as to which of the two was the bravest. He knew that Odysseus's cour-age could not always be depended upon and that Ajax was by far the better man; yet he gave judgement in favour of Odysseus. As for those famous law-givers, those brilliant intellects, those eminent scientists, the Athenians of the classical age, what sort of a verdict did they give in the case of Socrates whose wisdom was commended by the Delphic oracle above that of all living men? Am I not right in saying that by the treachery and jealousy of a wicked clique he was found guilty of corrupting young people—though the truth was that his philosophy was directed towards bridling, not inflaming, their passions—and sentenced to die by drinking the poisonous hemlock cup? This has left an indelible stain on the reputation of Athenian justice, because even today the best philosophers, those who aspire to the highest form of human happiness, regard his system as the most truly religious of all and swear by his name.

Forgive this outburst! I can hear my readers protesting: 'Hey, what's all this about? Are we going to let an ass lecture us in philosophy?' Yes, I dare say I had best return to my story.

As I was saying, Paris gave his verdict. Then Juno and Minerva retired from the scene, Juno in sorrow, Minerva in rage, each of them expressing in dumb-show her indignation at not having been awarded the prize. But Venus danced for delight, with the support of all her attendants. Then a fountain of wine, mixed with saffron, broke out from a concealed pipe at the mountain top and its many jets sprinkled the pasturing goats with a scented shower, so that their white hair was stained the rich yellow traditionally associated with the flocks that feed on Mount Ida. The scent filled the whole amphitheatre; and then the stage machinery was set in motion, the earth seemed to gape and the mountain disappeared from view.

After this, a soldier ran along the main aisle and out of the theatre to fetch the murderess who, though condemned (as I have already explained) to be eaten by wild beasts, was destined first to become my glorious bride. Our marriage bed, inlaid with fine Indian tortoiseshell, was already in position, and provided with a luxurious feather mattress and an embroidered Chinese coverlet. I was not only appalled at the disgraceful part that I was expected to play: I was in terror of death. It occurred to me that when she and I were locked in what was supposed to be a passionate embrace and the wild beast, whose part in the drama would be to eat her, came bounding into our bridal cage, I could not count on the creature's being so naturally sagacious, or so well trained, or so abstemious, as to tear her to pieces as she cuddled close to me, but leave me alone.

While Thyasus was busy inside the cage putting the last touches to the bed, and the rest of his household staff were either admiring the voluptuousness of the scene or getting things ready for the hunting display which was to follow our interlude, I planned an escape. I had such a reputation for tameness and gentleness that nobody was keeping an eye on me. I edged towards the outer gate, which was quite near. Once outside I bolted off at top speed and went six miles at full gallop until I found myself at Cenchreae, the most famous of all Corinthian boroughs, which is washed on one side by the Aegean Sea and on the other by the waters of the Gulf of Corinth.

Cenchreae has a safe harbour and is always crowded with visitors, but I wanted to keep away from people. I went to a secluded beach and stretched my tired body in a hollow of the sand, close to where the waves were breaking in spray. It was evening. The chariot of the sun was at the point of ending its day's course across the sky; so I too resigned myself to rest, and was presently overcome by a sweet, sound sleep.

*

Not long afterwards I awoke in sudden terror. A dazzling full moon was rising from the sea. It is at this secret hour that the Moon-goddess, sole sovereign of mankind, is possessed of her greatest power and majesty. She is the shining deity by whose divine influence not only all beasts, wild and tame, but all inanimate things as well, are invigorated; whose ebbs and flows control the rhythm of all bodies whatsoever, whether in the air, on earth, or below the sea. Of this I was well aware, and therefore resolved to address the visible image of the goddess, imploring her help; for Fortune seemed at last to have made up her mind that I had suffered enough and to be offering me a hope of release.

Jumping up and shaking off my drowsiness, I went down to the sea to purify myself by bathing in it. Seven times I dipped my head under the waves—seven, according to the divine philosopher Pythagoras, is a number that suits all religious occasions—and with joyful eagerness, though tears were running down my hairy face, I offered this soundless prayer to the supreme Goddess:

'Blessed Queen of Heaven, whether you are pleased to be known as Ceres, the original harvest mother who in joy at the finding of your lost daughter Proserpine abolished the rude acorn diet of our forefathers and gave them bread raised from the fertile soil of Eleusis; or whether as celestial Venus, now adored at sea-girt Paphos, who at the time of the first Creation coupled the sexes in mutual love and so contrived that man should continue to propagate his kind for ever; or whether as Artemis, the physician sister of Phoebus Apollo, reliever of the birth pangs of women, and now adored in the ancient shrine at Ephesus; or whether as dread Proserpine to whom the owl cries at night, whose triple face is potent against the malice of ghosts, keeping them imprisoned below earth; you who wander through many sacred groves and are propitiated with many different rites—you whose womanly light illumines the walls of every city, whose misty radiance nurses the happy seeds under the soil, you who control the wandering course of the sun and the very power of his rays—I beseech you, by whatever name, in whatever aspect, with whatever ceremonies you deign to be invoked, have mercy on me in my extreme distress, restore my shattered fortune, grant me repose and peace after this long sequence of miseries. End my sufferings and perils, rid me of this hateful four-footed disguise, return me to my family, make me Lucius once more. But if I have offended some god of unappeasable cruelty who is bent on making life impossible for me, at least grant me one sure gift, the gift of death.'

When I had finished my prayer and poured out the full bitterness of my oppressed heart, I returned to my sandy hollow, where once more sleep overcame me. I had scarcely closed my eyes before the apparition of a woman began to rise from the middle of the sea with so lovely a face that the gods themselves would have fallen down in adoration of it. First the head, then the whole shining body gradually emerged and stood before me poised on the surface of the waves. Yes, I will try to describe this transcendent vision, for though human speech is poor and limited, the Goddess herself will perhaps inspire me with poetic imagery sufficient to convey some slight inkling of what I saw.

Her long thick hair fell in tapering ringlets on her lovely neck, and was crowned with an intricate chaplet in which was woven every kind of flower. Just above her brow shone a round disc, like a mirror, or like the bright face of the moon, which told me who she was. Vipers rising from the left-hand and right-hand partings of her hair supported this disc, with ears of corn bristling beside them. Her many-coloured robe was of finest linen; part was glistening white, part crocus-yellow, part glowing red and along the entire hem a woven bordure of flowers and fruit clung swaying in the breeze.* But what caught and held my eye more than anything else was the deep black lustre of her mantle. She wore it slung across her body from the right hip to the left shoulder, where it was caught in a knot resembling the boss of a shield; but part of it hung in innumerable folds, the tasselled fringe quivering. It was embroidered with glittering stars on the hem and everywhere else, and in the middle beamed a full and fiery moon.

In her right hand she held a bronze rattle, of the sort used to frighten away the God of the Sirocco; its narrow rim was curved like a sword-belt and three little rods, which sang shrilly when she shook the handle, passed horizontally through it. A boat-shaped gold dish hung from her left hand, and along the upper surface of the handle writhed an asp with puffed throat and head raised ready to strike. On her divine feet were slippers of palm leaves, the emblem of victory.

All the perfumes of Arabia floated into my nostrils as the Goddess deigned to address me: 'You see me here, Lucius, in answer to your prayer. I am Nature, the universal Mother, mistress of all the elements, primordial child of time, sovereign of all things spiritual, queen of the dead, queen also of the immortals, the single manifestation of all gods and goddesses that are. My nod governs the shining heights of Heaven, the wholesome sea-breezes, the lamentable silences of the world below. Though I am worshipped in many aspects, known by countless names, and propitiated with all manner of different rites, yet the whole round earth venerates me. The primeval Phrygians call me Pessinuntica, Mother of the gods; the Athenians, sprung from their own soil, call me Ce-

* Part of this sentence has been displaced in the Latin text and an early editor has corrected it unintelligently.

cropian Artemis; for the islanders of Cyprus I am Paphian Aphrodite; for the archers of Crete I am Dictynna; for the trilingual Sicilians, Stygian Proserpine; and for the Eleusinians their ancient Mother of the Corn.

'Some know me as Juno, some as Bellona of the Battles; others as Hecate, others again as Rhamnubia, but both races of Aethiopians, whose lands the morning sun first shines upon, and the Egyptians who excel in ancient learning and worship me with ceremonies proper to my godhead, call me by my true name, namely, Queen Isis. I have come in pity of your plight, I have come to favour and aid you. Weep no more, lament no longer; the hour of deliverance, shone over by my watchful light, is at hand.

'Listen attentively to my orders.

'The eternal laws of religion devote to my worship the day born from this night. Tomorrow my priests offer me the first-fruits of the new sailing season by dedicating a ship to me: for at this season the storms of winter lose their force, the leaping waves subside and the sea becomes navigable once more. You must wait for this sacred ceremony, with a mind that is neither anxious for the future nor clouded with profane thoughts; and I shall order the High Priest to carry a garland of roses in my procession, tied to the rattle which he carries in his right hand. Do not hesitate, push the crowd aside, join the procession with confidence in my grace. Then come close up to the High Priest as if you wished to kiss his hand, gently pluck the roses with your mouth and you will immediately slough off the hide of what has always been for me the most hateful beast in the universe.

'Above all, have faith: do not think that my commands are

hard to obey. For at this very moment, while I am speaking to you here, I am also giving complementary instructions to my sleeping High Priest; and tomorrow, at my commandment, the dense crowds of people will make way for you. I promise you that in the joy and laughter of the festival nobody will either view your ugly shape with abhorrence or dare to put a sinister interpretation on your sudden return to human shape. Only remember, and keep these words of mine locked tight in your heart, that from now onwards until the very last day of your life you are dedicated to my service. It is only right that you should devote your whole life to the Goddess who makes you a man again. Under my protection you will be happy and famous, and when at the destined end of your life you descend to the land of ghosts, there too in the subterrene hemisphere you shall have frequent occasion to adore me. From the Elysian fields you will see me as queen of the profound Stygian realm, shining through the darkness of Acheron with a light as kindly and tender as I show you now. Further, if you are found to deserve my divine protection by careful obedience to the ordinances of my religion and by perfect chastity, you will become aware that I, and I alone, have power to prolong your life beyond the limits appointed by destiny.'

With this, the vision of the invincible Goddess faded and dissolved.

18

The Ass Is Transformed

I ROSE at once, wide awake, bathed in a sweat of joy and fear. Astonished beyond words at this clear manifestation of her godhead, I splashed myself with sea water and carefully memorized her orders, intent on obeying them to the letter. Soon a golden sun arose to rout the dark shadows of night, and at once the streets were filled with people walking along as if in a religious triumph. Not only I, but the whole world, seemed filled with delight. The animals, the houses, even the weather itself reflected the universal joy and serenity, for a calm sunny morning had succeeded yesterday's frost, and the song-birds, assured that spring had come, were chirping their welcome to the queen of the stars, the Mother of the seasons, the mistress of the universe. The trees, too, not only the orchard trees but those grown for their shade, roused from their winter sleep by the warm breezes of the south and tasselled with green leaves, waved their branches with a pleasant rustling noise; and the crash and thunder of the surf was stilled, for the gales had blown themselves out, the dark clouds were gone and the calm sky shone with its own deep blue light.

Presently the vanguard of the grand procession came in view. It was composed of a number of people in fancy dress of their own choosing; a man wearing a soldier's sword-belt; another dressed as a huntsman, a thick cloak caught up to his waist with hunting knife and javelin; another who wore gilt sandals, a wig, a silk dress and expensive jewellery and pretended to be a woman. Then a man with heavy boots, shield, helmet and sword, looking as though he had walked straight out of the gladiators' school; a pretended magistrate with purple robe and rods of office; a philosopher with cloak, staff, clogs and billy-goat beard; a birdcatcher, carrying lime and a long reed; a fisherman with another long reed and a fish-hook. Oh, yes, and a tame she-bear, dressed like a woman, carried in a sedan chair; and an ape in a straw hat and a saffron-coloured Phrygian cloak with a gold cup grasped in its paws—a caricature of Jupiter's beautiful cup-bearer Ganymede. Finally an ass with wings glued to its shoulders and a doddering old man seated on its rump; you would have laughed like anything at that pair, supposed to be Pegasus and Bellerophon. These fancy-dress comedians kept running in and out of the crowd, and behind them came the procession proper.

At the head walked women crowned with flowers, who pulled more flowers out of the folds of their beautiful white dresses and scattered them along the road; their joy in the Saviouress appeared in every gesture. Next came women with polished mirrors tied to the backs of their heads, which gave all who followed them the illusion of coming to meet the Goddess, rather than marching before her. Next, a party of women with ivory combs in their hands who made a pantomime of combing the Goddess's royal hair, and another party with bottles of perfume who sprinkled the road with balsam and other precious perfumes; and behind these a mixed company of women and men who addressed the Goddess as 'Daughter of the Stars' and propitiated her by carrying every sort of light—lamps, torches, wax-candles and so forth.

Next came musicians with pipes and flutes, followed by a party of carefully chosen choir-boys singing a hymn in which an inspired poet had explained the origin of the procession. The temple pipers of the great god Serapis were there, too, playing their religious anthem on pipes with slanting mouth-pieces and tubes curving around their right ears; also a number of beadles and whifflers crying: 'Make way there, way for the Goddess!' Then followed a great crowd of the Goddess's initiates, men and women of all classes and every age, their pure white linen clothes shining brightly. The women wore their hair tied up in glossy coils under gauze head-dresses; the men's heads were completely shaven, representing the Goddess's bright earthly stars, and they carried rattles of brass, silver and even gold, which kept up a shrill and ceaseless tinkling.

The leading priests, also clothed in white linen drawn tight across their breasts and hanging down to their feet, carried the oracular emblems of the deity. The High Priest held a bright lamp, which was not at all like the lamps we use at night banquets; it was a golden boat-shaped affair with a tall tongue of flame mounting from a hole in the centre. The second priest held an *auxiliaria,* or sacrificial pot, in each of his hands—the name refers to the Goddess's providence in helping her devotees. The third priest carried a miniature palm-tree with gold leaves, also the serpent wand of Mercury. The fourth carried the model of a left hand with the fingers stretched out, which is an emblem of justice because the left hand, with its natural slowness and lack of any craft or subtlety, seems more impartial than the right. He also held a golden vessel, rounded in the shape of a woman's breast, from the nipple of which a thin stream of milk fell to the ground. The fifth carried a winnowing fan woven with golden rods, not osiers. Then came a man, not one of the five, carrying a wine-jar.

Next in the procession followed those deities that deigned to walk on human feet. Here was the frightening messenger of the gods of Heaven, and of the gods of the dead: Anubis with a face black on one side, golden on the other, walking erect and holding his herald's wand in one hand, and in the other a green palm-branch. Behind, danced a man carrying on his shoulders, seated upright, the statue of a cow, representing the Goddess as the fruitful Mother of us all. Then along came a priest with a box containing the secret implements of her wonderful cult. Another fortunate priest had an ancient emblem of her godhead hidden in the lap of his robe: this was not made in the shape of any beast, wild or tame, or any bird or human being, but the exquisite beauty of its workmanship no less than the originality of its design called for admiration and awe. It was a symbol of the sublime and ineffable mysteries of the Goddess, which are never to be divulged: a small vessel of burnished gold, upon which Egyptian hieroglyphics were thickly crowded, with a rounded bottom, a long spout, and a generously curving handle along which sprawled an asp, raising its head and displaying its scaly, wrinkled, puffed-out throat.

At last the moment had come when the blessing promised by the almighty Goddess was to fall upon me. The High Priest in whom lay my hope of salvation approached, and I saw that he carried the rattle and the garland in his right hand just as I had been promised—but, oh, it was more than a garland to me, it was a crown of victory over cruel Fortune, bestowed on me by the Goddess after I had endured so many hardships and run through so many dangers! Though overcome with sudden joy, I refrained from galloping forward at once and disturbing the calm progress of the pageant by a brutal charge, but gently and politely wriggled my way through the crowd which gave way before me, clearly by the Goddess's intervention, until at last I emerged at the other side. I saw at once that the priest had been warned what to expect in his vision of the previous night but was none the less astounded that the fulfilment came so pat. He stood still and held out the rose garland to the level of my mouth. I trembled and my heart pounded as I ate those roses with loving relish; and no sooner had I swallowed them than I found that the promise had been no deceit. My bestial features faded away, the rough hair fell from my body, my sagging paunch tightened, my hind hooves separated into feet and toes, my fore hooves now no longer served only for walking upon, but were restored, as hands, to my human uses. Then my neck shrank, my face and head rounded, my great hard teeth shrank to their proper size, my long ears shortened, and my tail which had been my worst shame vanished altogether.

A gasp of wonder went up and the priests, aware that the miracle corresponded with the High Priest's vision of the Great Goddess, lifted their hands to Heaven and with one voice applauded the blessing which she had vouchsafed me: this swift restoration to my proper shape.

When I saw what had happened to me I stood rooted to the

ground with astonishment and could not speak for a long while, my mind unable to cope with so great and sudden a joy. I could find no words good enough to thank the Goddess for her extraordinary loving-kindness. But the High Priest, who had been informed by her of all my miseries, though himself taken aback by the weird sight, gave orders in dumb-show that I should be lent a linen garment to cover me; for as soon as I regained my human shape, I had naturally done what any naked man would do—pressed my knees closely together and put both my hands down to screen my private parts. Someone quickly took off his upper robe and covered me with it, after which the High Priest gazed benignly at me, still wondering at my perfectly human appearance.

'Lucius, my friend,' he said, 'you have endured and performed many labours and withstood the buffetings of all the winds of ill luck. Now at last you have put into the harbour of peace and stand before the altar of loving-kindness. Neither your noble blood and rank nor your education sufficed to keep you from falling a slave to pleasure; youthful follies ran away with you. Your luckless curiosity earned you a sinister punishment. But blind Fortune, after tossing you maliciously about from peril to peril has somehow, without thinking what she was doing, landed you here in religious felicity. Let her begone now and fume furiously wherever she pleases, let her find some other plaything for her cruel hands. She has no power to hurt those who devote their lives to the honour and service of our Goddess's majesty. The jade! What use was served by making you over to bandits, wild dogs and cruel masters, by setting your feet on dangerous stony paths, by holding you in daily terror of death? Rest assured that you are now safe under the protection of the true Fortune, all-seeing Providence, whose clear light shines for all the gods that are. Rejoice now, as becomes a wearer of white linen. Follow triumphantly in the train of the Goddess who has delivered you. Let the irreligious see you and, seeing, let them acknowledge the error of their ways. Let them cry: "Look, there goes Lucius, rescued from a dreadful fate by the intervention of the Goddess Isis; watch him glory in the defeat of his ill luck!" But to secure today's gains, you must enrol yourself in this holy Order as last night you pledged yourself to do, voluntarily undertaking the duties to which your oath binds you; for her service is perfect freedom.'

When the High Priest had ended his inspired speech, I joined the throng of devotees and went forward with the procession, an object of curiosity to all Corinth. People pointed or jerked their heads at me and said: 'Look, there goes Lucius, restored to human shape by the power of the Almighty Goddess! Lucky, lucky man to have earned her compassion on account of his former innocence and good behaviour, and now to be reborn as it were, and immediately accepted into her most sacred service!' Their congratulations were long and loud.

Meanwhile the pageant moved slowly on and we approached the sea shore, at last reaching the very place where on the previous night I had lain down as an ass. There the divine emblems were arranged in due order and there with solemn prayers the chaste-lipped priest consecrated and dedicated to the Goddess a beautifully built ship, with Egyptian hieroglyphics painted over the entire hull; but first he carefully purified it with a lighted torch, an egg and sulphur. The sail was shining white linen, inscribed in large letters with the prayer for the Goddess's protection of shipping during the new sailing season. The long fir mast with its shining head was now stepped, and we admired the gilded prow shaped like the neck of Isis's sacred goose, and the long, highly-polished keel cut from a solid trunk of citrus-wood. Then all present, both priesthood and laity, began zealously stowing aboard winnowing-fans heaped with aromatics and other votive offerings and poured an abundant stream of milk into the sea as a libation. When the ship was loaded with generous gifts and prayers for good fortune, they cut the anchor cables and she slipped across the bay with a serene breeze behind her that seemed to have sprung up for her sake alone. When she stood so far out to sea that we could no longer keep her in view, the priests took up the sacred emblems again and started happily back towards the temple, in the same orderly procession as before.

On our arrival the High Priest and the priests who carried the oracular emblems were admitted into the Goddess's sanctuary with other initiates and restored them to their proper places. Then one of them, known as the Doctor of Divinity, presided at the gate of the sanctuary over a meeting of the Shrine-bearers, as the highest order of the priests of Isis are called. He went up into a high pulpit with a book and read out a Latin blessing upon 'our liege lord, the Emperor, and upon the Senate, and upon the Order of Knights, and upon the Commons of Rome, and upon all sailors and all ships who owe obedience to the aforesaid powers.' Then he uttered the traditional Greek formula, 'Ploeaphesia', meaning that vessels were now permitted to sail, to which the people responded with a great cheer and dispersed happily to their homes, taking all kinds of decorations with them: such as olive boughs, scent shrubs and garlands of flowers, but first kissing the feet of a silver statue of the Goddess that stood on the temple steps. I did not feel like moving a nail's breadth from the place, but stood with my eyes intently fixed on the statue and relived in memory all my past misfortunes.

Meanwhile, the news of my adventures and of the Goddess's wonderful goodness to me had flown out in all directions; eventually it reached my own city of Madaura, where I had been mourned as dead. At once my slaves, servants and close relatives forgot their sorrow and came hurrying to Corinth in high spirits to welcome me back from the Underworld, as it were, and bring me all sorts of presents. I was as delighted to see them as they were to see me—I had despaired of ever doing so—and thanked them over and over again for what they had brought me: I was especially grateful to my servants for bringing me as much money and as many clothes as I needed.

I spoke to them all in turn, which was no more than my duty, telling them of troubles now past and of my happy prospects; then returned to what had become my greatest pleasure in life— contemplation of the Goddess. I managed to obtain the use of a room in the temple and took constant part in her services, from which I had hitherto been excluded. The brotherhood accepted me almost as one of themselves, a loyal devotee of the Great Goddess.

Not a single night did I pass, nor even doze off during the day, without some new vision of her. She always ordered me to be initiated into her sacred mysteries, to which I had long been destined. I was anxious to obey, but religious awe held me back, because after making careful enquiries I found that to take Orders was to bind oneself to a very difficult life, especially as regards chastity: and that an initiate has to be continuously on his guard against accidental defilement. Somehow or other, though the question was always with me, I delayed the decision which I knew I must sooner or later take.

One night I dreamed that the High Priest came to me with his lap full of presents. When I asked: 'What have you there?' he answered: 'Something from Thessaly. Your slave Candidus has just arrived.' When I awoke, I puzzled over the dream for a long time, wondering what it meant, especially as I had never owned a slave of that name. However, I was convinced that whatever the High Priest offered me must be something good. When dawn approached I waited for the opening of the temple, still in a state of anxious expectation. The white curtains of the sanctuary were then drawn and we adored the august face of the Goddess. A priest went the round of the altars, performing the morning rites with solemn supplications and, chalice in hand, poured libations of water drawn from a spring within the temple precincts. When the service was over a choir saluted the breaking day with the loud hymn that they always sing at the hour of prime.

The doors opened and who should come in but the two slaves whom I had left behind at Hypata when Fotis by her unlucky mistake had put a halter around my neck. They had heard the tale of my adventures and brought me all my belongings. They had even managed to recover my white horse, after its repeated changes of hand, by identifying my brand on its haunch. Now I understood the meaning of my dream: not only had they brought me something from Thessaly, but I had recovered my horse, plainly referred to in the dream as 'your slave Candidus'; for Candidus means 'white.'

Thereafter I devoted my whole time to attendance on the Goddess, encouraged by these tokens to hope for even greater marks of her favour, and my desire for taking holy orders increased. I frequently spoke of it to the High Priest, begging him to initiate me into the mysteries of the holy night. He was a grave man, remarkable for the strict observance of his religious duties, and checked my restlessness, as parents calm down children who are making unreasonable demands, but so gently and kindly that I was not in the least discouraged. He explained that the day on which a postulant might be initiated was always indicated by signs from the Goddess herself, and that it was she who chose the officiating priest and announced how the incidental expenses of the ceremony were to be paid. In his view I ought to wait with attentive patience and avoid the two extremes of over-eagerness and obstinacy; begin neither unresponsive when called nor importunate while awaiting my call. 'No single member of the brotherhood,' he said, 'has ever been so wrong-minded and sacrilegious, in fact so bent on his own destruction, as to partake of the mystery without direct orders from the Goddess, and so fall into deadly sin. The gates of the Underworld and the guardianship of life are in her hands, and the rites of initiation approximate to a voluntary death from which there is only a precarious hope of resurrection. So she usually chooses old men who feel that their end is fast approaching yet are not too senile to be capable of keeping a secret; by her grace they are, in a sense, born again and restored to new and healthy life.'

He said, in fact, that I must be content to await definite orders, but agreed that I had been foreordained for the service of the Goddess by clear marks of her favour. Meanwhile I must abstain from forbidden food, as the priests did, so that when the time came for me to partake of their most holy mysteries I could enter the sanctuary with unswerving steps.

I accepted his advice and learned to be patient, taking part in the daily services of the temple as calmly and quietly as I knew how, intent on pleasing the Goddess. Nor did I have a troublesome and disappointing probation. Soon after this she gave me proof of her grace by a midnight vision in which I was plainly told that the day for which I longed, the day on which my greatest wish would be granted, had come at last. I learned that she had ordered the High Priest Mithras, whose destiny was linked with mine by planetary sympathy, to officiate at my initiation.

These orders and certain others given me at the same time so exhilarated me that I rose before dawn to tell the High Priest about them, and reached his door just as he was coming out. I greeted him and was about to beg him more earnestly than ever to allow me to be initiated, as a privilege that was now mine by right, when he spoke first. 'Dear Lucius,' he said, 'how lucky, how blessed you are that the Great Goddess has graciously deigned to honour you in this way. There is no time to waste. The day for which you prayed so earnestly has dawned. The many-named Goddess orders me to initiate you into her most holy mysteries.'

He took me by the hand and led me courteously to the doors of the vast temple, and when he had opened them in the usual solemn way and performed the morning sacrifice he went to the sanctuary and took out two or three books written in characters unknown to me: some of them animal hieroglyphics, some of them ordinary letters protected against profane prying by having their tops and tails wreathed in knots or rounded like wheels or tangled together in spirals like vine tendrils. From these books he read me out instructions for providing the necessary clothes and accessories for my initiation.

I at once went to my friends the priests and asked them to buy part of what I needed, sparing no expense: the rest I went to buy myself.

In due time the High Priest summoned me and took me to the nearest public baths, attended by a crowd of priests. There, when I had enjoyed my ordinary bath, he himself washed and sprinkled me with holy water, offering up prayers for divine mercy. After this he brought me back to the temple and placed me at the very feet of the Goddess.

It was now early afternoon. He gave me certain orders too holy to be spoken above a whisper, and then commanded me in everyone's hearing to abstain from all but the plainest food for the ten succeeding days, to eat no meat and drink no wine.

I obeyed his instructions in all reverence and at last the day came for taking my vows. As evening approached a crowd of priests came flocking to me from all directions, each one giving me congratulatory gifts, as the ancient custom is. Then the High Priest ordered all uninitiated persons to depart, invested me in a new linen garment and led me by the hand into the inner recesses of the sanctuary itself. I have no doubt, curious reader, that you are eager to know what happened when I entered. If I were allowed to tell you, and you were allowed to be told, you would soon hear everything; but, as it is, my tongue would suffer for its indiscretion and your ears for their inquisitiveness.

However, not wishing to leave you, if you are religiously inclined, in a state of tortured suspense, I will record as much as I may lawfully record for the uninitiated, but only on condition that you believe it. *I approached the very gates of death and set one foot on Proserpine's threshold, yet was permitted to return, rapt through all the elements. At midnight I saw the sun shining as if it were noon; I entered the presence of the gods of the under-world and the gods of the upper-world, stood near and wor-shipped them.*

Well, now you have heard what happened, but I fear you are still none the wiser.

The solemn rites ended at dawn and I emerged from the sanc-tuary wearing twelve different stoles, certainly a most sacred cos-tume but one that there can be no harm in my mentioning. Many uninitiated people saw me wearing it when the High Priest or-dered me to mount into the wooden pulpit which stood in the centre of the temple, immediately in front of the Goddess's image. I was wearing an outer garment of fine linen embroidered with flowers, and a precious scarf hung down from my shoulders to my ankles with sacred animals worked in colour on every part of it; for instance Indian serpents and Hyperborean griffins, which are winged lions generated in the more distant parts of the world. The priests call this scarf an Olympian stole. I held a lighted torch in my right hand and wore a white palm-tree chaplet with its leaves sticking out all round like rays of light.

The curtains were pulled aside and I was suddenly exposed to the gaze of the crowd, as when a statue is unveiled, dressed like the sun. That day was the happiest of my initiation, and I cele-brated it as my birthday with a cheerful banquet at which all my friends were present. Further rites and ceremonies were performed on the third day, including a sacred breakfast, and these ended the proceedings. However, I remained for some days longer in the temple, enjoying the ineffable pleasure of contemplating the Goddess's statue, because I was bound to her by a debt of gratitude so large that I could never hope to pay it.

19

At the Bar

AT LENGTH the Goddess advised me to return home. I had thanked her not so much as she deserved but as much as I could, and took time over my leave-taking, because I found it hard to wrench myself away from a place that I had come to love so dearly.

I fell prostrate at the Goddess's feet, and washed them with my tears as I prayed to her in a voice chocked with sobs: 'Holiest of the Holy, perpetual comfort of mankind, you whose bountiful grace nourishes the whole world; whose heart turns towards all those in sorrow and tribulation as a mother's to her children; you who take no rest by night, no rest by day, but are always at hand to succour the distressed by land and sea, dispersing the gales that beat upon them. Your hand alone can disentangle the hopelessly knotted skeins of fate, terminate every spell of bad weather, and restrain the stars from harmful conjunction. The gods above adore you, the gods below do homage to you, you set the orb of heaven spinning around the poles, you give light to the sun, you govern the universe, you trample down the powers of Hell. At your voice the stars move, the seasons recur, the spirits of earth rejoice, the elements obey. At your nod the winds blow, clouds drop wholesome rain upon the earth, seeds quicken, buds swell. Birds that fly through the air, beasts that prowl on the mountain, serpents that lurk in the dust, all these tremble in a single awe of you. My eloquence is unequal to praising you according to your deserts; my wealth to providing the sacrificial victims I owe you; my voice to uttering all that I think of your majesty—no, not even if I had a thousand tongues in a thousand mouths and could speak for ever. Nevertheless, poor as I am, I will do as much as I can in my devotion to you; I will keep your divine countenance always before my eyes and the secret knowledge of your divinity locked deep in my heart.'

I went to the High Priest Mithras, now my spiritual father, clung around his neck and kissed him again and again, begging him to forgive me for not being able to return his kindnesses as they deserved. This goodbye took me such a long time that he must have feared that I would never stop saying, 'Thank you, oh, thank you!'

I had decided to go straight home to Madaura after my long absence, but a few days later the Goddess warned me to pack up my things in a hurry and take ship for Rome. As was to be expected, the wind blew fair throughout my voyage and I was soon at the port of Ostia, where I took a fast gig and reached the Holy City on the evening of December 13th. I made it my first business to visit the Goddess's temple in the Field of Mars, which gives her the local title of 'Our Lady of the Field'. I attended her daily services there and though I was a foreigner the priests gave me the freedom of her temple because of my initiation into her Corinthian mysteries.

The sun had completed his course around the Zodiac when the kind Goddess, who was still watching over me, visited me in a dream and warned me that I must be prepared for a new initiation and a new vow. I could not make out what I was intended to do, what was supposed to happen. Surely I was fully initiated already? I pondered the question deeply and consulted the High Priest; when it occurred to me with the force of a surprise, that so far I had been initiated only into the mysteries of Isis, not yet into those of the supreme Father of the Gods, the invincible Osiris. Though their divine natures are linked and even, in a transcendental sense, united, there is certainly a great difference between the rites of initiation into their separate cults. I guessed that the Great God needed me as a servant, and my guess was confirmed the very next night. I dreamed that a priest of Osiris clothed in white linen came into my room with fir-wands, ivy-chaplets, and certain other holy objects which I am not allowed to mention, and placed them among my household gods. He then sat down in my chair and told me to order a religious banquet. I noticed that he walked with a limp, his left ankle being slightly crooked; which I took for a sign that would allow me to recognize him again when I saw him in the flesh. The will of the gods had now been plainly expressed. I went off to the temple to pay my daily respects to the Goddess, and no sooner had I finished than I looked closely at the priests, to see whether any of them resembled the one about whom I had dreamed.

Almost at once I recognized the man. He was one of the Shrine-bearers, and not only was his left ankle crooked but his height and general appearance corresponded exactly with my vision. It turned out that his name was Asinius Marcellus, and the Asinius part of it seemed to refer to my transformation into an ass. I went straight to him, and found that he knew exactly what I was going to say, because he had been given instructions that matched mine. It seems that, the night before, while he was placing chaplets on the statue of Osiris he had heard an oracle pronounced by its holy mouth: namely, that he was being sent a man of Madaura who, though poor, must be initiated at once into the sacred mysteries. The God added that under his divine care this man would achieve fame in a learned profession and that Asinius himself would be richly rewarded for his trouble.

This was how I was dedicated to the mysteries; unfortunately, much to my disappointment, I could not be initiated as yet because I had not money enough to pay for the ceremony. The expenses of my voyage had eaten up what small funds I still possessed on leaving Corinth, and I found life at Rome far more expensive than in the provinces. To be baulked of my wishes by poverty distressed me; in the words of the proverb I felt like a victim caught 'between the altar top and the descending flint.' Worse, the God continued to appear from time to time in visions of the night and remind me of his commands. At last he ordered me to take the robe off my back and sell it. I did so without hesitation and, though it was not a particularly good one, managed to scrape together enough money to pay the initiation fee. The God had said: 'If you wanted to buy something that gave you true pleasure, would you hesitate for a moment before parting with your clothes? Then why, when about to partake of my holy sacrament, do you hesitate to resign yourself to a poverty of which you will never need repent?'

I made all preparations, spent another ten days without eating meat and submitted to having my head completely shaved; after which I was admitted to the nocturnal orgies of the Great God and became his illuminate. I took part in his service and sacrifices with the confidence that my knowledge of the corresponding rites of Isis gave me. This initiation consoled me for my enforced stay in a country that was not my own and at the same time enabled me to live less frugally: because Osiris, as the God of Good Fortune, put briefs in my way and I made quite a decent living as a barrister, even though I had to plead in Latin, not Greek.

Not long afterwards, would you believe it, I was granted yet another vision in which my instructions were to undergo a third initiation. I was surprised and perplexed, not being able to make head or tail of the order. I had already been twice initiated, so what mystery still remained undisclosed? 'Surely,' I thought, 'the priests have failed me. Either they have given me a false revelation, or else they have held something back.' I confess that I even began to suspect them of cheating me. But while I was still puzzling over the question and driven nearly mad by worry, a kindly god whose name I did not know explained the case to me in a dream. 'You have no reason,' he said, 'to be alarmed by your order to undergo still another initiation, or to suspect that something has been held back in the previous rites. On the contrary, you ought to be overjoyed at the repeated marks of divine favour shown you, and feel exultant at having been three times granted a favour that few receive even once. Rest assured that the holiness of the number three spells an eternal blessing for you and that it is necessary for you to undergo a third initiation. You have only to consider that the stole of the Goddess with which you were invested at Corinth is still laid up in the temple there and that even if you had brought it with you, no instruction to wear it here even at a rogation ceremony would be given you: it is a Greek vestment and cannot be recognized as conferring on you the dignity of a priest of Our Lady of the Field. Therefore if you wish to enjoy health, happiness and good fortune, treat the great gods as your counsellors and once more, as joyfully as before, submit to initiation.'

This holy vision convinced me that I had better obey. Without either neglecting or deferring the business on hand I went straight to the High Priest and reported my vision. Then once more I fasted, this time voluntarily extending the usual period of abstinence from meat, and paid all the costs out of my own pocket, the scale being dictated by my religious zeal rather than by the requirements of the temple.

I had no reason to repent of the trouble and expense, because by the bounty of the gods the fees that I earned in the courts soon compensated me for everything. Finally, a few days later, the God Osiris, the most powerful of all gods, 'the highest among the greatest, the greatest among the highest, the ruler of the greatest', manifested himself to me in a dream. In the previous vision he had disguised himself, but now he deigned to address me in his own person, with his own divine mouth. He came to assure me that I was soon to become a famous barrister and that I must not fear the spiteful slanders to which the learning acquired by my difficult studies would expose me; also that he wished me to assist in his sacred rites in the company of his other priests, and had therefore chosen me not only as a member of his Order of Shrine-bearers but as a Temple-Councillor for the next five years.

Once more I shaved my head and this time kept it shaved and

happily fulfilled the duties of that ancient college, which was
founded in the time of the Dictator Sulla. Making no attempt to
disguise my baldness by wearing a wig or any other covering, I
displayed it without shame on all occasions.

APPENDIX

HERE is the beginning of Lucian of Samosata's *Ass*, which continues in the same bald style all the way through. I stop at the point where his sexual humour becomes offensively crude. The whole book runs to only about an eighth of the length of Apuleius's.

This sample should be enough to acquit Apuleius of the charge of plagiarism except according to the jealous rulings quoted in modern copyright disputes. He has touched nothing of Lucian's which he has not transformed.

LUCIAN'S ASS

I ONCE travelled into Thessaly. The fact was that I had family business there with a man of those parts. A single horse carried me and my baggage, a single slave accompanied me, I followed the route I had determined upon. Some other travellers, too, happened to be going to Hypata, a Thessalian town of which they were natives, so I joined their company. It was a difficult road but at last we arrived within sight of the town. I asked the Thessalians whether they knew a man of Hypata named Hipparchus. I was carrying a letter to his house in the hope of being given a lodging there. Yes, they said, they knew Hipparchus and they knew in what part of the city he lived. They said that he had a deal of money but lived with nobody except a single slave-girl and his wife. They described him as extraordinarily miserly. When we were close to the city they pointed me out his orchard and a pleasant little house where he lived, just inside the gates. They then said goodbye and went off. I approached the house and knocked at the door. After a long time the slave-girl heard me and came to the door. I asked: 'Is Hipparchus at home?'

'Yes,' she said, 'but who are you, and what's your business?'

'I have a letter here for him,' I said, 'from Decrianus, the philosopher of Patra.'

'Very well,' she answered, 'wait here for me.'

She shut the gate and went inside again. Presently she returned and asked me to come in. I entered, found Hipparchus reclining on a narrow couch, greeted him and handed him my letter. He happened to be on the point of having supper. His wife was sitting close to him on the same couch and the table before them was still empty. He read the letter and said: 'Why, this is a great kindness on the part of Decrianus, the dearest and most distinguished of all Greeks, to send me his friends in such confidence in my hospitality. Well, you see my cottage, Lucius. It is very small, but big enough to lodge a guest.' He called the slave-girl: 'Palaestra, show my guest his bedroom and take along there any baggage he may have. Then conduct him to the public baths, for he has come from quite a distance.'

Palaestra then took me along to a very pretty bedroom. 'Here,' she said, 'is your bed and over there I will put your slave's mattress, and here is a pillow for you.' Then I went off to the baths and gave her money to buy barley for my horse. She took all my baggage inside and laid it in my bedroom. When I returned from the baths I entered the house at once. Hipparchus embraced me and asked me to recline at the table with him. The supper was none too frugal, the wine was smooth and old. After supper we toasted each other's health and chatted as guest and host usually do. When we had spent the evening over our drinks we went to bed.

In the morning Hipparchus asked where I was going next, or whether I intended to remain in Hypata. 'I am going on to Larissa,' I said, 'but I think that I shall be staying here for from three to five days.' This was not quite true; I had a strong desire to remain in Hypata and find some woman skilled in the black art. I wanted to see some wonder of magic, either a man who could fly or someone who had been turned into stone. This obsession set me walking through the streets of the city; I did not know where I should begin making enquiries about witchcraft but I walked through them all the same. Presently I saw a woman coming towards me, still fairly young, and quite well-to-do to judge by the way she sailed down the street. She had embroidered clothes, gold jewellery, plenty of slaves. As she drew near she greeted me and I returned her greeting.

'I am Abroea,' she said. 'You must have heard your mother talking about her friend Abroea, and I am prepared to love any child of hers as well as if I had borne it myself. Why not come and stay with me, my son?'

I replied: 'I should be delighted, but I fear that I could not possibly explain to my host why I am deserting him. Still, dear lady, I will stay with you in the spirit, if not in the body.'

'Who is your host, then?'

'His name is Hipparchus.'

'What, that miser?' she asked.

'Mother,' I replied, 'you do him an injustice. He has been hospitality itself. In fact, he might almost be charged with extravagance in his treatment of me.'

She smiled, took me by the hand and led me aside to whisper: 'Be very careful of anything that Hipparchus's wife does. She is a witch of the worst sort, lecherous too, always setting her cap at young men and if any of them refuses to do what she asks him she revenges herself on him by magic. She has changed many of them into animals, others she has destroyed out of hand. As for you, my son, you are a handsome young man of the sort that would immediately please any woman; and though you are her guest, nobody feels much obligation to guests.'

When I heard that the very thing of which I had been so long in search was waiting for me at home, I spent little more time listening to Abroea. I soon said goodbye, and on my way home this was how I addressed myself: 'Come, come, man, since you say that you are so anxious to witness these magical sights, rouse yourself, pray, and invent some clever plan which will allow you to achieve your heart's desire. And since you must keep the wife of your generous host at arm's length, I advise you to make a dead set at the slave-girl Palaestra. With her as your companion, instructress and bed-fellow you will quickly perfect yourself in the black art. Slaves pick up their masters' knowledge, whether it be good or evil.'

Talking with myself in this strain I re-entered the house. I found neither Hipparchus nor his wife at home, but Palaestra was busy at the stove preparing our supper and I at once addressed her: 'Lovely Palaestra, how prettily you bend and wriggle your hips as you stir the pot. Your sinuous motions send a shiver down my spine. He'll be a lucky man whom you allow to stick his fingers into your stew . . .'

FSG CLASSICS

Passage to Ararat
by Michael J. Arlen
Introduction by Geoffrey Wolff

The Dead Father
A novel
by Donald Barthelme
Introduction by Donald Antrim

The Dream Songs
Poems
by John Berryman
Introduction by W. S. Merwin

Geography III
Poems
by Elizabeth Bishop

House of Mist
A novel
by María Luisa Bombal

My Sister's Hand in Mine
The Collected Works of Jane Bowles
by Jane Bowles
Introduction by Truman Capote;
  Preface by Joy Williams

The Kingdom of This World
A novel
by Alejo Carpentier
Introduction by Edwidge Danticat

Wise Children
A novel
by Angela Carter

Break It Down
Stories
by Lydia Davis

Play It As It Lays
A novel
by Joan Didion
Introduction by David Thomson

Slouching Towards Bethlehem
Essays
by Joan Didion

The Old Gringo
A novel
by Carlos Fuentes

Sophie's World
A Novel About the History of Philosophy
by Jostein Gaarder

Darkness Visible
A novel
by William Golding
Introduction by A. S. Byatt

The Family Markowitz
A novel
by Allegra Goodman
Introduction by Jane Hamilton

Fierce Attachments
A Memoir
by Vivian Gornick
Introduction by Jonathan Lethem

The Man with Night Sweats
Poems
by Thom Gunn
Introduction by August Kleinzahler

Hunger
A novel
by Knut Hamsun
Introduction by Paul Auster;
  Afterword by Robert Bly